# ENCOUNTERS
## *with the*
# CHRIST

## DR. STEVEN A. JIRGAL

**CORE.**

Unless otherwise indicated, Scripture quotations in this book are taken from the *New American Standard Bible*®, Copyright © 1960, 1962, 1963, 1968, 1971, 1972, 1973, 1975, 1977, 1995 by The Lockman Foundation. Used by permission.

Published by The Core Media Group, Inc., P.O. Box 2037, Indian Trail, NC 28079.

Printed in the United States of America.

*This work is dedicated to all the hard working and dedicated pastors in my life. You are making a difference with your words and with your life!! Continue in the relentless pursuit of His pleasure! The harvest will one day come! Stay close, stay focused, stay true!*

*I Peter 2:21*

*In His Steps,*
*Steve*

# Table of Contents

# Introduction

What does a real encounter with Jesus look and feel like? What happens when the Master visits a person bringing peace, forgiveness, love, and healing? If a life is heading one way and a person runs into Jesus how does one walk from that point on? Without question there can be as many different answers as there are people who are asked. But one thing is certain. When a person genuinely encounters the Christ there will be change. Their life will never be the same again. God never intended for it to be.

Things were going well for Matthew Stiles. He was the Pastor of a stable church, had a solid marriage, and was anxiously awaiting the arrival of his first grandchild. But somehow life got off track. He lost his enthusiasm for his calling. Deep and haunting questions began creeping in. He felt the unnerving feeling of his faith dissolving before his eyes.

# Chapter 1
# The Pull

Frayton, Virginia was a good place to live. It was a small city just south of the Pennsylvania line and a short distance from West Virginia. The air was clean and the beauty of the mountains with their flowing streams, massive trees, and natural valleys took the edge off the harsh winters.

For the most part sixty-three-year-old Matthew Stiles was happy, even fulfilled. But somehow he felt uneasy lately. He was the Pastor of a small but healthy church in a semi-urban section of town. The people were faithful and the ministries fairly engaging. They had a food pantry, soup kitchen, and after-school program. Each fall the church would band together to bring blankets and coats to their neighbors in the hills of West Virginia. In his twenty-four years as Pastor of Fortress Baptist Church he saw little growth in numbers but he, and everyone else in the congregation understood that because of where the town and the church were located, the opportunity for membership growth was very limited. And it was because of the recognition of this reality, little pressure was put on Matthew to *make the church grow*.

But still, as Matthew sat on a bench near the edge of the church property he couldn't shake the feeling that something was missing. He stared out into the woods and was filled with the feeling that something just wasn't right. This was not a mid-life-crises. His marriage was as strong as ever. Melissa was the woman he had always prayed for. She was beautiful. She was slender and only four inches shorter than the six-foot-tall Matthew. Her long and flowing brunette hair always seemed to shine in the light of any room. Their college romance had blossomed into a healthy relationship leading them to the altar for their traditional marriage vows. Their daughter and her husband lived near by, and he was thrilled with the news of a baby on the way. He didn't feel burned out. Maybe he was a little overwhelmed with ministry. It wasn't a matter of health issues either. He was particularly healthy and strong for a man his age. He exercised almost daily and kept his diet in mind for the most part. He didn't even wear glasses except on certain occasions when words were small or the lighting was dim. Maybe he had his hands in too many activities but he always seemed to function better when he was very busy. He found himself wondering more and more about issues he had long settled in his mind. He remembered the season of his life when he felt himself being *called* into the ministry. He was a volunteer youth worker in the town he grew up in about a hundred miles south of Frayton. He was thirty-years old and worked for an accounting firm. He was well established and comfortable. He enjoyed the time he spent with the youth pastor as well as pouring himself into the lives of the young people. He also enjoyed his role as a Sunday school teacher and felt fulfilled in his walk with the Lord.

He had found himself in more and more conversations about the Bible and a personal walk with Christ. At one point, the pastor asked him to preach in his absence. He enjoyed his time of study in preparation for this opportunity and the sermon seemed to go very well and be received enthusiastically by the congregation.

As Matthew sat watching a ball game after church, he remembered the conversation he and Melissa had. She entered the room, plopped down on the couch beside him and waited for a commercial break.

"Can I ask you something?"

With his eyes still on the T.V. he said,

"You just did."

She smiled slightly and regained the lead in the conversation.

"O.K. but you didn't answer."

Seeing that she didn't buy into his cleverness and realizing she was right he said,

"Yes you can ask me a question."

"Good" she said as she pulled the remote from his hand, waved it toward the T.V. and hit the mute button.

"Is there any chance that you're being called into the ministry full time?"

Now she had all his attention and he turned to face her.

"You think that maybe God is calling me to be a pastor?"

Melissa smiled slightly. "Well, I see how much you enjoy being with the kids and I know how excited you get when you teach Sunday school. But when I watched you prepare to preach this week I saw another level of excitement in you. And when you preached today there was something inside me that saw you fit in so well. I just felt like this was your "sweet spot" then she made small quotation marks with her fingers.

"I gotta tell you" he said smiling. "I felt comfortable and really enjoyed all of it. I have been thinking lately about full-time ministry but I know that it *has* to be a call from the Lord. I don't want to run ahead of God and I don't want to do anything outside of his will for me, for us."

She gave a heavy sigh, "Well you know I never signed on to be a preacher's wife. I know that it's not an easy life, but if you are called then my plans are to go with you every step of the way.

"Well let's just put it to prayer" he said taking her hand and kissing it.

"Yup that's the plan" she said as she stood up, flipped the remote into his lap and sauntered out of the room. The game continued but Matthew missed the next several minutes. His eyes were on the T.V. but his mind was on his wife and her comments. Her supportive words stirred something deep in his heart-somewhere on the soul level. A few short minutes later a smile came to his face. He found himself thinking "I know God doesn't have favorites, but I sure feel like one!"

He remembered leading a Bible study during his senior year in college. It was the highlight of his week. The group had grown from three to more than thirty and they moved from meeting in his room to meeting in the dorm lobby. When the study was over, Kelli, a girl that he was interested in dating (but never did) approached him. She was a year younger than him and very popular. She had a spiritual maturity about her that added to her attractive face and smile. She gave him a gentle punch in the shoulder and simply said, "You should be a preacher!" He wanted to talk to her about it (or anything else), but before he could respond she was enveloped by the others in the room and his attention was drawn to someone else.

As a sat on the bench, a gentle breeze kicked up and played with his hair. He found himself thinking of the summer after his junior year in college when he went to visit his grand-father in Richmond. They sat on the swing in the back yard looking at the humming birds and watching the rabbits play in the tall grass. He had such love and respect for his grandfather who had been a preacher for over fifty years. The conversation meandered through college classes, creation, dreams, goals, and desires. At one point the conversation came to a comfortable silence and his grandfather looked up toward the clouds and said, "Matthew, if God ever calls you to be a minister, don't stoop to be a king." Matthew nodded showing his understanding of the statement. Then a call from his grandmother summoned the men for dinner.

His mind bounced to a very strange encounter he had shortly after he had joined his third accounting firm. Melissa had thrown him a wonderful surprise party for his thirtieth birthday. The house had been full of friends and Matthew glowed with a sense of richness in his heart. Family finances were good and the recent news of a baby on the way spun over and over in his mind. He and Melissa had been to a *life session* at the church with the youth. They stopped by a small diner on the way home for a cup of coffee and were engaged in a light conversation about their plans for a short vacation to the beach. It was to be a welcomed time of rest and escape and they each were looking forward to their time away.

As Matthew was sharing his thoughts about their upcoming respite he noticed Melissa's eyes wander to his right and he felt someone standing next to him. He turned slightly and was mildly surprised to find a man standing next to him. He was an elderly fellow who looked to be about eighty years old. He carried a cane and donned a long white beard and wire rimmed glasses. His clothes were very neat and pressed and showed no signs of wear. He gently yet firmly placed his left hand on Matthew's shoulder. This surprised both he and Melissa but for some reason neither of them felt a need to panic. His voice was firm and strong and lacked the slightest quiver. He looked down at Matthew and Matthew looked into his eyes. They were gentle eyes but ones that in a very strange way displayed wisdom. Without hesitation this aged one said, "When He calls, you must answer and follow without fear."

And just as suddenly as the words started, they ended. Before either of them could respond he turned and walked away. In silence the couple watched this old man exit the diner, gently negotiate the steps and moments later disappear into the darkness.

Without trying Matthew had tucked these comments and encounters away in the recesses of his mind. Every once in a while they would come forth as if awakening from a deep slumber and he would muse over them for a short time. But today they seemed to visit him with particular strength and life.

Matthew sat still and continued his memories of the early years in ministry. He remembered how excited his parents and grandparents were when he shared with him his plans to follow the Lord's leading and enter into vocational ministry. Not everyone, however, shared his excitement about ministry. Nick who worked for the same accounting firm as Matthew, always seemed to have a critical comment about everything. His reaction wasn't surprising when he learned about Matthew's departure from the firm to go to seminary.

Matthew was at his desk when Nick poked his head in. Nick had been with the firm about two years longer than Matthew. He was good at his job but beyond that, Matthew saw very few redeeming qualities. He was known to be harsh and direct and almost uncaring in his relationships. He had a sarcastic personality and seemed to criticize everything. Matthew knew he was married and often wondered how that could have happened. His relationship with Nick was cordial but not close. Leaning on the doorframe Nick said, "Seminary huh Bible Boy?" "That's right" Matthew replied turning halfway to face him. "Well" Nick said as he rubbed three fingers of his left hand together, "Get ready for the poor house." With that, he pushed away from the door and was gone. Matthew wasn't surprised. That was just Nick. He just sat there, gave a mild sigh and gently shook his head.

He reflected on the years he spent in seminary. Classes were challenging but interesting. They lived in a small apartment on the edge of campus. Melissa worked as a teacher's aid in a nearby elementary school. Matthew worked for a landscaper and did fill-in work in area churches. They didn't have much, but they had a strong faith in God and His word, and a deep passion for the lost and hurting. In those days he spoke with such conviction and enthusiasm. His energy level was surprising even to him. The ideas and dreams for ministry never seemed to end. He was enveloped in activities and reveled in the opportunities that continued to present themselves. Bible study came easily and prayer was almost automatic.

But somehow all of that had faded. In its place came thoughts and ideas that seemed so strange to him. He found himself dwelling on issues that he had put to bed so many years ago. His mind was filled with doubt and he questioned the validity of his beliefs. He wondered about the authority of the Bible, the forgiveness of sin, the power and involvement of God, the deity of Christ. Sometimes during the night, he would lie awake and even wonder about the very existence of God. Was there a God? What if all of this was just a cosmic joke? What if they were just part of a spiritual chess game? Was Karl Marx right when he said religion was "the opiate of the people?" Were all his beliefs a result of what felt good and gave him comfort? He believed in miracles but when it came to being absolutely honest with himself, he admitted he had never actually seen one. If there was a God, was Matthew mistaken about His character? These and so many more questions and doubts led Matthew to one over-arching question: Had he wasted his life following and teaching about a God who was not really there? Matthew had counseled so many people in these and many other areas but now he was the one in need of answers.

It seemed like Matthew had been sitting on the bench nursing these thoughts for fifteen minutes, but when he looked at his watch he realized he had been there for over an hour. The temperature had dropped several degrees making him feel chilled. He rubbed each of his arms, gave a heavy sigh, rocked forward and stood up. Looking deep into the woods he said aloud, "Show me Lord! Just show me!"

Matthew didn't remember the ride home. He walked quietly from the car port and into the house. As always he was greeted by Buddy their hyper-energetic miniature colie. Buddy was a friend to everyone who came in the house. The family often wondered what Buddy would do if there were an intruder. They joked about him showing the stranger where the silver was. But everyone was equally aware that Buddy was Matthew's dog. Matthew went for walks with him and groomed him and sat for lengthy times petting him as they filled the oversized recliner. Normally Matthew would place whatever he was carrying on the small hall table and drop to one knee and tussle Buddy's face and head. But that evening he somehow just wasn't in the mood. Buddy sat before him wagging his tail and waiting for his routine attention. All Matthew could muster up was a "Hey pal" and a soft pat on the head.

Melissa came from the study holding a finger in a book she had been reading. "Hey Honey! I didn't expect you home yet" she said as she made her way across the living room toward him.

"Hey Babe" was all Matthew could come up with.

Melissa immediately knew something was wrong.

"Are you okay? What's wrong?"

"Nothing. I just have a lot on my mind that's all."

Melissa knew better. She put her arms around his waist and gave him a hug. Matthew's arms encircled her and he kissed her on side of her head.

"How'd a guy like me get a girl like her?" he thought as he held her close.

Her hug felt so good to him. He wanted to hold her longer but the lifting of her head off his chest was the unspoken signal that it was time to end the embrace.

She looked up at him. "Someone give you a hard time today?"

"No" he managed. His eyes began to fill with unexpected tears.

"You know I'm always here for you."

"I know. Thank you Babe. I'm just trying to figure some things out that's all." With that he gave her another hug and wandered into the den and sat down. Predictably, Buddy jumped up and found his place on his lap.

For the next couple of days Matthew found himself "going through the motions" of his job and calling. More and more it felt like a job instead of a calling. He wasn't a person given to depression but he knew enough to sense that he was heading there. He felt dry spiritually and noticed that his prayer life had waned. But in an unusual way he didn't want to change. This wasn't self-pity, it was more a feeling of numbness. He had always been a man of prayer. *Pray without ceasing* had been an unspoken mantra for his Christian life. He often found himself in conversation with God and it seemed so natural for him to talk out loud to the Lord. But lately he found himself surrounded by his doubts and dwelling on his misgivings about God and himself.

It wasn't any one thing that brought Matthew to this *tipping point*. It was a culmination of things. Lack of sleep, attitudes of church members, the overwhelming weight of the calling, even natural disasters all added up to attack him at the deepest level.

A particular chance encounter came to Matthew's mind. He and his friend Jim had made plans to meet at a downtown diner for coffee early one Saturday morning. While Matthew sat alone nursing a cup he got a call from Jim. Jim's car wouldn't start so he would not be able to make it. Matthew figured he would finish his coffee and head home.

It was then that he focused on a man in the booth next to his. The man was sitting alone reading a newspaper. He was a middle-aged man with spots of gray in his hair. He had a neatly trimmed mustache and a loose fitting sweat suit.

At one point, the man sneezed and Matthew instinctively said, "God bless you." The man looked over his paper and said, "I doubt it" and went back to reading. Matthew took another sip from his coffee and without thinking about it said, "Good morning! My name's Matthew."

The man slid his paper down, nodded his head to one side and without much emotion said, "Jerry."

"What did you mean by 'I doubt it?'" Matthew asked.

Jerry put down his paper and sighed. Then he began a long explanation that he undoubtedly had shared several times before.

"Look, I used to go to church regularly and was very involved with religion. In fact, I used to be a believer." He used his fingers to make quotation marks in the air. "But a bunch of stuff happened that made me doubt if God was interested in blessing me."

Matthew was unfazed and asked, "Like what??

Jerry took a deep breath. "Like when my son died because of a drunk driver. Like when my boss walked into my office and told me I was fired." Then he added, "For no good reason!" "Like when our house was struck by lightning and almost burned completely to the ground." Jerry looked down. Matthew knew he wasn't through. He said quietly, "Like when my wife died two years ago from a brain aneurism. That's like what." He looked at Matthew without flinching.

Without invitation, Matthew grabbed his half-filled cup of coffee, stood up and slid into the booth across of Jerry. "Sorry man!" was all he could manage. Jerry spoke up again, "Listen, I got a real problem in believing that God is in control of everything. If that's true, why would he allow my son to die? If our car had been one mile-an-hour faster or slower that accident wouldn't have happened and my son would be alive today. I struggled through that and the loss of our house but then my wife died." Jerry paused as if to settle his emotions. "I wasn't even home. My daughter who is in high school came home and found her dead in the kitchen. She's scarred for life. Do you know what that's like?"

Matthew knew to be very careful with his words, "No. No I don't. but I know what God's like." Jerry broke in and raised his voice. "Me too! Please don't tell me that he's loving and in control. Don't tell me he has a wonderful plan for my life. Don't give me Romans 8:28 or any other verse from a book that some men wrote several centuries ago."

He paused as if he needed to let it all settle in Matthew's brain. Then he said, "Yesterday the doctor called and said I need to come in for testing. The x-rays showed a mass in my left lung that looks suspicious." Jerry leaned in and rested the palms of his hands on his paper. "Look. You seem like a nice guy and maybe you think it's your job to teach all that religious stuff to people. I get that. But the reality is I do believe there is a God. I believe he made the world and all that's in it." He shook his head slightly, "But from a personal standpoint I don't see his hand moving in mine or anybody else's life."

Matthew felt helpless. What happened to all the Bible verses he had memorized? What about the training he had? Where were the answers he had given to so many others? He breathed what he had labeled a *flare prayer* but nothing came. "Well" he began but the words refused to come. All he could manage was, "I'm sorry."

Jerry's voice softened. It almost seemed like he was the one bringing comfort to Matthew. "Listen, I'm not trying to ruin your faith or wreck your day. I do think Jesus was a good man who did good things. I think it's good to love your neighbor and forgive others and all that stuff." He made quotation marks with his hands again, "Miracles either didn't happen or could easily be explained away."

Matthew wanted to say something but couldn't. He felt like he was standing in front of a Gatling gun and the bullets of anger, resentment, mistrust, and bitterness were flying.

After a brief pause Jerry began again, "From what the Bible says, I know I'm a sinner. I hate, lust, and envy. I've stolen things, cursed, and lied. But for me to believe that one man's death could make up for me and billions of people's sins…that's too much for me to handle."

Matthew could only manage, "But what if it's true?" and even when he said it he saw the weakness in his response. Jerry countered with, "But what if it's false? What if so much of what you believe about God, the Bible, and Jesus is false?" Matthew was about to respond but Jerry cut him off. "What if most of what you thought was true was actually made up by men over all these years? Christians believe that other religions are false or only partially true, that they're made up by men."

Jerry had made a good point. The conversation ended amiably but that night Matthew found himself wrestling with doubts like never before. He was assailed by questions about so many things he thought he had settled in his heart and mind years ago.

He slept little that night. He just couldn't turn his mind off. He bounced from one idea and argument to the next. The morning brought no clarity. He was as unsettled as the night before. He picked at his breakfast and nursed his mug of coffee. He arrived at his office and didn't remember one detail about the trip.

Matthew's faith was being assaulted. He sensed it but somehow couldn't sidestep it. He felt discouraged and wondered if he was depressed. He went about his studies in a semi-stupor. He kept returning to his conversation with Jerry and felt a stronghold of doubt taking hold of his heart. Questions kept coming to his mind. The authority and accuracy of Scripture, the life of Christ, heaven, hell, and a relationship with God all stood on center stage as his doubts grew and he stumbled through his day.

He was a man of faith, a Bible teacher and preacher. How could these doubts ever become so strong? Where was his faith? Where was his security and confidence in the God he had trusted so many decades ago?

Life in the church wasn't perfect but it was good. Likewise, his home life wasn't ideal but it was satisfying and fulfilling. So where did this uneasiness, this crises of belief come from? How did the claws of doubt dig so deeply into his heart and mind? His week plodded along following the same path.

His Bible study has suffered as well. He prepared his sermons as usual. In his twenty-four years as the senior pastor of Fortress, never once did he enter the pulpit unprepared. It just wasn't in his wiring or *spiritual DNA* not to have a ready word from *the book of books*. But lately he found himself preparing for a sermon but neglecting his own time of study. The Bible simply didn't attract him as it had for so many years. It was like a movie that had been his favorite and he enjoyed so much, but after seeing it three times, it had lost its luster and appeal.

Time in prayer came with great effort. It wasn't that he didn't have time to pray. His well-established routines gave no evidence to that argument. It was just that he didn't want to pray. Somehow he felt that his prayers never went beyond the distance of his breath. When he did pray he felt himself pulled again and again to the words, "Show me

Lord! Just show me!"

Sunday morning came and he preached the sermon he had prepared and he felt himself struggle through it the entire time. Back at home he sat silently at the kitchen table while Melissa stood at the counter preparing lunch. He untied his tie and slid it a couple of times back and forth across the back of his neck. He gave a heavy sigh slowly letting the air escape from his lungs. He wanted to ask her what she thought of the sermon, but he had a fear of her honesty. Melissa heard more than noise. She heard the downcast heart of her husband.

"You okay?" she said walking toward him with a plate holding a sandwich, chips, and a pickle.

"I guess so" he said looking down. "What did you think of the sermon?"

"Not your best, but it was okay."

Melissa was always more gentle and kind with the truth. If the quality of something called for a five, she would give it a seven. He felt that she was rating it a five so he knew it was a two or three. Words like *disaster* and *train wreck* came to his mind.

"I felt it was terrible!" he said still looking down as she moved toward the fridge to put water in their glasses. She placed the glasses on the table and sat down placing her hand on his shoulder.

He continued to stare at the floor. "I don't know how much more of this I can take. I feel like a hypocrite. I'm not preaching with any power because I'm not living with any power. I feel like I'm preaching about things I'm not sure I believe any more.

The alarm of that comment could easily been seen on Melissa's face. She had never seen him voice many doubts before. Her husband had always been a man of strong conviction. She saw in him as a man who carried a faith that would sustain him and all those around him. His faith had carried him through countless storms and seasons of struggle. And now he was conveying to her that the *solid rock* he had been standing on was *sinking sand*. Tears filled her eyes. Her heart was breaking for the soul of her husband. What could she do? How could she help? What was happening to him?

She slid her chair next to his and wrapped one arm across his shoulder, placed the other hand on the side of his head and pulled him close to her. "We'll get through this my love."

"I..." He was about to say "I know" but somehow he couldn't force the words out. He didn't know. Just another thing placed on the growing pile of uncertainty. He felt a tear running down the side of his nose and watched it drop to the floor. He didn't try to stop its fall because he simply didn't care. Melissa issued a silent but heartfelt prayer. "Lord, please help my husband. He's a good man, but he's hurting now and I don't know what to do. Please give him strength!"

With no activities scheduled for the church that evening, Matthew spent the afternoon on the couch in front of the T.V. Nothing on the box appealed to him. He normally didn't watch much television and had often mentioned that T.V. stood for *time vacuum*. He had been known to say, "The problem with television was that there is too much *tell*, and not enough *vision*." A good bit of the time he spent in and out of slumber.

The next morning, he slept a bit longer than usual. He normally went to the office later on Mondays but that day he struggled to pull himself from bed. On the fifteen-minute drive to the church thoughts assailed him that were so foreign to him that he felt violated. He wanted to quit. He wanted to run. He wanted to simply disappear. But what would he do? Where would he go?

As he worked his way down highway 19, he found himself strongly tempted to steer his car directly into oncoming traffic. He played it out in his mind. He had a life insurance policy that would take care of Melissa for several years. It had to look like an accident and it had to be quick and complete. He didn't want to feel any pain. He had enough of that inside him already. If he slipped his seat belt off it might increase his chances of a quick death. If the air bag were disconnected it would raise suspicions so that idea was quickly dismissed. He wanted to tell Melissa how much he loved her and how much she meant to him but that would also point to the plan. These thoughts were so ironic to him. "I love you but I'm leaving you." They brought conversations and sermons back to his mind. He had often told his congregation, "Suicide is a permanent solution to a temporary problem." He had also asked the question, "Is it reasonable to think, 'I'll punish them by killing me?'" He reflected back on the several funerals he had done over the years and saw the pain and struggle in the hearts and minds of loved ones left behind. Funerals were always hard. They were hard on everybody. Even when an older person dies an *expected* death it's tough. It's even tougher when someone dies when no one sees it coming. But the absolute toughest deaths to endure are those where the loved one ended their own life.

He remembered receiving a call late one Sunday night. He had just settled in bed and was thinking about the events of the day and what was in store the next day. A phone call at night always alarmed him. It never brought good news. He picked up the bedside phone and heard a rasping shaking voice.

"Matthew?"

"Yes, this is Matthew."

"Matthew it's George. I need your help."

"Yes. What's going on George?" Matthew asked sitting up.

"It's Jordan. My nephew."

George's voice trailed off and the line went silent. Matthew thought he had hung up and his mind raced in a dozen directions. Jordan had come to live with George and his wife Patti a year ago. He was nineteen and brought with him a bag full of struggles. The bag included drug abuse, a violent home life, and an arrest record. George and Patti had agreed with George's brother that a change in Jordan's life might be just what he needed to turn himself around. He arrived under the conditions that he get a job, attend church with them each week, and be drug and alcohol free. Jordan found employment at a poultry plant and seemed to be doing well. He made a couple of friends at church, bought a used car, and it looked like the turn he needed was happening. On one occasion he did come home and George could tell he had been drinking. He pressed Jordan on it and after a while Jordan confessed that he and a friend had a *couple* of beers together. Jordan knew that he had disappointed his Aunt and Uncle and seemed repentant so they chose to dismiss the incident.

Matthew was about to hang up and look for George's number when he heard he man breathing.

"Patti and I came home from a weekend in the mountains. We thought Jordan was in his room. Patti went upstairs to check on him. When she came down she was crying. She had a note and a liquor bottle in her hand. Among other things The note said that he was tired of being a failure and that he was done with the struggle. We both panicked. We searched the rest of the house but couldn't find him. Patti got on the phone and started calling people who knew Jordan. I went to look outside. I noticed the shed door open. When I went inside…."

His voiced trailed off again.

Matthew waited patiently fighting his own tears as he knew what was coming next.

"Then I found him. He shot…himself."

That funeral was so hard on George and Patti and their friends. It took its toll on Matthew as well.

These thoughts made Matthew wonder what would be said at his funeral. His experience told him that Melissa and their daughter Terri would really struggle. They both would cry for days. Friends and family would do their best to bring comfort but the loneliness Melissa would feel would overwhelm her. He was certain that an extended season of depression would envelop her.

Then one word came to mind as if it was presenting itself in bold letters. *SELFISH!*

Matthew had always seen those who had committed suicide as selfish. He was careful with who he shared that with not wanting to add more pain to those left behind. But he held a certain amount of contempt to those who quit life and heaped a life-time of pain on those left behind.

It was with those latter thoughts that he chastised and rebuked himself out loud. In a somewhat surprising move he found himself yelling, "Matthew, you're such a selfish jerk! Knock it off! What about the person you hit? What happens to them? What if they're hurt or killed? What about their family and friends? If there really is a God, this is NOT His plan for your life. Now get your act together and quit being such a baby!" The temptation exited as fast as it entered.

Matthew finished the drive to the office deeply stunned by the thoughts he had allowed to permeate his mind. He entered his office, made his *to do* list and began his weekly routine. But progress was slow and motivation quickly dried up. By eleven-o'clock he closed his computer, told his secretary he was going out to run and errand and exited the building.

Moments later he found himself driving out of town and headed to a place he'd been to countless times. A few minute later he had entered *Denegan National Park* and was working his way up a one-mile trail to the top of Mount Lee. The air was cool and crisp and he imagined the freshly produced molecules of oxygen fighting to enter his lungs and he welcomed them in by taking several deep breaths. The sky was clear and he found himself thinking, "If you don't label this a beautiful spring day, you're not paying attention." Matthew guessed Monday morning as the reason why no one was on the trail and he was grateful to be alone. As he hiked he deliberately kept his pace slow. He didn't want to simply conquer the climb, he wanted to enjoy the journey. He had spent too much of his time on the conquering side of the ledger. Too often he saw his tasks as a competition to be won. College, seminary, ministry, home repairs, sports, even a visit at the hospital had all become competitions to be won instead of processes to enjoy. He stopped several times along the way to enjoy the view and catch his breath. Eventually he reached the top. Except for one time when it was overcast the mountain had never failed to provide a stunning view. He could see across the borders to West Virginia and Pennsylvania. For several minutes he simply sat on a bench and stared out at the majestic view.

This place had become a special retreat for him. It was where he and Melissa had come when they were seriously contemplating going into full-time vocational ministry. They had trekked up the trail so many times with special friends. He remembered leading the group in receiving *The Lord's supper* at this place. It was where he remembered coming with Terri when she was such a little girl. Ah Terri!

She was so excited to be hiking with her Mom and Dad. She was only four but she hiked a good bit of the trail and he carried her the rest of the way. Near the top he put her down to finish the hike and reach the top. Her face lit up as they rounded the corner at the summit, and the majestic scene came into full view. She gasped and said, "This is so beautiful! We should live here!" Matthew and Melissa both laughed and Melissa said, "I'm good with that!"

Scenes of Terri came flooding to Matthew's mind. She had been such a compliant child. She was a people pleaser but also held an adventurist spirit. She always made good grades and they didn't have to spend much time encouraging her to get on her assignments. Even during her years in middle school she gave them little cause for concern. She was outgoing and friendly and made friends easily. Matthew reflected on the night she had made her personal commitment to Christ.

She was about eight-years-old and had been asking Melissa lots of questions about Jesus and how to go to heaven. Patiently, Melissa had walked her through the Bible and explained to her how a person becomes a Christian. Then one night after going to bed she came into the living room. Matthew and Melissa were watching a movie and were surprised to see her.

"Honey, what are you doing up? Are you okay?" Melissa asked.

"It's time for me to become a Christian" Terri said.

Matthew and Melissa looked at each other fighting the desire to smile.

Matthew said, "Okay, sweetheart. Come sit with us."

He slid away from his wife making room for their daughter between them.

"Why do you want to become a Christian?" Matthew asked.

"Jesus wants me to." Terri answered.

"Baby, tell us what you know about sin?" Melissa asked.

"Sin is what I do when I don't listen to you and Daddy or when I have bad thoughts. God doesn't like sin. It makes him sad.

"That's right" Matthew told her. What does it mean to be a Christian?"

"It means that I ask Jesus into my heart and he forgives me for my sins and cleans me up. Like taking a bath and getting all the dirt off me."

Matthew could hear Melissa's words coming through his daughter's voice. His mind wandered slightly. "I wish more adults understood that."

He looked at his wife and saw her grin and nod slightly. Then he came back to her.

"Okay, Darling. Why don't we pray? Why don't you tell Jesus you're sorry for your sins, ask him to forgive you and come into your heart and be the Lord of your life."

The three of them knelt by the couch and in a voice so sincere and pure they listened as their little girl surrendered herself to the Lord. Matthew could still feel the tears of joy sliding down his cheeks.

As she grew her faith grew and so did her friends and desire for adventure. She was very good at sports and played volleyball and ran track throughout her high school career. Matthew's dreams of an athletic scholarship never materialized but he didn't spend much time dwelling on it. She wasn't reckless but enjoyed the rush of adrenaline often accompanying her exploits. She enjoyed mountain biking, hiking, white-water rafting, and scuba diving. During her junior year in college Matthew was surprised when she called to tell him about her weekend.

The call was not the surprise. The fact that she and two of her friends had gone "bungee jumping" was. He was careful not to admonish her, but only said, "Well that proves that you really are crazy!"

Terri just laughed and went on to describe how "awesome it was."

When Matthew informed his wife what *her daughter* had done, she gave a heavy sigh and made the comment, "I'm glad I didn't know about this beforehand! I'd be a nervous wreck."

As Matthew sat at the edge of the vista he realized he was smiling. He knew he was a blessed man. He realized he had a good life. He had a solid marriage, a good job, plenty of friends, and sound health. Soon he would become a Grandfather. So why was he so troubled in his soul? Why would he want to put an end to all of that? Why was he plummeting downward? The feelings he had about God came flooding back to him and he felt the roots of doubt begin to grow in his heart again. In such a strange way he could feel his soul sinking within him. It was as if the scene before him was slowly changing. He thought he saw the bright lush of the colors before him begin to fade to black and white. Several times he wiped his eyes hoping to clear both his mind and vision with little success. He knew he was alone physically, but he felt deeply alone spiritually. St. John of the cross called this the *dark night of the soul*. Henry Blackaby labeled it, *the crises of belief.* Both those descriptions fit so well with what Matthew was going through.

"There has to be a way out of this" Matthew thought. "I keep trying to climb out of this but I keep getting dragged back into it. What's wrong with me?"

Matthew looked around making sure no one was coming up the trail. With the assurance that he was alone he stood and shouted through his tears, as loud as he could, "C'mon God! Help me out of his! Why won't you make yourself real?" He heard his voice echoing through the trees below. Then the the sound died out and his aloneness crept back in. He found himself whispering through a cracking voice the words that were becoming all too common for him, "Just show me Lord. Show me!"

The drive back to the office was uneventful as was his progress for the rest of the day. He had skipped lunch but just didn't seem to care. He tried to concentrate on the tasks before him but found himself alternating between staring at the floor and the walls. He looked at the shelves of books that lined the walls of his office. Over the years he had collected a healthy library that fed his love for reading. He thought,

"You would think that a man surrounded by so much information would have a few ideas about life and God." He gave a heavy sigh and shook his head slightly.

The afternoon dragged on and finally he felt comfortable in heading home. He would spend some time talking with Melissa, grab some supper and head back to the office for a counseling session with a young couple struggling in their marriage. The last thing he wanted to do was to try to fix someone else when he felt so broken himself. But duty demanded it and he knew he would throw himself into their lives and try to help them with their ongoing problems.

Melissa was clearly concerned when she saw her husband. His face looked drawn and filled with worry. He looked like a man who hadn't slept in days. She greeting him as he put his keys and I-Pad on the counter near the door. She hugged him and held him tighter and longer than normal. Without moving her head from his chest she said,

"Matthew, I'm so worried about you. I'm not used to seeing you like this. How can I help you?"

"I'll be okay. I just need some rest. I've got a lot on my mind."

"Well, tell me about it. Let me help you."

"Just some things I have to work out."

She lifted her head from his chest and looked up into his face, "Matthew, I'm your wife. I want to help you through whatever it is that's bothering you but I feel like you won't let me in. You know I'm here for you."

"I know. And I appreciate it more than you realize. I just need some time to work through some of my thoughts that's all."

"Do you need to talk to someone."

Matthew knew what she was saying. She was asking him about counseling, professional counseling. It was probably his pride that caused that suggestion to bother him slightly. He knew she was just trying to help, but he was the one who gave counsel to others. He was the one who fixed people when they came his way. He was the one who was close to God (or so he thought), and could point people in the right direction. Matthew didn't respond immediately, but then quietly said "Maybe. We'll see."

Melissa knew that was a comment of appeasement and that was Matthew's way of saying "Probably not."

Melissa ended their hug by gently letting go of him. She stepped away slightly, looked into her husband's face, and said, "Maybe we should get away for a short while. We haven't been away in a couple of months. Let's go to the beach."

"Yeah, maybe we should do that" was all that Matthew offered.

"You got anything to eat. I missed lunch today and I've gotta get back to meet with the Martins at 6:30."

"Sure. What do you want."

"Doesn't matter. Whatever you got is fine."

# Chapter 2
# The Downpour

On the ride back to the office Matthew was amazed at how cloudy it had become. The afternoon was clear and free of clouds, but now the sky was covered by rolling black clouds. He felt the wind press against his mid-sized car and it surprised him how strong it was. It made him grip the wheel tighter and focus his attention on driving. By the time he had gotten to the office a mist began to fall. He had an umbrella in the back seat but didn't bother with it as the rain was insignificant and the wind was very strong. He got into the office without being too wet and waited for the Martins to arrive.

Mike and Tammy Martin were a young couple who met at another church. A friend invited them to Fortress when they began dating and they never left. Matthew had developed a good relationship with Mike as did Melissa with Tammy. Mike worked as a carpenter and Tammy taught seventh grade English. They were in a small group study and rarely missed Sunday morning worship. Matthew had done their premarital counseling and officiated at their wedding. Everything seemed to be lining up well for them as they moved along in their married life.

But somehow they had reached an impasse. They were suffering from what Matthew labeled *marital drift*. Mike worked long hours and often arrived home late. When they were home together, Tammy was either grading papers or working on her graduate school assignments. They spent so much time working on their careers that they had nothing left to pour into their marriage. As Matthew was commonly heard to say, "They were so busy earning their salt, that they forgot their sugar."

Matthew helped them see that they needed to make some adjustments and gave them an assignment to begin *dating* again. They agreed to put more effort into their marriage and left after Matthew prayed over them.

For a few minutes Matthew remained in his office. His spirit was still downcast and that lost feeling he had resurfaced stronger than ever. He gave a slight smile when the thought came to him, "You're telling them how to keep their marriage together when you can't even keep your life together." Then Melissa's urgings came to him, "Maybe I do need some professional counseling. I'll have to look into that tomorrow."

He grabbed his keys and made his way down the hall. Through the glass door and with the help of the parking lot lights, he could see that the rain had picked up significantly. The wind was still blowing hard and the rain pounded in big drops. He thought about returning to his desk to wait it out but the idea of sitting alone held no appeal to him. He chose to make a run for it and deal with the consequences later. As always, his car was locked so he found the correct key while still inside and sprinted his way to the car wondering why he never bought a remote door lock. Moments later he sat in his car soaked and questioning his sense of judgment. He paused a few moments, shook the rain off his face and hands and started the car and a journey that would forever transform his life.

The rain seemed to increase as he made his way down highway 19. Even with the high beams on, he struggled to see much further than the hood. He could barely make out the yellow lines in the middle of the road and couldn't see the white line on his right. He found himself following the tail lights of the car in front of him. Thankfully the traffic was very light and Matthew reasoned it was because *they had some sense*. The storm was predicted but he couldn't remember being in a storm as strong as this one. The radio was on, but the pelting rain made it impossible to hear. Every once in a while the sky would light up with a lightening bolt followed closely by a booming thunder clap. Had he been inside he would have enjoyed the show on nature's stage but driving in it was unnerving. He passed a couple of cars parked under a bridge and felt himself judging them as wise. Still he plunged on through the storm.

A long streak of lightning completely lit up the sky and it seemed like the thunder sounded at the same time. Then a sight flashed on the side of the road. Just to his right and on the edge of the road, Matthew saw an unmistakable figure standing. It was an old man in a long robe. He had a long white beard and was holding a staff in his right hand.

His left hand was pointed skyward and his staff was raised over the road. "What in the world?" Matthew thought surprised by the sight. "What's he doing out in the storm?" He only saw the man for a very brief moment and the thought of stopping to help the old fellow flew through his mind.

Then the unthinkable happened. While rounding a gentle curve he saw a large puddle covering half the road. The car in front of him plowed through it sending a wave of water off the road. But the water returned as quickly as it had been expelled sending a *tidal wave* under his tires. In a fraction of a second he felt his car begin to spin. He tried to turn into the skid but it changed nothing. He had lost complete control and was at the mercy of the laws of physics. He knew it wasn't possible but he felt that the car was picking up speed as it left the pavement. He went over an embankment and was airborne.

The car came down with a loud crash. He never saw it coming but felt the airbag punch him soundly in the face. Matthew looked over the deflated bag to see the outline of a large tree the front of the car was pressed against. The rain was letting up and he could see steam coming from the hood. He did a quick body check and determined that he was hurting but for the most part uninjured. As best as he could tell, he was not bleeding but he did feel some soreness on his chest probably caused by the seat belt. His head ached and there was a loud buzzing in his ears. He looked down for his phone but in the darkness couldn't tell where it had flown. His eyes searched the dash and scanned the floorboards but saw no sign of it. He reached behind him and found the umbrella he had ignored earlier that night. Instinctively, he popped the button for the seat belt, lifted the handle to his left, and was surprised to find the driver's side door opened without trouble.

He stepped out of the car slightly stunned and eased himself upright. He didn't know much about cars but the fact that the front end was in a *V* shape told him the vehicle was totaled. He heard a loud hissing coming from under the hood and didn't even venture a guess as to what it was. He was somewhat surprised at how far off the road he had traveled. The highway was about thirty yards away up a slight hill. He was about to open his umbrella but realized it might hinder him from traveling on the little trail back to the road. He took a deep breath and began what seemed like a long trek toward the road and the help he needed. Even though there hadn't been much traffic, he felt that surely someone had seen him or would be traveling down the road shortly.

As he moved away from his car he was relieved that the buzzing in his ears had dissipated and almost stopped. He was equally relieved that the rain had stopped entirely. Then came the recognition that stunned him. The sun was poking up on the horizon. He stopped and stared. How could that be? He had only been there a few minutes at the most. He felt certain he hadn't been knocked out and there was no way he was in the car all night. His surprise continued as he looked at the ground and noticed that it was dry. But while he was looking down, his eyes focused on something that made him stop in his tracks. He was wearing sandals! Along with that realization came the fact that he had a long robe on.

"I must have hit my head" he thought. "Now I'm imagining things."

He placed his left hand on a small tree to steady himself. He had to figure out what was going on. When he lifted his arm he felt something on his wrist. Pulling back the sleeve of his robe he found a small leather bag hanging from a thin strap. Opening the bag revealed several foreign coins. "Where did this come from?" he wondered.

Matthew leaned against the tree. His mind was spinning and he was very confused. He ran his hand through his hair and then placed his hand on his chin. It was then that he noticed a short beard.

"What's going on?" he said quietly.

He turned back toward the car to get a look at himself in the mirror and found that the car was gone.

"That can't be!" he whispered. "I know it was just here a second ago. "This is unreal. I've got to get to some help."

He made his way up the knoll toward the road. But when he came from behind some bushes he saw what looked like a completely different world. The highway he had been on just minutes before was now a dirt road. Houses that he had passed were gone leaving in their place a series of small clay homes or dusty hills. Matthew had to sit down. He had to figure out what was happening to him.

He found a large rock to his left and leaned against it. His mind raced over the events of only a few minutes ago. He left the church. It was pouring rain. He couldn't see. An old man in a robe was by the road. He hydro-planed, spun around, and went off the road hitting a big tree. That's it. That's all that happened. But now, here he was wearing sandals and a robe which weren't his, and donning facial hair that sure wasn't his. He looked down and was stunned to see that his umbrella was gone. In its' place was a long and very old staff. With his left hand, he reached for the staff and it was then that he noticed something that caught his breath: his watch was gone! And his ring! His wedding ring was missing. "That's impossible! How could both of them be knocked off at the same time. What is happening to me?" Somehow he managed a private moment of humor when he quietly said, "I don't think we're in Kansas anymore Toto."

# Chapter 3
# Levi

As he sat pondering these things, he noticed a lone figure coming around the bend. It was a man. Surely he could shed some light on what was going on. As the man approached Matthew noticed that he was small in height but stocky. He wore a brown robe with an off-yellow band at the bottom. A rope that was knotted in the front held the cloth piece tight to his waist. His skin was deeply tanned and he had a long beard peppered with dark and light hair. His head was covered with a white cloth that was rimmed with dried sweat stains. He carried a walking stick in one hand and a small cloth bag over his opposite shoulder. As he approached he smiled in Matthew's direction.

"Shalom" he said lifting his staff toward Matthew. Then he said something that Matthew couldn't understand.

"Morning" was all Matthew could manage. Before he moved he found himself asking, "Do you speak English?"

The man paused and tilted his head, "English? I do not know what that is my friend. I speak only Hebrew, Greek, and of course Aramian."

Realizing he now understood the man Matthew thought, "How can I understand this guy? And more than that, how can he understand me?"

Years ago he had taken both Hebrew and Greek in seminary but he had never become conversant. How is it that he understood what this stranger was saying?

With these thoughts bouncing through his head he said, "How do you understand me?"

Shrugging his shoulders, he answered, "Because you are speaking Greek. You have a strange accent but my ears are not so dull that I cannot understand. Are you traveling to the city my friend?" the small man asked.

"Yes" Matthew answered though he really didn't know what city it was and his mind was struggling to keep up.

"Come! Let us walk together. The distance may grow a friendship" he said smiling.

Matthew pushed himself from the rock. He didn't see that he had much choice. Before they had taken two steps together the bearded man asked, "What is your name?"

"Matthew" was all he could bring out.

"I am Levi. I lived in the city for many years but my wife and I moved to the house of my father after he died. I am going to see my brother and his family. They have lived in *Jerusalem* for many years. My brother and I buy and sell together. I go to deliver to him some money."

Matthew stopped. He was aware that the Levi paused before he said Jerusalem and noticed that he nodded his head as he said the word. While he was wondering over this strange movement, his mind reached back and he blurted out, "Jerusalem?"

"Yes, Jerusalem" he said turning to face him.

Again he noticed the man's head bob slightly over the name.

"The city of peace. Have you been there before?"

"No" Matthew answered while at the same time thinking, "Am I in Israel?"

This wasn't entirely true but for some reason he thought it was. Fortress Baptist Church had given Matthew and Melissa a trip a to Israel in celebration of their twenty years of ministry to the church and community. So, he had in fact, been to the holy land several years before. But somehow in all the confusion Matthew had answered "No" and for some reason decided to stand by his response.

"Are you well my friend?" Levi asked.

"Yes. Yes. I'm fine I think" Matthew said slowing his walk and looking in the direction of the city in disbelief.

"How can this be happening?" he thought. "Is this a dream? How can it be a dream? Everything seems so real!"

"Perhaps you are hungry. I have dates" Levi said stopping and leaning his staff against his chest in order to free his hands to open the bag that was slung over his shoulder. Reaching in, he pulled out a smaller bag and extended it toward Matthew. Matthew pulled out two dates while his mind struggled to keep up with what was going on.

"Thank you" he said quietly.

He slipped a date in his mouth. It was soft and very sweet and seemed to melt as his tongue pressed it against the roof of his mouth. Slowly he chewed it and swallowed.

"How could this be happening?" he thought again. "If this is a dream how can I be tasting food? How do I get out of this?"

"Come. The day does not wait for us" Levi said stepping in the direction of the city.

"How far is the city?" Matthew asked as he stepped to keep up with his guide.

"It is not far. We will see it as we crest this hill and turn with the road."

The two men began to walk together with Matthew's eyes taking in everything as his mind fought to process anything.

"Do you have family?" Levi asked.

A long pause followed. Finally, he answered, "Yes" seeing no harm in telling him that. "I have a wife named Melissa and a daughter name Terri. She and her husband are to have a child soon."

"Ah, that is exciting!" Levi offered. "Where is it that you are from?" he asked.

Before Matthew realized it he answered, "Frayton" then he coupled it with, "It's a very small town many miles west of here.

"You carry no bags?" Levi asked.

Matthew searched for an answer. "What do I say? I can't tell him about the car, the church, the accident." Without much thought, Matthew said, "I had bags but in my travel, I lost them."

"I am sorry to hear that my friend" said Levi. "I am sure that Jehovah will meet your needs."

"Yes, I am sure as well" Matthew said not really understanding what he was saying.

"Do you have business in the city Matthew?"

"No. I am just going to see what it is like" was all he could manage. "I am on a long journey discovering what the Lord would show me." Then he thought, "That's for sure!"

"Have you a place to stay?"

"Not yet" he said shaking his head slowly.

"Then you will come with me. We will visit my brother who will be blessed to see me." Levi smiled and winked at Matthew.

"Then we will go to the temple and we will be blessed to see it. It will be a good day for all of us."

"*THE* temple?" Matthew thought. "We're going to *THE* city of Jerusalem and we're going to *THE* temple?"

Matthew's knowledge of biblical history reminded him that the temple had been destroyed in A.D. 27. In its place or at least very close by stood a mosque.

"This is all too weird" he thought. "I think that this is the place in the movie where I say, 'I need a drink!'"

They passed small houses with flat roofs built very close together and Matthew noticed that as they walked the houses increased in number. When they topped the hill and rounded the bend, the city came into view.

Matthew stopped and stared. Up on the adjacent hill stood *The City.* It was massive, majestic, and mesmerizing. His eyes scanned from one end to the other. Most of the buildings were white and the formidable wall surrounding it shone in the bright sun.

Matthew stood still and breathed heavily. He tried to take it all in but struggled to conclude that all this was real.

"She is beautiful yes?" Levi broke in.

"Incredible" was all Matthew could say.

"Come. Let us enter the city of our God."

# Chapter 4
# The City

A half hour later Matthew and Levi were entering the city through the main gate. Matthew was beside himself with the wonder that began when he met Levi. "Could this really be happening? Am I going into *the* Jerusalem city? Did I really go back in time or is this the strangest dream anyone has ever had?" The gateway was lined with men sitting on either side of the entrance way. The men were dressed very well with colorful turbans or head pieces. They donned long robes of various fabrics and colors. All of the men had long beards and sideburns which were equally long and curled. He saw several the men bearing what he knew to be phylacteries. Some of the men had dozens of them rimming the bottom of their robe. He knew they must be Pharisees or some other kind of holy men. The men had been engrossed in conversation but all was quiet when the two strangers made their way through the gauntlet.

Matthew could feel their eyes on them. He normally didn't become intimidated easily but in this venue he found himself feeling extremely self-conscious. Levi how, ever didn't seem to be bothered at all. He smiled and took Matthew by the arm, leaned into him and whispered, "My friend, we are in the company of nobodies who tell everybody and anybody that they are somebody. Do not be alarmed." With that he escorted Matthew through the opening and into the city square.

The entire city was alive with activity. Every part of the streets was paved with cobble stones that seemed centuries old. Vendors had their carts lining the edges of the street. They were filled with fruit, vegetables, fish, bread, fabric and a host of other things. And the noise! Each of the vendors was shouting to all who would listen advertising their wares. Matthew found it hard to think but was enjoying all the activity just the same. When he looked up he saw plants on the edges of balconies and clothing hanging over the sides of the white-washed walls. "My brother and his wife live only a short walk from here. They are expecting me but they will be glad to meet you" Levi shouted above the crowd.

As they made their way along the bustling street they saw a commotion up ahead. People were shouting and Matthew noticed the crowd begin to part as some horses came down the street. From in front of Matthew, Levi used his arm to brush Matthew back and to the side. Moments later Matthew saw several soldiers whom he knew were Romans guide their steeds through the throng. As they went by Matthew could hear the people jeer and curse shaking their fists and spitting on the ground. The soldiers paid them no attention but kept moving among the angry mob.

As the soldiers went past the two men, Levi turned slightly to Matthew winked and said, "More nobodies who want to be somebodies. But these have weapons my good friend. We must be careful! More and more of the soldiers are in the city ever since the Savior died."

"The Savior?" Matthew surprised himself with the question.

"Yes. The Savior. Have you not heard of Jesus?"

"Well, yes I have. In fact…" Matthew was about to say more than he knew Levi could handle.

Levi continued, "Ever since that horrible day the Romans have been in the city in large numbers. There have been several uprisings and threats of more crucifixions. Everyone is nervous. Even the religious leaders are on guard. Several of them have been brought in before the authorities. We do not know where all this will lead."

"Were you there?" Matthew asked before he had a chance to stop himself.

Levi looked down. "Yes. I was there. And I have never lived such a terrible day. I will never forget it. Come, let us sit a few moments."

He led Matthew around a corner and into what Matthew would call a café. The two men sat down and Levi's face took on a sudden mixture of sadness and caution. A young woman working at the café approached the table immediately. Levi held up two fingers and ordered something Matthew had never heard of. The woman nodded and retreated. Levi looked around a couple of times and then began.

"I first met the Master two years ago. I had heard of him but never took much interest in another teacher out in the hills. I kept hearing of miraculous healings and other signs. I heard of some of the sayings he was sharing and great explanations of the sacred writings. A few confrontations were reported between Jesus and his followers and the religious leaders." Matthew leaned in. Levi again looked around seeming to be less cautious and continued.

"I remember when I first saw him. My brother and I were traveling to my home after spending the night in the city. Up ahead we saw a large crowd. As we got closer we could see many scribes and Pharisees gathered around a man we had never seen before. It was Jesus. I am not sure what I was expecting but he somehow looked different than I thought he would be. He looked strong, like a man who was no stranger to hard work. He was of average height and somewhat handsome but plain. He did not dress as the Rabbi's do. He wore a simple white robe with a brown sash. His head was uncovered and his beard was shorter than most of the teachers."

Matthew nodded encouragement to his new friend. "My brother and I got closer and we could hear the leaders yelling at Jesus. We were surprised that Jesus did not yell back. He simply waited until they were finished and responded. We only heard a few words but whatever he said seemed to please some and anger others. We heard several comments from the crowd. Some were amazed and began discussing his comments. Others, like the Pharisees, seemed disgusted and shook their heads. Jesus moved toward the city and some walked away. But a large group followed him as he walked."

"We walked with him a short distance as well. We heard him talk about righteous living, caring for the poor and faith. He said that a small amount of faith would bring great results." Levi paused a moment as the young woman brought their order. The drinks were in a small cup. Like a coffee cup without a handle. He leaned over the cup and smelled it. It had the aroma of sweet tea but looked dark. Cautiously he sipped the mixture. It was sweet but Matthew detected a very slight flavor of mint. It was very good and Matthew tried to hide his surprise and acted as normal as possible. The woman asked the men if they desired anything else then walked away when Levi shook his head. He began again.

Levi pointed to a wall a few feet away and said, "We were this close to Jesus and we could hear every word he said." Matthew nodding in understanding. "While he was comparing faith to a mustered seed a woman beside us called out. I still remember her words. She said, 'Jesus! Can you help my son?' Jesus stopped talking and looked in the woman's direction. I could see on his face that he had located her and he nodded in her direction. The crowd parted, stepping away from the woman and Jesus extended his hand motioning the woman to come forward. The woman approached the Master with her arm around her small son. He looked to be seven or eight years old. His right arm was poorly bandaged and he walked toward Jesus staying close to his mother.

She explained to Jesus that her son had injured his arm a couple of weeks ago while helping his father repair the wheel on their wagon. Something had slipped cutting him with a piece of jagged metal. They had seen the physician and had it treated. At first it seemed to get better but now it was much worse. Jesus nodded that he understood and extended his hand toward the injured arm. The boy lifted his arm and Jesus began to unwrap it. I was close enough to see that the wrappings were stained with blood and that the wound was still raw." Levi leaned toward Matthew, rubbed his beard and his face took on the look of nausea. "Then I smelled it. It was horrible. I could see the wound clearly and knew that the boy's flesh was rotting. Several others in the crowd noticed it too and I watched many of them take a step back and shake their heads." Matthew grimaced with the description. He never felt comfortable around the sight of blood and it showed on his face.

"But Jesus never flinched. He threw the bandages away as if to say, 'We will not need these again.' I could not hear him speak but I watched him look upward and saw his lips move. He turned the boys arm over and rubbed the uninjured side three times. Then my friend, he turned the arm over again and it was healed. I have never seen anything like it in my life. Some of the crowd gasped while others cheered. My brother and I stood there in silence trying to understand what we had just seen." Levi clapped his hands and sat back in his chair. "It was a miracle. It was a genuine miracle! The woman fell at Jesus' feet and kept saying 'Thank you, thank you, thank you!' The boy hugged the Master and the crowd moved on with Jesus toward the city."

"My brother and I wanted to join them but decided to continue on home. We talked about it the entire way. I couldn't wait to tell my wife what we had seen. We both wished we could have heard more of what the Master was saying and agreed that we would go to hear him again when we learned where he was." Levi picked up his cup with both hands, raised his eyebrows, and sipped. The men sat there for several seconds in silence. Matthew felt pangs of jealousy creep into his heart. "To actually talk to someone who saw Jesus. This is incredible!" he mused keeping his thoughts to himself.

The men finished their drinks with Matthew wishing for more. They stood and Levi reached into his sleeve and slid the cord of a small bag over his wrist and hand. He opened the sack and removing two small coins. He stacked them on the table and Matthew followed him out thanking Levi as they walked. The streets were as busy as ever and the noise seemed to grow as they moved along.

# Chapter 5
# Isaac & Miriam

Shortly, they reached the house where Levi's brother and his wife lived. It was more of an apartment than a house. Like all the other dwellings it was whitewashed and shared a common wall with the two homes on each side. Levi knocked but then opened the door leading into the house. A man rose from the table immediately and strode across the room. He was thin and average height and wore a robe that was more of a house coat. Matthew noticed that it did not have the common sash he had seen on so many men. His beard was shorter than Levi's and didn't carry as much grey. "Levi!" The two men embraced and while holding Levi close he said, "How good it is to see you! You are too much a stranger my brother!" Levi returned the comment with a hug. "And these tired eyes are so glad to see you too, my brother and my friend." Matthew stood by the door enjoying the scene when a woman came from another room. She was short and slightly on the plump side. She had a round face that seemed to light up when she entered the room. Her robe was blue and she donned a matching kerchief on her head. "Levi! How good it is to see you!" He released his brother and hugged the woman. "Ah, Miriam! The woman the world is blessed to have!"

"Such love and affection. Such a greeting" Matthew thought. He remembered that Levi mentioned that he had not seen his brother or wife in a couple of weeks and smiled as he thought, "They make it seem like years since they've been together."

Matthew watched Miriam turn to him. Her smile never left her face as she asked, "And who is this man you have brought with you?" Levi turned in Matthew's direction extending a hand toward him. "This is my new friend Matthew. We have traveled on the road together." Miriam gave a single nod in Matthew's direction while still smiling. "You are with Levi and will always have a place here." Levi stepped toward the man, put his arm around his shoulder and patted his chest with an open hand. "And this. This is my favorite brother Isaac." Isaac walked over to Matthew and gave him a hug. "My brother failed to mention that I am his only brother and that I am his younger brother." Then turning to Levi he said, "And I always will be!" Levi joined his brother in laughing then Levi answered, "When I was born our parents were so overjoyed they wanted to have another one of me and that is how Isaac came to be." Isaac chuckled shook his head and said, "When Levi was born our parents thought 'We can do better than this!' And that is how I came to be." The two men continued their embrace chuckling over their much used comments.

Miriam broke in. "Matthew, we are honored to have you here. While these two fools chatter on would you like to sit down? I have some fresh fruit from the market. Matthew looked around but saw no chairs in the room. In fact, he only saw a short table in the middle so he made his way to a side room that held a bench, three chairs and a small table. He sat down on the edge of the bench in what was obviously the kitchen. Shortly, Miriam placed a wooden bowl of fruit in front of him. The bowl was filled with grapes, figs, dates, and what looked like oranges. When Matthew tasted each of them he thought, "So fresh! I have never tasted fruit like this before."

Miriam stood near the opposite wall. She smiled as Matthew pressed an entire date in his mouth. "Tell me Matthew, where are you from?" The question caught Matthew off guard but the food in his mouth bought him a few seconds to think. He gave her the same answer he had shared with Levi earlier that day. "My wife and I live in a small town called Frayton. It is many miles west of here." Hoping to cut off further questions he added, "We have a daughter who is also married and lives with her husband not far from our home. Miriam smiled. "Jehovah has been good to you."

"He sure has and I'm afraid I am guilty of not being thankful enough."

"I too am guilty of that" she added. "And what is it that brings you to the Holy City?"

Another question Matthew wasn't ready for. He thought of giving a witty answer and saying "My feet" but then realized she might not understand or be a fan of his sarcastic sense of humor. So he side-stepped an outright lie and said, "It has always been a dream of mine to see Jerusalem. Life is too busy and moves too fast so I thought that I must go before my legs are too old and weak to carry me." The thought of mentioning the words "bucket list" were quickly dismissed.

The woman smiled. "I understand. Too much water passes before we take time to drink." What an awesome comment" Matthew thought. "I should write that down."

Miriam stepped into the other room and Matthew heard their voices drop to the level just above a whisper. He heard words like "meeting, stranger, tonight and the Master." He knew they were talking about him and wasn't surprised. Every few seconds one of them would look in his direction and when his eyes caught those of Isaac he saw him smile. He knew soon he would discover the content of their conversation.

Moments later, the huddle broke up. The three came into the room and joined Matthew at the table. Levi began the conversation,

"My friend, we have something we must ask you. Please do not be offended, but we must know some things about you."

Matthew leaned in. His nod gave them permission to continue.

Levi took a deep breath and looked around more out of habit that necessity.

"You have told me that you have heard about the Master."

"Yes. Yes, I have."

"What do you know about Him?"

Matthew's mind cautiously raced. He wanted to tell them so much but knew they wouldn't, they couldn't, believe him. With all that was going on, he was struggling with his own concept of what was real. The reality was that he was now living two thousand years before he was born. He had to resist telling them that he had read the Bible and knew all the stories about Jesus. Being a preacher and going to seminary couldn't be mentioned. Even words like church, congregation, and ministry had to be left out. In a very creative way, he had to tell them the results of what happened without telling them the details of what actually occurred. This called for all the creative juices Matthew's mind could summon.

He started slowly with three pairs of eyes glued on him. "Several years, I mean months ago a friend of mine invited me to a meeting where a special speaker would be giving a message. I didn't have anything else to do so I joined him. The room was crowded but I saw several of my friends there. They had a group of people singing and someone prayed before the crowd. The speaker spoke about Jesus and told several stories about what Jesus did and what he taught. He spoke about sin and forgiveness and asked if anyone wanted to come forward and ask Jesus to rule his heart." That phrase brought confusion to the faces of his new friends so Matthew raced back into his mind and grabbed another phrase. "He asked if any of us wanted to surrender our lives to the obedience of Christ and be named a follower of his."

Isaac couldn't resist. He leaned forward and broke in, "And what did you do?" Matthew took a deep breath and said, "I knew I was a sinner in need of forgiveness and so I raised my hand. Several others did the same and we were asked to stand and go to a side room. In the room we broke into groups of two with a counselor, instructor in each group. We were shown what the Bible, I mean the word of God says about what we needed to do. The instructor led us in a prayer and that night I asked the Lord to be my Savior."

"I knew it!" Levi said clapping his hands. "I knew you were one of his followers! My heart told me so!" The broad smiles of the other two displayed equal joy and in a strange way brought relief to Matthew. Isaac put a hand on Matthew's shoulder and said, "We are brothers, yes?" "Yes we are!" Matthew said smiling as he nodded.

Miriam's voice still carried an air of celebration when she said, "Now you must find out where the meeting is tonight. We have a new family member who must come with us. "Yes" Levi said. "The meeting tonight." Matthew was a bit confused but felt no alarm.

Within an hour Matthew and Levi were back in the center of the city square. They spoke little as Levi moved to different locations among the crowd and Matthew followed. They would stand near a group and simply listen to the conversations. Matthew thought this was strange but there seemed to be no surprise or resistance from any of the groups. They heard comments about crops, family, the city, rain, the temple, the Romans. It was clear to Matthew that Levi was waiting for something to be said about Jesus but no comments were made regarding him.

When they reached the fifth group it seemed as though Levi was becoming impatient. The men were talking about the Romans. All of them evidenced disgust and were united in their anger toward them. Levi waited for a pause in the flow of comments and simply asked, "My friends, did you witness the crucifixion?" Without details, everyone knew which crucifixion Levi meant. None of the men seemed surprised and a couple of them nodded that they were there. Then the comments came. "He was another confused teacher" said a man who appeared to be the oldest in the circle. Another one commented, "I heard many of the things he said. None of them called for the loss of his life." Three men commented simultaneously about their feelings about Jesus. Then Matthew saw a man across from them look directly at Levi and slowly nod twice. Levi's eyes never left the man. He reached over to Matthew and grabbed his wrist, squeezing firmly. The pressure on his wrist told Matthew that they were on to something. The men stayed in the circle for a few minutes listening to comments about Jesus but not entering into the conversation. "He could have cost us our peace with the Roman dogs!" "The Pharisees and Sadducees were only jealous. They were anxious about their standing with the people." "His followers died out just like so many others." None of the comments appeared to be strange to Matthew. They were reacting exactly as he expected.

Tapping Matthew on the back of his arm, the two men left the group without a word. They made their way across the square and stood in the corner between two empty vendor's carts. The aroma around them was stifling. Fish! The cart had not been cleaned out and the former merchandise left its foul unmistakable scent. Matthew silently wished they had picked a different place to stand but Levi didn't seem to mind. "We will be free to talk here" was all Levi needed to say to clue Matthew in to his friend's choice of a waiting place.

Before long, the nodding man made his way across the square and approached them. He looked to be middle-aged and wore a white robe with a black sash. His head was uncovered showing long brown hair with a few streaks of gray. He had a slight limp and carried a cane which he leaned on as he strode toward them.

"Shalom my friends!"

"Shalom" the men replied.

"The day is warm, yes?"

"It is warm, but always a good day in the city of Jehovah" Levi countered.

Matthew knew his best posture was one of silence and said nothing as the men talked.

"I am Jonas."

The men shook hands. "Levi. And this is my friend Matthew."

"Do you live in the city?"

"No, my wife and I live in a small village a days' walk from here. I am here visiting my brother."

"Ah, family and friends" he said nodding in Matthew's direction, "Treasures to be sought and enjoyed."

"Yes" Levi said smiling.

"Friends and family can give you comfort and direction" he added.

Then he took the end of his cane in both hands and stepped back a half step. He leaned down slightly and drew a curved line in the dirt. "Friends and family can get you from here and help you get to there."

Matthew saw a broad smile come to Levi's face. He reached for the man's cane and said, "They can also help you go from here back to where you need to be." With that he scraped the ground with the end of the cane making a mark from one end of the curve downward and crossing the other end of the curve.

Matthew immediately recognized the figure. It was the outline of a fish and it came to be a symbol of the followers of Christ. He had read about it being used as a code but now he was actually seeing it in play. He fought to keep silent and to stifle his excitement. The man grinned, nodded, and touched Levi's shoulder. He looked over both shoulders quickly and turned back to the men. "Come" was all he said.

The three of them moved quickly through the crowd. They left the square and gathered by the wall of the city. People moved passed them but none of them very close to the trio.

"Tonight we meet again" Jonas said. "East of here, outside the city in the area called Bethahn. Do you know it?"

"Yes" Levi said. "And the time?"

"After sundown. When you enter the village you will go passed the well. You will walk until you come to a broken cart in the street. The handle of the cart will point to the house where we will be."

Levi nodded.

Jonas looked over both shoulders again.

"I will see you there my friends" he said shaking each of their hands.

Then he leaned forward and whispered, "He lives!"

Levi and Matthew both smiled and Levi said, "He lives!"

With that Jonas turned and limped away being lost in the crowd almost immediately.

Turning to Matthew and putting his hand on his shoulder, Levi smiled and said, "We have a place to be tonight my good friend!"

Matthew nodded, "I can't wait!" He had never spoken truer words. He felt his stomach move with excitement. He was going to *church* tonight! But he knew this would not be like any other church he had been to. "This is the real deal" he thought as the two men turned and began working their way back to Isaac and Miriam's place.

# Chapter 6
# The Meeting

Back at the house Levi was quick to tell the other two about their encounter. They shared his excitement and looked forward to the meeting that evening. Later that day they ate a simple meal of fish, bread, and figs. Matthew couldn't help but think that he had never tasted food so fresh, so good.

When it was time to leave for the meeting the four of them exited the home and then, to avoid suspicion they left the city through separate gates. Matthew and Levi through one and Isaac and Miriam through another. They met at the crossroads and traveled to the village together.

As they walked Matthew thought of all the *prayer meetings* he had been to over the years. So many times they were heavy in meeting and light in prayer. Often, during a time of sharing, it became a *top the testimony* time. Many times people carried a *look at me* attitude. He had a very strong feeling that tonight it would be a *look at Him* kind of meeting.

Levi knew that Matthew would not be familiar with the type of meeting they were to attend so he tried to fill in the blanks. "We will be in someone's house. It will not look like the synagogue and the Pharisees and Sadducees will not be there unless they have become part of *The Way*." Matthew had heard that term before and understood it to be used in describing the early formation of believers. He knew they would not be called *Christians* or *Little Christs* until the church was more formally organized. He also knew that it was at Antioch that the label was given and accepted by the followers of Christ.

Levi continued, "No one, not even the host will be recognized as more or less than anyone else. We will all be on the same level, men and women, old and young. Someone will have been invited to share though I do not know who. Then others may be invited to share their experiences with the Lord." If Matthew was unsure about what to expect, the words of Levi had put him at ease.

They found the well and the broken cart just as expected. The house the handle pointed to was average size. It had a flat roof like most homes and even in the fading light they could see that it was in need of repair. Some of the plaster had popped off and it was missing a couple of shutters. They approached the house and Isaac knocked gently. A woman opened the door slightly and peered out. "We have been invited by Jonas" Levi offered. Without speaking a word, the woman opened the door and the four of them entered.

To the left of the door was a small table that held a wash basin half filled with water. The room they entered was void of any furniture. It was obvious that it had been cleared to make room for those who would attend. And attend they did! The room was almost completely filled with people. It was impossible to move without bumping into someone. Even so, there seemed to be a welcoming air about those who were gathered. The four of them worked their way to the far wall and faced what looked like the front of the room. Everyone was talking though they were doing their best to keep their voices down to avoid attracting attention from the street. Matthew looked over and saw Jonas at the far end of the room. Their eyes met and they exchanged waves and smiles.

A few minutes later a man stepped to the center of the far wall. He looked fairly young and Matthew guessed he was in his late twenties. He was dressed in the traditional way with a loosely fitted brown robe, white sash, and sandals. His head was uncovered and he sported a close-cropped beard and shoulder length hair. When he began to speak immediately the room grew quiet.

"Shalom my friends!"

"Shalom!" the room responded in unison.

"My name is James and I come to you from the sacred city of Jerusalem."

"James" Matthew thought. "Could this be James, the brother of John, one of the disciples? This is incredible!"

"I want to welcome you to a gathering of The Called Out Ones. We come tonight simply to give account of the time we spent with the Master." He smiled broadly as the room gave him their full attention.

"My mind remembers meeting Jesus as if it happened yesterday. My brother John and I were with our father. We were all fishermen.

Things were going well and our father had just expanded his business to include another boat and some hired hands. In fact, our nets had become so full that they needed to be repaired in several places, a good problem to have but a problem nonetheless."

Matthew looked around the room. No one was moving and each stood in rapt attention as James continued.

"My brother was joking with me about tying better knots when he stopped in mid-sentence. He was looking over my shoulder and I saw his face take on a serious look. When I turned around, there stood, Jesus on the hill about ten yards from us. He had several men with him and even a few ladies. He had long flowing hair and a full, but short beard. We had heard a little about him and knew him to be a good teacher, even a Rabbi although he didn't look like the other Rabbis. His face was warm and friendly even inviting. He smiled at us and said, 'You work to find fish to fill men's bellies, but I work to find men and fill their souls.' We both dropped the net and stood to face him. He said, 'Come and follow me and I will show you how to fish for men.'

"Without us knowing it, our father had come up from the boat and joined us. Our father was a strong and good man, but not an outwardly religious man. He went to the synagogue on the Sabbath and the temple during required times, but for the most part he kept his beliefs to himself and worked hard all his life. He taught us to work hard as well, to obey the commandments, and to live honorably. He asked Jehovah for a good catch and thanked Him when it came."

"Jesus looked at him and nodded. I saw my father nod back to him slowly. Both John and I turned to our father. He must have seen the look on our faces and knew what we were thinking. Without a word he pointed his head in Jesus' direction signaling to us his approval and for us to go with the Master if we desired. John stepped toward Jesus and I followed. I didn't join Jesus because John did. I joined Jesus because something inside me drew me to him. Even as a young man full of hope and promise with work in the family business, I knew there was something missing. There had to be a greater purpose for my life than to work the boats on the lake and try to catch more and more fish. The boats, the net, the market were all we needed when we were young boys, but somehow they had lost their attraction. Later I learned that John felt the same way. We both knew that being with Jesus would give us what we secretly were looking for."

For just a few seconds, Matthew's mind raced back to the time when he surrendered to Christ. He was only fifteen at the time but he was certain he knew what he was doing. When the preacher asked if anyone wanted to ask Christ to forgive them for their sins he knew it was what he wanted. He raised his hand and moments later stood to join others in a side room to pray *The sinner's prayer* and invite Christ to be Lord of his life. He too felt the pull that James was describing. James continued and Matthew's mind immediately came back to his voice.

"We were not planning on joining Jesus permanently. We both thought that if we spent a few weeks, maybe a month with him we would learn about *fishing for men* and the inner needs of our hearts would be met. But the more time we spent with the Savior, the more we wanted to be with him and the deeper our relationship grew with him. Everywhere we went we heard teaching like we had never heard before. We laughed with him and learned from him. There was so much about him we found hard to explain. He was so loving and caring to everyone we met, yet he was confident when he spoke of the heavenly Father and the sacred book." A few voices called out quietly, "Praise Jehovah!" and "Glory to God!"

"And the things we saw him do, the miracles, they always got our attention and the attention of those around us. In fact, many were following him to see the signs that he would show us. I noticed that most times he would perform a miracle and follow it with a profound spiritual teaching. The sick would come to him, he would pray over them, place a hand on them, and they would be well. Then he would tell us a story of God's love for us, the importance of faith, or the way to find peace."

"One day we were walking along a path on the edge of a village. A woman approached us saying that she was a widow and in need of food. Jesus stopped and told the woman to hold out her hands. He bent down and picked up some small stones, three twigs, and a couple of leaves. He held them up took a deep breath and said, 'Thank you Father!' I was standing right next to him my friends. And when he placed them in the woman's hands they had become meat, lettuce, and bread. All of us, including the woman were without words. He placed his hand on her shoulder and looked at all of us and said, 'Do not be anxious. Do not fear. Only believe.'

The woman thanked him deeply and turned toward her home.

We all watched her leave. She moved as if her feet did not touch the ground. Jesus pointed to a small but beautiful flower along the path. He knelt down and pulled it up. He smiled as he held it up and said, 'My children. Our Heavenly Father has made each flower for his enjoyment and yours. And though they carry such beauty and show such care he has for them, you must know that he cares more for you and is more willing to provide for you.' Then he said those words again, 'Do not be anxious. Do not fear. Only believe.'"

Now the room was filled with "He is Lord, He is the Christ" and "Praise be to our God!" When things seemed to quiet down a bit James spoke up again. "Are there any others here who have walked with the Lord?"

For a few moments no one spoke. James did not show any signs of uneasiness as the silence settled over the group. Then an elderly man spoke. He had a cane and held it up as if to speak with more impact. "I saw the Master. I am Joell. I am by trade a physician. I had a man in my care who I sought with everything I knew to make well. He was not an aged man but he suffered from weakness, dizziness, and pains so great in his head they brought nausea. I treated him for many months but he only seemed to get worse. Even my associates could do little for him. He was quickly loosing hope. He lived in a village several miles from where I was. While on my way to his house one day I encountered Jesus just outside of my town. I had never seen him before but had heard so much about him that I knew this must be him. He was speaking to some children and was surrounded by a small crowd. I intended to walk past them but he looked up and caught my eye. I slowed down as I walked by but never took my eyes off of him. The entire group watched me as I moved. Then he spoke to me. He simply said, 'My friend, do not hurry. The man you go to see will be well when you get there. He is healthy and whole. Praise Jehovah for what he has done.'

The man looked down and seemed slightly ashamed. He shook his head slowly a few times and then with tears rimming his eyes continued. "I walked for over an hour wondering what his words could mean. As I walked up the small hill to the man's house he met me. He looked almost entirely different. His eyes had a life in them that I had not seen in many months. He was smiling and began laughing as he talked. He told me that less than an hour before he began to feel better. His wife prepared some food for him and he ate it and felt his strength return.

As the moments went by he felt his health return to him."

The physician looked at the crowd and paused a moment. It was clear that he desired to tell them something and wanted to choose his words carefully. "My friends, this was a man who had lost all hope of being healthy again. This was a man that I knew would not be alive much longer. This was a man I had no hope in curing. But because of the words of Jesus, this is a man who lives today and is healthy and strong. Jesus is *The Great Physician*!"

The room erupted in cheers and applause. The caution that had governed their excitement was lifted and all who were gathered there sought to give enthusiastic praise to God. Knowing that the volume of noise might attract those in the street, James motioned for silence.

"Another has come who has had the touch of the Master. "This is Zachariah. He is a fellow believer and has a testimony of what the Master did for him. The room was filled with applause. A man stood up, meandered through the crowd and joined James. James hugged him and sat down.

Zachariah smiled broadly. "I am Zachariah from the tribe of Judah. As you know, Judah means praise and I am here to testify to the name of my tribe. I have much about which to praise the Savior! For thirty-eight years I had no feeling in my feet and legs. When you are a certain way for so long you become accustomed to it. You accept it and give up on any hope of changing it."

"My family brought me each day to my normal spot by the pool near the sheep gate. We each had our own place. Many people would come down to the pool to bathe and some would often hand us a small gift. It was never much, just enough to help us a little and ease their minds a good bit."

"There was a tale that said when the waters stirred, Yahweh's Spirit was present and whoever got into the waters first, they would be healed. Because of my legs, I was never able to enter the water in time. It did not matter however, because I never knew of anyone being healed from it. Sometimes we believe things because we want them to be so."

"One morning, on the Sabbath, a group of men came by the pool. We noticed them immediately and had hopes that they would give us some alms. I didn't know any of them and thought they came to bathe. When they came closer my hope of a few coins was lost as I saw they were not wealthy men. In truth they looked more like beggars than some of us did."

"The group stopped in front of me. The leader asked, 'Do you want to be made well?' I thought it was such a foolish question. Of course I did! Or did I? My friends, begging is not a good life, but it is not the worst either. I was carried by my family to the pool. I was given food for the day. I had my place and my friends with their struggles by my side. I had no responsibilities, no appointments, no one to expect anything of me. It is truly not the worst life to be had."

"But all that changed when this man Jesus came to me. My only hope in healing centered around the pool so I told him I had no way of getting in. He bent down and leaned into me. I can still feel his breath and hear his words in my ear. He was simple and direct. He said, 'Get up! Pick up your mat and walk.'"

"Immediately, I felt my feet tingle. I had not felt anything in my feet for years. Then my knees began to vibrate. I bent my knees" He shook his head, "Without my hands! I sat up and then rolled to my side. Then I stood up. I stood up! Those by the pool and those with Jesus clapped their hands. I bent down and picked up my mat. I was crying with joy! There was a great celebration!"

"But there were two men watching from the steps on the other side of the pool. They were Pharisees and they were not happy. They came to me and told me that I was wrong to pick up my pallet on the Sabbath. That didn't matter to me. I told them that the man who healed me commanded me to and I obeyed. They wanted to know who it was but when I turned to point him out he was gone!"

"I went into the temple. It had been many decades since I had been there. Inside the court of the Jews I saw him! He turned to me when I came up behind him and just smiled. I fell before his feet and kept repeating to him, *Thank you! Thank you!* He brought me to my feet and encouraged me to live a sinless life. He said, sin can cause something worse to happen to me."

"I was not certain but perhaps somehow he knew what had caused me to lose the use of my legs. When I was but a boy, a friend of mine and I got into a potter's shed by climbing through the opening in his roof. We took two or three pots and sold them in the next village. Over several weeks we had taken many pots and vessels. One day he saw us on the roof and yelled. When I turned to run, I slipped and fell to the ground injuring my back and losing the use of my legs. For thirty-eight years I had been unable to walk."

Matthew immediately felt bad for the man. As a boy, he had his share of mischief. He thought of the time he and two friends siphoned gas from a neighbor's car. They also made a game of breaking out windows from the back of a warehouse one Saturday afternoon. They never got caught and never suffered for it. Here stood a man who was punished for thirty-eight years simply for being a foolish boy. It seemed unfair to Matthew.

But there was more to Zachariah's story. "Today I am a merchant. One of my clients from my village is the son of the old man we stole from all those years ago. He is still making and selling pottery. God has a sense of humor my friends!" Matthew smiled and whispered, "Yes he does my friend!"

Zachariah moved back to his place as the crowd applauded. James held his hands up again and the crowd quickly became quiet. He said, "My brothers and sisters, I have no doubt there are others here who have met the Savior. But the hour moves on and we must bring our time together to a close. As we end our time here I want you to know that the cross still saves, the tomb is still empty and still my friends, still he lives." Everyone in the room quietly yet firmly said, "He still lives."

Without prompting each person placed a hand on the shoulder of someone nearby. It was quiet for a moment as if they were waiting for someone to bring things to a close. Then one man in the corner began to sing. As he started a few others joined in until the entire group was singing the well known passage of Scripture, "Hear, O Israel. The Lord is our God. The Lord alone." They sang the phrase three times and all ended together. It was some of the most beautiful singing and heartfelt words Matthew had ever heard. Matthew knew the passage very well. It was known as *The Shammah*. But now he believed that it would have new meaning for him the rest of his life.

All those gathered began to hug one another and a great feeling of love and care filled the room. Then James held both hands above the crowd and broke in. "My friends, it is now time for us to depart. Please go with the blessings of our Lord and Savior, Jesus Christ. It was he who gave his life as a sacrifice for the sins of the world. And may his peace rule and reign in your hearts and minds. Amen and Amen." The crowd responded with a hearty "Amen" and the group exited in groups of two or three by way of both the front and back doors.

Matthew and his three new friends talked all the way home. The trip back to the house flew by. Before he knew it Matthew was under a sheepskin blanket on a makeshift bed on the roof of the house. The pillow his head rested on was filled with goose feathers and he sunk deep into it. His fingers were locked behind his head as he looked up at the stars. They were so clear and bright and so close. It looked as if he could just reach out and grab a handful. "How could all of this be happening?" Earlier today, or last night, or two thousand years from now he was in his office trying to keep a couple together. Now he was in Jerusalem a few weeks after the resurrection trying to keep his mind together. His brain argued within himself. "It has to be a dream! Maybe he was in a coma from the collision. Perhaps he would wake up in the hospital and he could get his life back to normal." But normal wasn't what he wanted. What was happening he knew was real even though he found no way to explain it.

His mind bounced back and forth between these and other thoughts. Finally, they settled on Melissa. "Oh, Melissa. I wish she could be here" he thought. "Unless this is in fact a dream, she must be wondering where I am. She must be worried." He felt his heart ache as he mused over his love for his wife. "I have to get back to her! There must be a way to wake up, move to another dimension, travel through time, or do whatever it takes to return to my bride!"

As he pondered these thoughts he moved his right hand from behind his head and stroked the side of his face. "And a beard!" Melissa never liked him to have any facial hair even when he neglected to shave while on vacation. He smiled as he thought, "What would she think of this?" His smile slowly faded as his heart felt the sting of missing the woman that he was so in love with. He moved his hand from his beard and wiped a small tear rolling down the side of his head and drifted off to sleep.

# Chapter 7
# The Master's Touch

The sun was working its way over the short wall and across the floor when Matthew awoke the next day. He opened his eyes expecting to see the usual sights in his bedroom. He was confused and had to quickly recall the former events which led him to the cot on which he lay. "It wasn't a dream! I'm still in Jerusalem" he thought as he gazed around the roof.

He made his way down the narrow steps and found the three sitting at the small table in the kitchen. They had been talking quietly and all turned and smiled at him as he entered the room. "Good morning!" he said returning their smiles.

"Shalom" the three offered.

"Are you rested?" Miriam asked.

"Yes. I slept well. I fell asleep with last night's meeting on my mind."

"I think we all did" Isaac replied.

Miriam rose and poured a cup of what looked and smelled like coffee and extended it to Matthew. He smiled and nodded a thank you and joined them at the table.

"Today I leave for my home. Will you join me Matthew?" Levi said.

"I would be honored" Matthew responded understanding that he had few options. "When will we leave?"

"We will have a bite to eat and go by the temple. We will depart from the city before the sun gets too strong."

Matthew nodded. "The temple!" He thought. "I'm actually going to the temple!" It was almost too much for him to take in and he hid a slight smile behind his hand and thought, "This is amazing! It shouldn't take too long to pack."

With hugs and rich blessings from the other two Matthew and Levi found themselves working their way through the crowd in the street.

Matthew was a step behind Levi as he led him to the gate. He was bumped a couple of times and thought "Rush hour!" The thought brought a smile that Levi couldn't see so he didn't bother to hide.

A half hour later they stood below the temple steps. They took their time in climbing up and stood on the platform connected to *the Court of the Gentiles*. Matthew did a poor job in hiding his excitement. The two of them stood and faced the city. "Only those blessed by Jehovah stand here my friend!" Matthew but said nothing.

They walked through a very large area where several officials sat examining some animals and exchanging regular coins for temple coins. For a short time, they stood and watched the activity of both the officials and the people who brought in animals for sacrifice and coins for exchange.

The two men turned and walked across the large stones passing through both *the Court of the Gentiles* and *the Court of Women*. Matthew knew that as a non-Jew, he was forbidden to go past the area designated for Gentiles but he pressed that out of his mind. They entered *the Court of the Jews*. It was a large open area filled with men even at such an early hour. They stood with their backs to several massive marble columns and Matthew kept looking around staring in wonder at everything he saw. The entire area was made of marble, silver, gold, large gems, and carved stone. At each corner was a large brass container sitting on top of a marble pedestal. Matthew's suspicions of what it was were confirmed when he saw several men pass by and drop a few coins in one of the bowls. It made a loud clanging sound that could be heard throughout the great room.

Matthew had read that a sort of *game* was often played among those wealthy enough to participate. It was called *rounding the temple*. Those of means would take a bag of coins and walk around the temple area. As they came to one of the containers they would drop a coin in to the applause of those gathered. Then they would go to the next one and do the same. The goal was to see who could make the most trips around the temple court dropping a coin as they passed each container. It was the height of pride and the idea always irritated Matthew. "So much for not letting the right hand know what the left hand was doing" he often thought.

At the far end of the court was an altar. Many were kneeling in front of it engaged in prayer. Behind the altar was a room that Matthew knew held the sacrificial altar. It is where animal sacrifices were made. He could only imagine how busy this place would be and how much blood flowed during the holy days.

A large curtain hanging from the ceiling marked off the area behind the sacrificial altar. This was *The Holy of Holies*. From his reading, Matthew knew the curtain to be at least four inches thick. That sight brought new meaning to the tearing of the barrier at the crucifixion of Jesus. He wanted to share this insight with Levi but was sure that would bring nothing but confusion. He also knew he was forbidden to be where he currently was, but understood that to enter that area, for anyone besides the High Priest, meant certain death by stoning. Still, his heart ached to pull back the massive curtain and look inside.

The men stood in the court for several minutes watching all the activity. After awhile, Levi stepped forward and approached one of the brass containers. Matthew watched him slip his purse from his sleeve and pull out three coins. He looked upward without saying anything. Then he dropped the coins in the container and walked back toward Matthew. "Perhaps a small amount of good will be done with that" he said as he patted Matthew on the back. The two men walked out of the temple area in silence.

When they reached the city gate, there stood some Pharisees, Sadducees and other city leaders. They didn't greet the men with the hard stares they encountered when they entered the day before and Matthew guessed it was because they were leaving and not coming. Still, he noticed the conversation died down as they passed. Again he felt some residual uneasiness.

Out on the road the two walked at a comfortable pace. The conversation mostly centered around the meeting the night before and the difference Jesus had brought into so many lives, including the two of them.

Up ahead they saw a man moving in their direction. As he approached they could tell it was a man and noticed that his pace slowed down. When he got close enough they could see a broad smile come across his face. He stopped in front of them, "Shalom good men!"

"Shalom" the two repeated.

Matthew could tell by Levi's face that he did not recognize the man. This fact did not stop the man from engaging them in conversation.

"Have you men been to the city?" he asked.

"Yes" they said together. Then Levi took over. "We have been there for two days and now we are on our way home."

"I am heading for the great city myself. I have much to tell those who dwell there."

Levi and Matthew looked at each other and Matthew spoke up.

"And what is it that you have to tell?"

"I must tell my story of who Jesus is and what he has done for me."

Now the two men were completely engaged and intent on hearing this man's story.

"I am Levi and this is my friend Matthew" Levi reported. We too are followers of Jesus and have been talking to people about Jesus while in the city.

"I am Judah although I am from the tribe of Benjamin. I believe my parents had a sense of humor yes?"

"I guess so" Matthew said gently.

Judah looked and noticed a log not far off the road. He motioned to the others to join him on the fallen tree. They walked a few yards and and sat down together with Levi and Matthew at one end and Judah at the other.

Without prompting Judah began. "Oh my friends, you do not know how strange it is to sit with you here. It is something that I am still getting used to. You see, for many years I lived as a leper."

At that single word Matthew leaned forward and Levi leaned back. Matthew had never met a person with leprosy and Levi had never desired to. Still, here they were sitting with a man who told them he had been a leper.

"I remember the day I bore the curse of a leper as if it happened yesterday. My younger brother and my cousin and I had been working in the fields with our father. The three of us went down to the river to bath before dinner. As I pulled my robe up and knelt beside the river, I heard my cousin gasp. He said, 'Judah, your leg!' I looked at the outside of my leg and saw a raw patch of skin. I speak the truth when I tell you that I had never seen it before. I thought that I had just scraped my leg as we worked that day. The next evening the rash was still there and I believed that it had gotten bigger. In the morning I showed my father. His face showed alarm but he said little. I heard him talking to my mother and then it was decided that I must go with them to see the priest."

Our priest was a very old man. But his eyes were as strong as his legs were weak. When I pulled up the side of my robe he looked at the spot and sat back in his chair. For a few moments he said nothing. Then he looked at my parents and said the word no one wants to hear, *leprosy*." Both men made no effort to hide the pity that was written across their faces. Matthew watched Levi's eyes meet the ground. The three of them sat there silently as Judah's story settled into their hearts and mind. Then he continued.

"I am certain that you do not know what life as a leper is like. When the priest labels you such you must leave society immediately. Your home and family are left behind in an instant and you may be driven out of town with sticks and rocks. The only place to go is the colony far from everyone you ever knew. It is there that you will spend the rest of your life. The village is made up of several small huts most of which are just a few feet from each other. There are several fire pits about which the homes are built. Each person must gather sticks from the hillside when they wish to cook. For the most part, each member has their own hut unless there is a family that enters. You never again may enter the temple, synagogue or anyone's home. If you are in away from the colony and someone walks in your direction you must yell *Unclean! Unclean!* or those around you will punish you with stones and drive you away. My friends, it is a difficult life when others label you. But when you are forced to label yourself, misery and discouragement are your constant companions. Your food comes at the mercy of others and you are never certain of having enough."

"I remember strongly the day I entered the village of the lepers. As I walked passed the first two or three huts those outside stopped what they were doing and stared at me. I did not look like them. The disease had not attacked the more obvious places. It was still confined to my leg and hidden from the surrounding eyes. Yet they knew that I was one of them. Why else would a man just walk into the midst of the colony? It was then that I noticed for the first time the smell. The stench of rotting flesh was unbearable. My stomach churned and I fought hard to keep from vomiting. "

"I walked toward a fire pit and just stood there looking down. I could not believe what was happening to me. Then an elderly man approached me. He told me his name was Gerrahn and I quickly learned that he was the village leader. He was kind to me and did his best to ease me into my new life among the others." "So misery does love company" Matthew thought. "He showed me to a small hut a few feet away and I entered it and sat down on a small cot. The thought that this was to be my new life broke my heart and I began to weep."

Both men listened quietly. Looking at him, it was difficult to believe that he had lived as a leper. He looked so healthy. His face shone like a man at peace with the world yet they had no outward reason to doubt him. He continued.

"Before a year had gone by, I had no fingers on one hand and only two on the other. My nose had rotted off, and I only had three toes on each foot. One of my ears was gone and I had to wear a cloth wrapping to keep anyone from seeing me. I was living a life, if that is what you would call it, that I would not wish for anyone to live." The two men nodded communicating both agreement as well as encouragement to continue. Judah took a deep breath and began again.

"If a leper is ever to leave the colony it is only to walk on the hillside perhaps to gather sticks or just to be away from the colony for a short time. He would never enter another village or go to any city." Judah nodded assuming the men saw this as obvious.

"One day, after I had been in the colony for a few years I left to gather wood. As I walked over a small hill a group of people approached me. I called out *Unclean! Unclean!* The group stopped immediately and most retreated. But one of them kept waking toward me. I had no idea who he was and why he did not stop like the others. I called out again, *Unclean! Unclean!* but he did not stop. He came right up to me and I raised my eyes to look at him."

At once when I saw his face I felt a peace come over me that had long been absent. His eyes were kind and loving. He showed no fear. And then he touched me!" Judah stood up and began to pace. "He touched me on the shoulder! Then he took his other hand and touched my other shoulder. It had been years since anyone had touched me. I can still feel the warmth of his hands and the wonderful way it felt to be touched by someone again. He did not speak at first. But as I stood before him he held his hands on my shoulders and looked into my eyes. I was tempted to look away but somehow I could not. He looked upward and stared into the sky. Then he looked at me again and spoke. I will never forget his words. He said, 'My son, the Father knows your pain. Be healed and walk in faith.' Then he took his hands off me. My knees gave way and I fell to the ground.

At first I could not rise. I do not know how long I had been there but while on the ground I felt the warmth of his touch cover my entire body. It started in my feet and moved upward through my legs and chest. I began to breath heavily. My head and face became very warm, almost hot and then my whole body began to tingle. It was such a strange sensation. I had not had any feeling in my hands and feet for a long time and in a very strange way I was enjoying the sensation."

"Then I heard several members of the group gasp. My head covering had fallen off and I believed they were sickened by my appearance. But at the same time I knew this was somehow different. Then the man touched my shoulder again and said one word, *Arise!* I obeyed and rolled to my knees. It was then that I noticed my hands. My fingers had returned. I stared at them for what seemed like several minutes. I kept opening and closing them in wonder. 'How could this be happening?' I wondered." Judah shook his head and turned his palms up looking at them. "These fingers that I had not seen in such a long time looked just like they had never been diseased. I began to get up and it was then that I saw my feet. The stubs of my feet now had toes. My eyes filled with tears. This was really happening! Several times after that I almost called out *Unclean* when people approached me." Matthew thought, "Old habits die hard." Judah continued, "But all I had to do was glance at my hands and feet and I knew that I was healed."

Judah clapped his hands. "I was healed my friends! I know you may not believe it but I was completely healed!" Levi stood leaving Matthew on the log. He put his hand on Judah's shoulder, smiled and said, "We believe my friend. We believe! To God be the glory!" "Yes!" said Matthew standing and putting his hand on Judah's other shoulder, "To God be the glory!"

"And now I must go my brothers! The story of who Jesus is and what he has done for me must be told. We will meet again my friends." "Yes we will" Levi said. Then Judah added, "Until then, may the words of Jesus richly dwell in your hearts and minds!" Levi smiled and said, "And with you too my friend." With that Judah hugged each of them and quickly continued his trip toward Jerusalem. Looking over his shoulder he called out, "He lives!" "He lives!" the two shouted back as they turned to begin their walk to Levi's home.

# Chapter 8
# **Gophna**

Little else was talked about as the two traveled along the dusty road. With great enthusiasm they relived the testimony of their newly found brother. After another hour of walking they crested a small knoll and paused at the top to look down on the little town Levi called home. It was small but not insignificant in size. Houses dotted the valley with small areas of farm land scattered along the hillside. Sheep and cattle grazed on the far hills and Matthew could see lush crops growing among the homes.

"Ah, Gophna!" Levi said as he inhaled deeply and pointed toward the shallow valley. The men made their way down the hill and worked their way along the main street of the town. Levi was greeted a few times by those they passed and soon they found themselves in front of Levi's home. His house, like so many others was small, square, and whitewashed. When they approached the dwelling the door opened and a woman stepped out. She was short and rather plump with long dark hair tied under a blue kerchief. When she saw the men she flashed a wide and inviting smile. "Levi!" He stepped toward her and they embraced. "Hannah, my love. I have missed you!" As he hugged his wife her eyes rose to notice Matthew. "And who have you with you my love?" she said nodding toward Matthew. "Ahh, this is my good friend Matthew. We met on the road to Jerusalem and have so much to tell you." "Well come in," Hannah said as she turned to go inside. The inside of the home looked surprising familiar. It had a somewhat large living and dining room combined and two bedrooms along with a small kitchen. If he didn't know better Matthew would have guessed they were back at Isaac and Miriam's place. They made their way to the kitchen and sat down at the low standing table. Hannah pulled a large scoop from a pot and filled a glass with water for each of them.

Levi filled her in on all the events of the past two days and she did nothing to hide her interest and delight. When he finished he asked her, "And where is my boy?" "He is outside. I'm sure he will be in when his belly calls to him" said said smiling. Levi looked at Matthew. "I cannot wait for you to meet my son Benjamin. He is only ten but has the mind of one much older. He also has the energy of a dozen horses" he said looking at Hannah and patting Matthew on the forearm.

While he was still smiling in bounced Benjamin. Immediately he ran to his father calling out "Abba!" Levi hugged the young one as the smile on his face grew back. He grabbed his son by the shoulders and turned him toward Matthew. "This is my friend Matthew. We have been in the city together." Benjamin stepped forward extending his hand. Matthew stood up, leaned over, and shook the young man's hand.

Matthew sat back down and Benjamin found a place on his father's lap. "Father" he said, "I saw some Roman soldiers yesterday!" Levi's face grew somber. "Tell me what happened." "They marched through our village. I counted ten of them. They were walking toward Jerusalem." "What did you do?" his father asked. "I did like you told me to. I stopped and looked down until they passed." "You did well my Son" Levi said giving his boy a squeeze.

Levi looked at Matthew. "Ever since the crucifixion the Romans have been making their presence known. Mostly they move through the cities but sometimes they come through the villages just to remind us that they are still here and they are still in charge. A friend of mine made the mistake of getting in their way once. He had a bad leg and struggled to move quickly. The Romans came around a corner and he did not get out of their way fast enough. He was knocked to the ground and felt the side of a sword on his back. No one moved. All we could do was watch and wait 'til they passed. He wasn't hurt badly but it united us all in our anger against those dogs." Levi's face was stern.

Matthew watched him as he looked down at the table. Then he saw a slight smile come to his face. "I have heard that Jesus taught us to love our enemies. That is not an easy thing to do. All my life I have learned to hate the Romans. Time and time again they have hurt our people. So many I know bear the scars of a Roman sword or spear. I know of an old woman who was bumped to the ground by a Roman horse. The soldier kept moving and never looked back. That was several years ago and still to this day she does not move well.And these people are the ones Jesus says we are to love?" he said giving a mild giggle.

"The law tells us that a Roman is allowed to require us to carry their pack up to one mile. I am told that Jesus taught that if a soldier requires us to carry his pack one mile we are to carry it two. I have never done this but I have been in a meeting where I heard a man speak who carried the soldier's pack two miles. He said that when they reached the one mile mark the soldier went to pull the pack from him and he told him that he would carry it another mile. He said the look on the soldier's face was worth the trouble. As they walked the man told him about Jesus. The soldier said little but when the second mile was over the soldier shook the man's hand. Perhaps there is some hope for those people." Levi chuckled again.

Hannah spoke up. "Speaking of meetings I have heard there is a meeting of the called out ones in a couple of days." The two men leaned forward. "Yes?" Levi said. "Yes. I do not know where or when but my friend Bellah told me so." Levi popped the table gently. It looks as though we have a meeting to attend my friends." The group smiled and Benjamin asked, "Me too Father?" "Yes my Son. It is time for you to come too." Benjamin gave his father a squeeze.

Matthew's bed that night was once again on the roof. The view was different than that of Isaac's but the cot and sheepskin blanket were the same. And the brightness of the stars rivaled any beauty he had ever seen. Once again his mind found its way to Melissa. He wondered where she was and what she was feeling. Did she even know he was alive? Was he in a hospital in a coma? How could he reach her? How could he let her know he was okay? These thoughts and more rattled around in his head as he felt himself float off to sleep.

The sun pounced on Matthew's face bringing its warmth and waking him up. He listened for a few moments and heard the sound of talking and digging. This was followed by a few words being sung. He stretched, yawned and swung his feet over the edge of the bed. He walked to the edge of the roof and looked over the short wall. Behind the house he saw Levi and Benjamin working in the garden. He made his way down the steps and found Hannah in the kitchen baking. She turned and smiled at him as he said, "Good morning." "Yes" she said as if he had asked her a question. "The men are in the garden gathering up a few things." Matthew slipped his feet into his sandals by the door and stepped out. He was greeted by Levi. "Good morning my friend.

Did you rest well?" "Yes" Matthew said. "Yes I did. And you?" Levi said, "Yes. I rested as I man rests who has so much to be thankful for" and he waved his hand over the house, the garden, and his son.

"We are blessed with a large garden. It gives us food to eat, food to share, and food to sell." Immediately Matthew's mind raced back to so many financial counseling sessions he had taught. Regarding money, he taught, "Save some, spend some, give some away." He looked at Levi and responded, "That is a blessing!"

Levi leaned on his hoe and pointed to the garden. "The sun comes heavy today my friend. We must give our young friends a drink." He motioned to Benjamin to pour some water from the bucket he held. "We give to them today and they give to us soon after. It is the way of our God, yes?" Matthew had never heard it put that way before but he knew it was true. He smiled and nodded in agreement saying "Can I help?" Levi pointed to a small bucket holding some rocks.

"Would you take that bucket of stones and put them on the village pile? It is down the street to the left."

"Village pile?" Matthew asked.

"Yes" Levi said. It is a pile of stones down the street. Anyone is free to take or leave stones. Some are used to build walls or paths. Some are even used to build houses."

Matthew gave an understanding nod, picked up the bucket and made his way around the house and into the street. When he reached the pile he saw a boy picking through the pile and putting stones in a small bucket. When the boy saw Matthew he stood, bowed, and said "Shalom." Matthew returned the greeting and noted, "This is a good sized pile."

"Yes" said the boy. "It grows and shrinks as it is needed. We are building a border around our garden. I have not seen you before." He extended his hand and said, "I am Simeon." Matthew took his hand and gave it a short pump.

"Where do you stay?" the boy asked.

"I am the guest of Levi" Matthew offered pointing toward Levi's house.

"Ah, Levi!" Simeon said. "He is one of the kindest men in our town."

Matthew was surprised at the way the boy handled himself. He looked to be about ten-years old, but talked like a boy much older. He was engaging and confident, even precocious.

"And where do you stay?"

Simeon waved his hand in the other direction. "I live with my mother and father right over there. I am good friends with Benjamin" He volunteered before Matthew had a chance to ask.

Matthew knelt down in front of the pile. He felt compelled to ask the young man even more. "Has anything special happened in this town?"

The boy looked down.

"No not here." Then his face lit up as he said, "But a prophet and teacher named Jesus came to my uncle's village and I got to meet him."

Now the boy had all of Matthew's attention. Matthew dumped his pile of rocks, turned the bucket over and sat down on it. He leaned his elbows on his knees and said to Simeon, "Tell me what happened."

"My uncle and aunt live outside of Gergossa on the east side of the Sea of Galilee. One day my uncle and aunt were going to the market in Gergossa. I got to go with them. From the road we saw a great crowd gathered on a hillside by the sea. I had never seen so many people in my life! We didn't know what was happening so we asked a man who was coming our way. He said 'The teacher from Nazareth is here.' We followed the man and when we got to where the teacher was, the crowd was even bigger than I thought." Simeon took his own bucket, dumped out the few rocks that he had and sat on it as well.

"We were far from the man but somehow we could hear everything he said." Displaying a proud look on his face Simeon patted his chest and said, "I was able to walk through the crowd and sat down toward the front. Jesus wasn't shouting but he was talking very loud, loud enough so his voice could reach those in the far back. I heard a man whisper to another man that Jesus had healed many that day. He said he healed a blind man, a man who had an injured arm, and a man who could not walk."

Using a finger to tap the side of his head Simeon said, "I remember everything he said. Jesus talked for a long time. He talked about heaven, the holy book, caring for the poor, honoring God, and all kinds of things." Matthew was amazed at how expressive and animated this boy was. "When he finished I saw him talk to some of the men up front. I don't know what he said but I watched them turn to some of the people up close. Whatever they asked, everyone shook their heads *No*. Then I heard one of the men speak loudly to those up close, 'Does anyone have any food?'"

"I had a small bag with our lunch. It was not much, just enough to keep us from getting hungry while we walked to Gergossa. I held my sack up and one of the men saw me. He came over to me and looked at my bag. Then he said to me, *Come* and led me to Jesus."

Simeon grinned and looked right in Matthew's eyes. "Jesus looked at me, knelt down, and smiled. I heard him say, 'And a little child shall lead them. Thank you young one!' He stood up and turned to some of the men near him and I heard him say something about baskets. Then he took my bag and looked inside. He looked up to the sky for just a moment and I heard him whisper, 'Thank you Father for this bounty of food.' Then things got exciting."

Matthew shifted on his bucket. He was very familiar with the story and somehow felt that he knew the boy just as well. He nodded both in agreement and for the boy to continue. "Jesus told everyone to sit down in groups. He took the fish and the bread and began to break them up. He put a few pieces in each of the baskets the men brought to him. Some of the men didn't have baskets so they used their robes to hold the food. Then they began to give the food out. I didn't understand what was going on but as they gave the food out, more was in their baskets or robes. One of the men came to me and the people around me. He held out the basket and I saw that it was full. We each took a piece of fish and a few pieces of bread and passed the basket around. When he took the basket back I looked in and saw that it was still full. One of the men in our group put a piece of bread in his mouth and said, 'We are in the presence of God!' and everyone nodded."

Matthew said, "That must have been amazing!" Simeon nodded to Matthew and said, "I'll never forget it. It took a long time for everyone to get some food. There were so many people around Jesus that I couldn't see him. Somehow he slipped away from the crowd and we learned later that he and his disciples were by the sea. The people around me kept saying things like, 'he came to save us from our sins' and 'he is the deliverer.' I even heard some say, 'we will never go hungry again."

Simeon stood up and righted his bucket signaling that the story was over. He went back to the task of gathering stones again starting with the ones he had dumped out. For several seconds Matthew stared at the ground saying nothing. He was letting everything his young friend said sink in. His words kept coming back echoing in his ears "We are in the presence of God."

Simeon's bucket was full enough and he grabbed the handle with both hands and yanked it off the ground saying, "Back to work." He leaned away from it and turned toward his home. He looked back at Matthew and said, "The Lord be with you." Matthew stood up and said, "And also with you my friend" and he bowed his head slightly in a *Thank you* gesture. Matthew stood there for a while watching the boy stride toward home. He gave a heavy sigh and breathed out, "The presence of God."

At dinner that night Levi explained that in the morning he had to travel South to Jericho to bring his neighbor's goods to a merchant. He said that his neighbor's back prevented him from making the sixteen-mile journey. He invited Matthew to go with him and Matthew nodded his acceptance of the offer. They would be riding on his neighbor's cart pulled by his neighbor's donkey and would be gone for a couple of days. "I would like to buy his old donkey but he will not let me pay with sandal dust, my good nature, and handsome features." Levi chuckled and smiled at Matthew while winking at his son. Hannah went to another room and returned with one of Levi's robes in her hand. She extended it to Matthew saying, "You will need an extra robe as you travel. Please take this as yours." Matthew took the robe and gratefully bowed and said, "Thank you." He was relieved that no one had asked him much about his loss of clothes and scarcity of money, but didn't spend too much time working up an answer.

While Matthew lay on his cot that night, he replayed his conversation with young Simeon. Levi had labeled him *The village celebrity* and mentioned that Jehovah has a reputation of taking what little we give Him and making more than enough. He finished with "He does that with us too! When we give all that we have of ourselves he takes it and makes more of us than we ever dreamed." Matthew remembered grinning and thinking, "That has the makings of a great sermon."

He thought of the church's food pantry and how they always had more than enough to share as hungry men and women would walk up asking for something. On more than one occasion, they scraped the bottom of the bowl giving the last person the food prepared for their Tuesday lunch for the homeless.

As he began to slip into sleep he thought, "I wish Melissa were here!

Lord, is this a dream?" On the heels of that he heard himself say quietly, "If she were here and this is a dream, I think that maybe I wouoldn't want to wake up" and he shifted on his cot and drifted away.

# Chapter 9
# Jericho

The next morning, sunshine blinking through a large tree on the hill woke Matthew up. He rolled from his cot, pulled on his robe and made his way downstairs. The family was up and the kitchen was filled with a mixture of smells floating from an iron skillet.

The meal was unusually large with hummus, fish, biscuits, dates, and figs. Matthew stifled a giggle as his mind asked, "What, no bacon?" Thankfulness swept over his soul. So many times in the past (or the future) he had remarked how blessed he was to know the satisfaction of a full belly. He had been on several mission trips and spent time among the hungry-the real needy. So often he prayed and gave thanks that hunger was such a foreign feeling and he had quietly admonished himself for using the phrase, "I'm starving!"

The family sat down. Levi lifted his head upward and simply said, "A table full of food Lord. Thank you!" With that he reached out for the plate of biscuits took one and passed the plate along. There was no discomfort in the silence that followed. Everyone was enveloped in the meal and shortly they had finished and left the table.

When Matthew and Levi walked next door, they found the cart packed and hitched to the donkey. They met no one but simply grabbed the harness and directed the unit to the front of Levi's house. Hannah and Benjamin came out to send the men off. Hannah handed Levi a bag of food and the two embraced. She turned to Matthew and handed him a head piece. "The sun will be strong. You will need this as you travel. It is yours to keep." Matthew took the kerchief, nodded and said "Thank you." Then he watched as Levi put his hand around his wife's shoulder and his other one on Benjamin's head. Then he heard him repeat what he knew as *The Mizpah*. "Now may the Lord watch between me and you as we are absent one from another. Amen."

Levi bent down and kissed his son's forehead. He embraced his wife again, whispered something to her, and delivered a gentle kiss on the cheek. With that the two men boarded the cart and pointed it Southeast toward Jericho.

The warmth of the sun was welcomed as the men made their way through the village. Levi pointed out several homes and seemed to have no end to the stories he told about those dwelling there. Growing up in this town had filled his coffers with stories and a constant search for boyhood adventure. Soon the town was behind them and they found themselves alone on the road.

After riding for some time, Levi announce that there was a village ahead where his cousin Elizabeth lived with her husband Thaddeus. "There we will wash and rest and visit." Matthew gave a nod of understanding and smiled.

When the wagon pulled up an elderly man came from behind the house carrying a broom. Levi slid off the wagon and moved toward the man. The eyes of the two men sparkled as they met and embraced. Matthew watched the men as they greeted one another. This was more than a hello. This was genuine affection as two hearts touched.

He was often amused at how he had seen so many others greet one another. He chuckled as he recalled people saying "How are you?" or "Howya doin'" but never waiting for a reply. He noted that it had become no more than a *Hi* and continued smiling as he watched the interaction of the men.

Thaddeus turned toward Matthew and said, "And who is this with you?" Levi extended his upturned hand toward Matthew motioning him over. "This Thaddeus, is my good friend Matthew." Thaddeus smiled, hugged Matthew and said, "Welcome friend." As he returned the hug Matthew thought, "These greetings! Such sincerity. Such kindness. Such affection! I don't think that I'll ever get used to it."

As the men turned toward the house the door opened. In the doorway stood a short but slender woman. Her head was partially covered but revealed dark hair streaked with gray. She smiled broadly as she reached for Levi and said, "Ah Lev! My cousin! You are my favorite, but don't tell the others!" Levi leaned over and hugged her saying, Elizabeth! My favorite cousin! I always tell the others!" She gave a short giggle and said, "Come in! Come in!" Then turning toward Matthew she said, "And your friend?" Thaddeus broke in and put his hand on

Matthew's shoulder saying "This is our new friend Matthew." Elizabeth smiled at him and bowed slightly saying "Welcome" as she led the three of them in.

The four of them entered the house. Matthew looked quickly around and thought "Same house, different location." Elizabeth opened a window and moved toward the kitchen. Immediately a gentle breeze blew in and caressed their faces in a refreshing way. The men sat on cushions on the floor and leaned on the small tabled in the middle of the room.

"Are you one of our Hebrew brothers?" Thaddeus said nodding toward Matthew. Matthew was about to answer when Levi jumped in, "He *is* one is one of our brothers." "Ah, yes!" said Thaddeus beaming, "Another one of the way! How long have you followed the Master?" Matthew almost said, "Since I was a boy" but then caught himself knowing he could offer no explanation. So without much forethought he said, "Since I was convinced that he was the Messiah and the only one to forgive me of my sins." The men laughed as Thaddeus patted Matthew's shoulder and said, "The same is true of us!"

Thaddeus' face grew serious and he leaned forward as if to share a secret. "I actually saw Jesus in the temple." Then he leaned back letting that thought settle in. "I was in Jerusalem for the feast and Elizabeth and I went to the temple with our sacrifice. We had brought two doves. It was the best we had. We showed them to the priests and I knew by the look on their faces that they were not acceptable. They never are!" he said patting Matthew on the hand. "We paid the fee to get temple coins and the exchange fee." Thaddeus held up his index finger and slowly shook it toward the men, "They have lots of ways to put their hands in our purses."

"We turned to walk away and there he was, standing right behind us!" Thaddeus used a thumb to indicate the direction. "I looked into his eyes but he looked right passed me. I had never seen eyes like that before. They were fixed on the priests and money changers. His eyes were focused and angry. He brushed past me and with one arm he turned the table over and with the other he grabbed the dividing cord between the tables. Money and birds flew everywhere. There was a knot in one end of the cord and he spun it over his head just missing the man behind the table. The man moved away and Jesus flipped over the next table and the next. All eyes were on him as coins spilled all over the floor. The animals ran in every direction." Out of the corner of his eye Matthew saw Elizabeth slide into the room and sit at the left side of the table. He knew she was there but couldn't pull his eyes off of Thaddeus.

Matthew knew the story and had even preached on it a couple of times, but didn't dare interrupt. "He was out of breath and I heard him yell, 'My house is to be a house of prayer, not a den for robbers.' He threw the cord to the ground, shook his head in disgust and he and his disciples walked out of the temple. None of the people moved but I could see on their faces so many of them wanted to cheer."

Elizabeth and I followed them down the temple steps. They were moving too fast for us but as we watched them leave we heard a Pharisee say to two others standing near, 'That is the one we've been talking about. We must do something soon!'" Thaddeus looked at both men and his face grew stern, "And even then I knew what they meant."

Both Matthew and Levi didn't move. Levi had heard the story and Matthew had read it several times before but it came to life through the lips of an eyewitness. Thaddeus wasn't done. "The next day we prepared to leave the city. As we walked down the main street we saw a crowd ahead. The crowd was growing but we were close enough to see what was going on. I will never forget what we saw. A woman was in the center of a circle of men. She was seated on the ground and leaning to her side. Her eyes were streaming tears and her face was covered with the dust of the road. Everyone was shaking their fists and yelling at her. I looked around and saw that several men of different ages were holding stones. I didn't know what she had done but I knew what the end would be for her."

I had only seen someone stoned one other time in my life. It was a brutal scene. A man had been caught stealing from the synagogue coffers. They drove him outside the village and surrounded him with men holding rocks." Thaddeus looked down and shook his head slowly as if he was seeing the scene again. "The older men started first. The first stone hit the man in the chest and he turned away and covered his head. But the others screamed and hurled their stones immediately. In seconds the man was on the ground covered in blood. The stones kept coming until there was no life left in him. The entire incident was over in a few minutes and the crowd of men walked away." He patted Matthew's arm and continued, "Then one of the younger man approached the man. He carried a large rock and stood over the man.

He raised it over his head and brought it down on the man's skull crushing it. I tried to look away but somehow I couldn't. I remember it like it was yesterday. It was horrible!"

Matthew felt his stomach turn and his jaw tighten. The men sat there in silence and Levi asked, "And the woman?" Thaddeus took a breath and continued. "I knew she was to follow the fate of that man. Then I saw the Master. He was on the opposite side of the circle from me. He brushed through the crowd and came to the edge of the circle. A Pharisee was next to him holding a stone the size of a man's fist and Jesus stared at him and the man looked away. Jesus stepped into the center of the circle and faced the men. I couldn't hear everything they said, but I did see one of the men point at the woman and say the word *Adultery*. Several of the men repeated the word to each other."

"Jesus didn't respond to them. I watched him kneel down in from of the woman. I do not know if he spoke to her or not. He touched her shoulder and stood up and walked to the edge of the circle of men. She never moved. He knelt again and began writing or making figures in the dust with his finger in front of one of the men. Then he stood up and looked the man in the eye. Then he did it again in front of another man. Then another. Each time he traced something he stood up and looked the man squarely in the eye. Each of the men stepped back a bit as he teacher stood before him." Matthew had always wanted to know what Jesus had written and said but understood that the answer would not be forthcoming. He nodded for Thaddeus to continue even though he knew the outcome.

"Then I heard his words, not just to the men with the stones but to all of us. 'He who is without sin let him be the first to cast a stone at this woman.' There was nothing but silence. I heard the thud of stones hitting the ground and one by one the accusers left. I wanted to leave too but I couldn't move. I had never seen anyone with such command of a crowd, especially one made of the religious rulers. The disciples gathered around the two of them and I watched him reach for the woman and help her to her feet. She still had tears streaming from her face but they were tears of relief. I don't know what he said to her but I saw her nod and give a slight smile. My friends, I did not know much about him but I knew he was a special man." Both Levi and Matthew nodded in agreement but made no comment.

Thaddeus pointed his finger in the air for emphasis, "But after the resurrection, after he rose from the grave I too became a follower. He is the Messiah!" Matthew smiled widely and nodded. Levi clapped his hands and said, "Yes! Yes, he is!" It was not until then that Matthew took notice of the tray of hummus and bread that Elizabeth had slid in front of them. Each of the men helped themselves and enjoyed their snack in silence.

After some lengthy good-byes and well wishes both men were seated back on the cart and road along for some time saying nothing. Finally, Levi broke the silence saying, "Now you can see why Elizabeth is my favorite cousin. And Thaddeus...you will not find a better man though you wander the village for days. Matthew smiled and nodded. His mind flew back to the story of the woman to be stoned. Again he wondered what Jesus had written in the dust. All he or anyone else could come up with was conjecture. No one knew and once again like so many other unanswered questions Matthew was forced to conclude, "If God wanted us to know he would have put it in the book." And like other times, he heard himself assign it to the list of "Theological chicken bones that we must choose to push aside to enjoy the meat."

For two more hours the men rode with intermittent conversation coupled with long periods of silence. They arrived at a town named Kaheel. They were still several miles from Jericho so they made arrangements to stay at an inn.

The inn keeper was a round man with fat hands. He asked the men where they were from and noted that he had not heard of it. The men climbed the stairs and found their way to their room. The room held two beds and a very small table with a lantern on it. Between the beds was a window with some sheer curtains for decorating purposes only. A small table with a wash basin and pitcher was by the door. The men took only a minute to look around and drop their belongings on the beds. They then made their way back down to enjoy some dinner.

To the side of the front door stood three tables. The tables had no decorations on them and no table cloth. A man with a white turban occupied a table in the corner of the room but for the most part, the two men enjoyed an extended time alone. During dinner the inn keeper approached their table and asked, "Are you members of the way?" Levi's eyes moved toward Matthew and with caution he said, "What is it you mean?" The large man leaned forward and said, "I've heard you speak of the Master and one of you said Jesus. Are you followers of Jesus?" A long pause fell over the three of them. Levi and Matthew looked again at each other and then at the man. He smiled and nodded. The tense moment was broken by his words, "I have become one of his followers." Matthew heard a loud breath come from Levi. "We are his followers too my friend. Forgive us for our silence but we know we must be careful." The man's smile widened, "I understand and I am not angry my brothers. "

He told them his name was Mordeccai and they introduced themselves as well. Then he asked, "Have you met Jesus?" "Not in a formal way" Levi offered, "But I have heard him speak and we have learned so much about him." The pride inside Matthew's heart almost caused him to say, "I have read all the stories in his book" but he was quick enough to change his comment to "I have read the prophesies of the Messiah and have heard the stories and have come to believe." Both men smiled at him, then Mordeccai leaned closer and whispered, "If you will come down after dark I will tell you of the time I met the Master." The men leaned forward and Levi said, "We will be here my friend."

Matthew could hardly wait for the sun to set. They lay on their beds resting but not sleeping. At the appropriate time they found their way back down to the dining area. They found Mordeccai seated at a table by the fireplace. He was nursing a cup of something warm and looked up as the men approached. A smile quickly came to his face and he stood motioning to the men to sit down in the two empty chairs. He pointed to a pot on the table and said the word *Bechai?* and without their response he poured each of them a cup of the warm liquid. The drink was slightly bitter but Matthew enjoyed it nonetheless.

Mordeccai dipped his head and said, "And now I will tell you my friends of the time that I met the Master." The two men leaned forward and it seemed as if the rest of the world faded away.

My wife and I were visiting my family in Gadara. The second night we saw him. "The Lord?" Matthew asked. "No, no my friend. Not the Lord. That came later. We saw a man called *Mob*. Some also called him *Legion*" Matthew knew this story as well. Looking around in the dim room Mordeccai continued, "His was a tortured soul. I never knew his real name but he was filled with so many demons that those around him called him *Mob* or *Legion*. We had heard stories about him and at night we could hear him in the hills howling."

My cousin had told me that this man once was maker of fine fabrics.

He was not wealthy but was a man of some substance. He lived alone in the village but had many friends. The story is told that he began to visit the pagan temple in a village a few miles from here. Someone said that one time while visiting him, they noticed a small statue of Baal in his home. One evening two priests from the pagan temple came to visit him at his home. No one knows what they talked about, but they stayed with him for several hours. They left and those close to his home heard him yelling several times during the night. The next day, he continued to yell. Then the howling started. He became violent with all those around and before the week was completed, he had set fire to his house and it burned to the ground. From that point on he lived among the tombs.

One afternoon my father and I were walking back from the market. We heard several people shouting and as we came up over a hill we saw him. He was standing in the road blocking the way. He was naked and covered in filth. His body had many open sores and he had a horrible odor. As the crowd stood there he screamed, threw dust in their direction and ran away over the hill. My father told me that he lived out in the open among the tombs. Several people had tried to clothe him and restrain him but he tore them all off and ran away. Many in the village were angry and wanted him driven out of the area. They claimed it was keeping people away and hurting their business. They said it was frightening their families and demanded that the town leaders do something about it. They tried to restrain him with ropes and even chains but he always seemed to escape and slip away. And the howling continued."

"Then one day it seemed as if the entire town was gathering outside the village in the hills. All we heard was that the teacher was there. My father and I joined the crowd and we heard his words. He spoke with such great authority and explained the teachings of Jehovah in a way we had never heard before. Then from behind the crowd the howling started. The crowd parted and he was standing right there." Mordeccai pointed to the far wall indicating *Mob's* location. Matthew's eyes followed Mordeccai's hand and he nodded. He came right up to Jesus and they were face to face. *Legion* looked like he was about to scream but Jesus raised his hand. He said, 'What is your name?' I was standing close to them and was surprised at how calm the crazed man was. He simply said, 'My name is legion for we are many.' He began to cry and then he fell at the Master's feet. A very strange voice came from him. It was deep and raspy. He said, 'Oh Holy One, do not torture us before our time. We beg you to send us into the herd.' Jesus put his hand on the man, pointed to the far hill, and said, 'You must leave this man!' The man shrieked and fell face down on the ground. He didn't move. Then behind us we heard the tremendous squeal of pigs. The pigs began running and jumping all over the place. Then all of a sudden they began running in our direction. For just a second I thought we we going to be trampled. Then all of a sudden they turned and raced over the hill and off a cliff."

"Everyone looked back at Jesus. The man was smiling and crying and standing next to Jesus. I was close enough to look in his eyes." Mordeccai leaned in toward the other two and whispered for emphasis, "Peace. All I saw was peace." He sat back in his chair and engaged in his normal voice again. "My friends, this was a man who was out of his mind. Just minutes before he was running throughout the hillside screaming at people and cutting himself. Now he just stood there next to the Master with nothing but peace on his face. Jesus pulled a wrap from one of the men nearby and put it on the naked man. He just patted the man on the shoulder and smiled."

The table was silent as the two let the story sink in. Matthew thought, "Jesus, the prince of peace" and nodded slowly. Then Mordeccai patted the table as if he needed to regain their attention. "I wish that was the end of the story my friends. But there is more. That was all the village talked about for the rest of the day. Everywhere we went the subject of Jesus' encounter with *Mob* came up.

The next day the city leaders found Jesus with many people on the hillside. The man who had been delivered was with him. He was clothed and simply sat with Jesus. Many people wanted Jesus to stay." Mordeccai's face grew angry and his voice became harsh. "But because of the loss of the pigs-pigs! Unclean detestable pigs that were to be used in pagan sacrifice the leaders told Jesus that he was not welcome in their village." Mordeccai shook his head. "Money was more important to them than the poor man's soul. They told the Master to leave!" "Money trumps the man" Matthew thought. "It always has and it always will."

Mordeccai continued, "I never saw him again but I heard often about the signs he showed and the words he spoke. I was in Jerusalem the week after he arose and I met one of his disciples. It was then that I became a believer."

Both men nodded and smiled slightly reviewing in their minds Mordeccai's experience. They enjoyed a lively but guarded conversation for over an hour but then agreed that it was late and time to retire for the night. After exchanging words of blessing and peace the two worked their way up the stairs to their room.

The sun found the men on the road early the next morning. The conversation was light and mutually enjoyable. A few hours later they were moving their cart through the main gate of the city of Jericho. Matthew was actually tempted to sing the childhood song, "Joshua fought the battle of Jericho" but he knew it would not be well received.

The city reminded him of Jerusalem with it's bustling atmosphere and crowded square-and the noise. They slowly moved the cart through the crowd and found themselves outside a small shop very close to the center of town. The owner came out and he and Levi exchanged greetings. Matthew learned that his name was Demitri. He was a tall thin man with a strong face and a pleasant attitude.

"And how is my friend Nathaniel?" "Aging like the rest of us, but he is well" Levi chuckled. His back continues to trouble him but he complains little." "Nathaniel is a good man!" Demitri smiled. "Yes" Levi agreed. "He is a good friend and neighbor and one you would do well to buy from" Levi was smiling and holding up the edge of some fabric. Demitri smiled. "Yes this is true." Then turning towards the shop he called, "Eleena. Please come." In a moment a short wide woman appeared. She nodded at the men and looked at her husband. "This is Levi and Matthew. They are neighbors of Nathaniel. Please look over these fabrics for me." She nodded and Demitri turned to the men. "Come let us leave the dust and noise and sit in the back." He led them through the shop and into a dimly lit room. The room had a small lantern that was burning, a few odds and ends on a table and four chairs. He waved them into the room and all three men sat down.

He patted an open hand in Matthew's direction and said, "Now my friend, tell me about your life." Matthew hesitated but began, "I am from a small town called Frayton a long way west of here." Matthew smiled slightly thinking that at least he was telling the truth.

"And how is it that you earn your living?"

Matthew was stumped. How could he answer that without sounding ridiculous? He leaned forward, nodded slightly, and said, "I am a teacher." Then he added, "I met Levi on the road to Jerusalem."

"Ah a teacher!" Demitri exclaimed. "It is good to meet a man who teaches!"

Matthew was silently relieved that he didn't inquire about the subject he taught.

Then turning to Levi he asked, "And you my friend?"

Levi spoke up, "I buy and sell in the city of Jerusalem where my brother lives." Again Matthew noticed Levi's nod in respect of the city.

"I also look around for friends who need my help" he said putting a hand on Matthew's shoulder.

Then in a move that caught the men by surprise Demitri leaned forward and asked, "Have you heard of *the* Teacher?" When he emphasized the word *the* both men knew exactly what he meant. But he followed it with *the Messiah* In an equally surprising move Levi responded without hesitation, "Yes we've heard of him. He is Jesus the Messiah and we are both followers of his. And you?"

Demitri nodded strongly. "Oh, yes. He is my Savior and Lord!"

"Is everyone in Israel a follower of Jesus?" Matthew thought. As if to answer Matthew's question Demitri explained, "So many have come to follow him. Some of us came to know him personally as I did, while others have surrendered to his Lordship after the resurrection. Eleena and my son have not yet come to know the Savior, but they are close. They are close my friends." He smiled, nodded, and winked.

"I was a friend of John." "The Disciple?" Matthew jumped in. Demitri shook his head, "No. John the Baptizer. We grew up together and were schooled together under the teacher Jameel. We spent much of our childhood together but as we grew, he being a Nazarite, went his way and I went mine. Years later, I heard of John. He was living in the hills in the Negev. He was a teacher or maybe a Rabbi and was calling all to repentance and baptism. I went to see him a few times but was never baptized. His teaching and way were true and right and many followed him."

"One day I watched him baptize many in the waters of the Jordan. He spoke such true words with authority. In an age of *taking* he preached that we are to *give*. He said, 'He who has two cloaks and sees his neighbor with none should give one to him. He spoke of love, respect, and service."

"While John spoke I looked around. All of a sudden I saw Jesus on the hillside. I didn't see him coming, he was just there. He walked toward John and their eyes met. John stopped and pointed at Jesus. He shouted, 'Behold, the Lamb of God. It is he who takes away the sins of the world.' Then he turned to his own followers and said, 'He must gain and I must lose.' He was speaking of Jesus' popularity and the growth in numbers of his followers. Many of John's disciples left to follow Jesus from that day on. I didn't go with Jesus but I sat with him a few times. He too spoke with authority but but somehow it was different. I don't know how but his words stayed with me long after I left the Master."

"I didn't see him for a long time but I kept hearing stories of his teaching and healings. I even heard about some of the confrontations he had with our religious leaders. Something always seemed to draw me to him. One of the most fascinating things that I noticed was the change that came over people after spending time with him. Wherever Jesus goes, people are changed." The men sat in silence as the truth of that statement settled over them.

Suddenly Demitri popped the table with his hand and stood up. "Come! I will bring you to one who has been changed. Eleena met him in the doorway. "The fabric is very good." Demitri smiled. "As expected. We will settle shortly when we return.

He hurried the men down the street telling them, "You are going to meet a man who was one of most hated men in all of Jericho. He was a stubborn, cheating, selfish, and wealthy man. But the Messiah changed all that."

They stopped in front of a home looking like all the others. Demitri reached up and pulled on a rope ringing a bell. Moments later the door opened. There in front of them was a short chubby man. Matthew was too afraid to guess but didn't have to as Demitri exclaimed, "Zaccheus!" "Ah, Demitri my friend! Come in! Come in!"

He motioned the men to follow him and they obeyed. Inside Matthew noticed that the home was larger than any of the other ones he had been in. There were two hallways leading to three or four rooms each. It was well decorated and comfortable. "These are my friends, Levi and Matthew." "Welcome friends" Zaccheus said grabbing each of their hands as he bowed.

The men saw a woman emerge from an adjoining room. She was slender with long dark hair showing no signs of gray. Without question she was beautiful. Matthew fought against the question rising in his mind, "How did *he* get *her*?" Zaccheus swung his hand in the woman's direction "My lovely wife, Meesha." She smiled and the men each bowed in her direction. From another room a young girl appeared. A daughter? No, more like a servant girl. She was not introduced but spoke up, "I will fix something for you." With that she moved through the room and into the kitchen.

"Please sit down" Meesha said motioning with her hand. The men found places on the floor and sat on pillows around a short table. There was a slight breeze wafting through the room and each of the men turned their faces up to enjoy it. Zaccheus sat opposite Matthew. He was leaning to one side and his face bore a slight grin. When Matthew looked at him, one word came to his mind, *peace*.

Dimetri turned to Zaccheus. Nodding his head in their direction he said, "I told my brothers" and he emphasized the word with a nod, "how the Messiah had come and changed your life." Needing no other prodding, Zaccheus jumped in. "Ah yes!" He said nodding and beaming. It seemed as if his face took on a slight glow. "A day as if it was yesterday, but it was over a year ago."

"I was not a man at peace. I grew up in this city and came to think only of myself and what I could possess. When the ancient city came to be rebuilt my grandfather and father served with the planners. Our family was well-known throughout the region. As a boy I learned the value of money and began to pursue it early on. I had little time for family and friends and as my hunger for more grew I had more things and less friends. I was not worthy of friends." Matthew was waiting for the common sign of quotation marks made with the hands but none came.

Zaccheus looked down at the table. He seemed to hesitate while recalling his earlier life. "I found those who were struggling and lent money at a good return. I began to trade farther and farther from the city and began to import goods. I even traded with the Gentiles-enemies of our people. This made no difference to me. If they had a few shekels I made sure to get to know them. My wealth brought me into circles that increased my opportunities to make more. The day I decided to become a tax collector is the day I chose money over our very people. I rose through the ranks and became the leader of those who did the same. A few years later I married Meesha." He smiled and whispered, "Still the most beautiful woman in the city. But I found no peace and little happiness."

His smile disappeared and he seemed to take on the role of a teacher. "My friends, when you chase only money, you may catch it. But you must be aware of all that you lose in the race. The only friends I had were my fellow tax collectors. And even then I am certain that they would have nothing to do with me had it not been for my position or wealth. We had joined hands with the Romans and had become enemies of our people. Because of this it was not safe for me in the city or the country. I could go nowhere alone and began to live in fear. There were many Zealots around, and I am sure they would have loved to use one of their daggers on me."

"One day a large crowd began to gather in the street. I learned that Jesus, the teacher was coming. I had heard so much about this man. I heard about his teaching, and the way he had healed so many. I even heard about his prophesy and the way he dealt with the religious leaders. I just wanted to see him, to get a glimpse of what he looked like. The crowd got bigger and bigger and as he and his disciples approached the noise increased. The closer he got, the more excited I got. But with all the pushing and shoving I couldn't get close enough to see him, and no one was eager to give me a place."

"I moved away from the street and walked quickly along the buildings. I was going to wait up ahead, in the middle of the street, but I knew the crowd would be moving with him. I thought of going up to a rooftop but everyone was in the street. I ran farther ahead and found a large tree." He smiled and patted his belly saying, "I'm not one who is built for running or climbing, but I did the best I could." The three men smiled back.

Matthew wanted to break out in the children's song, "Zaccheus was a wee little man..." but he dismissed the thought as quickly as it came. The portly man continued, "I climbed as quickly as I could but really wasn't very high. Then I saw him! He was coming straight toward me! The crowd was so noisy. People were shouting and trying to touch him. He stopped directly under me. When he stopped the noise died down. It was almost as if everyone expected him to speak. I watched him look down for a moment. No one spoke to him but I saw him nod."

"Then he looked up at me and called my name." Zaccheus' eyes rimmed with tears. He paused and gathered himself. "I can still hear his voice today. It was so clear and so direct. I didn't know how he knew my name but he did. He told me to climb down and that he would come to my house...my house for a meal. The noise of the crowd grew but I tell you truly, I never heard them. I only heard him! He was coming to my house!"

"When we walked into the house and Meesha met him, she began shouting orders to the servants and everyone was scrambling to make things ready for the Master. In moments we had a feast prepared. Jesus said very little. He smiled a great deal and his face made me feel so strange inside. He talked of the love of God, forgiveness, and heaven."

I'm not sure what came over me, but while Jesus was speaking I interrupted him. I promised to give away half of all that I had. I also told him that I would give back four times the amount I wrongly took from others. When I looked over at Meesha she had her hand over her mouth in surprise. I'm sure I was more surprised than she, but I knew what I said was right."

"Jesus called me a Son of Abraham! I had not heard that phrase in many years and never was it used to address me! He told me that he was what I was seeking because I was lost." Zaccheus patted his own chest, "Deep in my heart I knew all was well. I had such peace, such assurance, such joy, all that I ever longed for! I have never been the same since I spent time with him. My whole life had been centered around *getting*. He showed me the joy and fulfillment of *giving*. I will never forget that day, and I will never stop following Jesus the Messiah!"

The room was cloaked in silence. Zaccheus wiped a small tear from his eye and gave a confident smile. Dimetri reached over and patted his friend's arm. Matthew watched as Meesha came from behind and put her arm around his chest gently hugging him. When he looked at Dimetri's face it carried a somewhat smug smile. He could almost hear him say, "I told you so!" and Matthew didn't blame him.

The next day found the two men seated on an empty cart heading for home. Meesha had a snack prepared for the journey and they were enjoying some fruit. The day was warm and clear but not too hot. After riding for a few hours they made their way to a large village and stopped at an inn for a meal. While Matthew was tying the donkey to a post he made the comment, "It is amazing to walk in the steps of Jesus and to meet so many who have met him." Levi laughed lightly, "Yes! These are wonderful days we are living in!" Out of the corner of his eye Matthew saw a man get up from a bench and approach them. By his robe and phylacteries, he knew him to be a religious leader, maybe even a Pharisee or Sadducee. The man met Levi as he was coming off the cart. He moved close to Levi, too close Matthew thought. "You mention Jesus. Do you mean the Galilean?" Levi didn't pause. "Yes. Jesus from Galilee." The man spit on the ground. "This man Jesus has caused our people much trouble. He has disturbed so many with stories, lies and false signs." Levi turned to face the man and Matthew came closer. "What about all the people he healed? What about all the miracles?" Levi said. "Miracles?" the man said loudly. "Magician's tricks. Slight of hand and no more. He was a deceiver and blasphemer and nothing beyond that." Levi steadied himself and squared his shoulders with the man. He simply said, "He lives." The man's face reddened. "He does not live! You are a fool! His followers continue to cause trouble but they will be stopped!" The man turned away abruptly and walked toward the synagogue.

Levi looked at Matthew who's face was frozen in surprise. He smiled at him and said, "Not everyone who looks sees, and not everyone who listens hears." With that he patted Matthew on the back and the two entered the inn for lunch.

They were finishing a plate of fish, bread and hummus when the door behind them opened. The religious leader stood there with another leader and two synagogue soldiers. They strode over to the table and the man they met earlier pointed a finger at Levi and spoke up. "Are you a member of *the way*?" Levi answered without hesitation. "I am a follower of the risen Lord Jesus Christ!" "Enough!" the man shouted. "Take him!" Matthew tried to stand up but two hands on his shoulders kept him in his seat. The other soldier grabbed Levi's arm and pulled him from his chair. As the men began to leave Matthew stood up and was met with an elbow in the ribs doubling him over. A large hand on the back of his head pushed his face into the table. His ear was filled with one loud word, "Stay!" Out of the corner of his eye he saw Levi leave the room and he heard Levi shout "Yeshua ha Messhia." Matthew whispered, "Jesus the Messiah."

Matthew left the inn and quickly made his way to the synagogue. Two guards stood on the steps barring his entry. By the sounds from inside, he could tell they were in a room close to the front of the building. He felt that maybe they believed it would defile the synagogue to bring a "blasphemer" too far inside. He heard words like "Fool! Troubler! Blasphemer" being yelled from inside. Matthew sat on the steps and quietly prayed for his friend.

An hour later the doors of the synagogue burst open and Levi was thrust outside. Matthew caught him before he tumbled all the way down the steps. Matthew helped him sit up. Blood trickled from his nose, one of his eyes was swollen, and his lip was bleeding "Are you hurt my friend?" he asked. "Not badly my Brother. I will be better in time." Then he looked at Matthew with a sly grin and said, "Yeshua ha Messhia." Matthew grinned, shook his head, and repeated, "Yeshua ha Messhia."

He helped Levi to his feet and then back down the street and onto the cart. "Reminds me of the bullies back in Junior High" Matthew thought. The men turned the cart around and began their long ride back home. "This is not a surprise" Levi said, "The Master said 'If they hated me, they will hate you.'" Matthew nodded without smiling and the two rode on in silence. After awhile Levi turned to Matthew and said, "When I told you back at the synagogue that I will be better in time I did not know how soon that would happen." Matthew looked at him in disbelief and struggled to understand. Sensing Matthew's mental struggle, Levi said, "I am better because I just realized what an honor it is to suffer for the sake of the Master." Matthew nodded his head in understanding.

# Chapter 10
# **Choices**

Late that afternoon the men reached a large town. Like the cities, it was very busy and only a little less noisy. On the far side of the market stood a man with two servants. He was looking over some merchandise in a wagon. Levi pointed him out and said, "I know that man. He is very wealthy and he actually spoke to Jesus one-on-one." Let us go talk to him." They made their way across the square and approached the man. "Shalom Anthonius!" Levi said. The man looked up at him knowing that there were many who did not know him but acted as if they did. Levi bowed to the man. "I am Levi and this is my friend Matthew." He smiled and nodded to the men. "Are you a merchant?" the man asked. "No, just a sojourner. I have heard that you spoke with the teacher Jesus."

Anthonius put down what he was holding. In a low voice he said, "Speak to me truthfully. Are you one of our religious leaders?" "No we are not" Levi said. "Are you a synagogue or temple official?" "No. I tell you the truth. We are just men who are followers of the Messiah." "Then yes, I have spoken to Jesus." Will you share with us what he told you?" Levi asked. Anthonius looked around. Turning to his servants he said, "We wish to be alone." The man closest to him bowed his head and said, "Of course." The two men departed. Anthonius pointed and said, "Let us go inside."

The two men followed him to a room in the back of the store and sat down at a small table. Without hesitation Anthonius began his story. "It is not to everyone that I tell this story. I must be very careful." Levi grinned, waved his hand over his face and said, "We know. Not everyone is friends with the followers of Jesus." Anthonius put his hand on Levi's shoulder as if to say, "I understand."

He took a deep breath and leaned back in his chair. "I lived in my father's house about a mile to the South of town. My father was a very wealthy man who owned much property and had many servants. He was very well known throughout the region. My brother and I worked for my father in the family business. The plan was that one day we would take over the business and run things for our father. My father was a driven man who worked very hard and demanded complete loyalty."

One day my father sent me to a town to examine some goods that had just arrived. A servant rode with me and as always I did what I was told. On the way back we came upon a crowd just outside the village. Jesus was in the middle of the crowd. We stopped and stood in the back listening to him teach. He was talking about Jehovah's love for us and spoke of many things concerning heaven. He told us the value of heaven and said we should trade whatever we have for it. He told us that whatever we needed to give up to enter heaven, it would be worth it. I listened to every word he said and like everyone else I wanted to go to heaven. I don't know why, but at one point I asked him a question about heaven. I said, 'Teacher, what must I do to enter into heaven?' He turned and looked at me and it felt like the rest of the crowd disappeared. He answered my question with a question. He said, 'What are the commandments that are written in the Torah?'"

"I knew the Torah. My brother and I had personal Rabbis when we were growing up. I had read the Torah many times and my teachers required me to memorize parts of it. I said, 'Do not kill, do not steal, do not commit adultery' I could have listed all of them but the Teacher held up his hand for me to stop. I attended the synagogue regularly and I sacrificed at the temple two or three times a year. He said, you have answered well. Do all of these and live.' But something in his voice told me there was more. I was confident and told him, 'I have kept the commandments of our people since I was a boy.'

His next words startled me. He said, 'One thing you lack...' These were strange words to me. I could think of nothing that I lacked. I always did what I should do and I always possessed what I wanted. How could I be lacking anything? I had priests, Rabbis, Pharisees, Scribes, and Sadducees as friends. They always invited me to the festivals and celebrations. I was known in the local synagogue and in the temple. How could I lack anything?"

Anthonius leaned toward the men. "He said, 'Go, sell, and give everything to the poor. Then come, follow me.' I was very familiar with the first two words. My entire life was about going and selling. But I was always going and selling to get, not to give. And the the last part? Give it all to the poor and follow him? How could I do that? Friends, I *did* give. I gave to the synagogue and to the temple. Often I would round the temple and drop coins in the brass container."

Matthew's mind jumped back to his visit to the temple. He remembered the brass containers and the *game* the wealthy played. Anthonius continued, "Sometimes I would round the temple two or three times. I GAVE! People knew I gave and recognized it. I gave to the synagogue and sometimes to the poor. But give everything?" He let the air rush through his lips to emphasize the absurdity of the request.

I looked down at my robe. It alone was worth more than the Teacher and his followers had. How could I give everything? What would my father say? What would my friends and family say?" He paused and looked down. Matthew understood clearly what Jesus meant about a camel and the eye of a needle.

Anthonius continued, "I walked away with his words burning in my heart... 'one thing you lack, go, sell, give.' I want to. I want to follow his teaching, but at this point I can not." Matthew thought, "Nothing has changed. People still struggle with holding on to things. We let go of one thing only to grab for another." He himself felt the strong pull of materialism. "Go, sell, give...still the call of Jesus!"

Anthonius looked down. He looked so sad. "Maybe some day, when I am older I will be able to follow, but not now." Levi wanted to console him, to comfort him. He wanted to tell him that he didn't really have to give everything but that would directly contradict the words of the Master. The soreness of his own cheek served as a reminder of the call to sacrifice. He leaned forward and put a hand on Anthonius' shoulder and said, "I hope one day you will find the strength my friend." In a whisper Anthonius replied, "I hope so. I really do."

The men sat back in their chairs for a moment letting the time they spent together soak in. Then Anthonius stood up and the other two followed his lead. They came to the street and found the servants standing by the door with bundles in their hands. Anthonius turned to the two and said, "Shalom my friends. Jehovah be with you." And with that he was gone.

# Chapter 11
# The Visitor

After a quick bite to eat, the men were once again, heading home. The remainder of the ride was uneventful but full of conversation. Levi and Matthew talked of boyhood days, family, and the good news of salvation. They each quoted what they heard (and read) of the words of the Messiah with Matthew being careful with the way he shared.

Hannah met the men as they came through the door. Immediately, she noticed Levi's face and she was filled with concern. Levi tried to act as if it was nothing but Hannah would have none of it. She wanted to know all the details of what happened and was visibly angry at the way her husband was treated. She instructed him to sit down as she got a wet cloth and began gently cleaning his face. Levi tried to lighten the mood by saying, "It is a good thing that you were not there. We are commanded not to kill." Hannah only shook her head and gave a loud sigh.

Matthew went to bed that night with so many thoughts in his head. He missed Melissa terribly but somehow felt that he was on a trip out of town for a few days. Deep inside he had the feeling that he would be returning home again soon. With these images and the review of the past few days Matthew drifted off to sleep.

He stretched as he awoke to the smell of biscuits and fish. A strange combination but a great taste. Matthew celebrated a great night's sleep and attributed it to *holy air*. He made his way downstairs and joined the family for breakfast. Having enjoyed breakfast, he joined Levi in the garden.

Benjamin returned from the well and said, "Father, there is a man at the well who has been with Jesus. He is talking to the people of the town." Levi stood up and smiled. "Let's go to him and see what he has to say." Walking through the house he told Hannah and the four of them walked toward the center of town and the well. Under a couple of large trees by the well, they found several dozen people seated around a man.

The man looked to be about forty years old. His clothing was very simple as expected. His head was uncovered and he leaned on a walking stick. His face was beaming as he talked and he had a very strong voice. Levi and the other three joined the group and sat down to listen.

They learned from the others that his name was Demarcus. He had traveled with the Master though he was not of *the twelve*. He and a large group of others were sent out in pairs to share the news of the Messiah. Their message was simple: The kingdom of God is at hand! The Messiah has come! Repent of your sins! Love God and love each other!

"My friend Tershahn and I left with words to share but never dreamed of what would happen on our journey. We left the Master and simply began walking East. Everywhere we went we simply shared the message Jesus had given us. There was some resistance from the religious leaders but mostly they were curious. They could offer little argument."

"But one time Tershahn shouted to a crowd, 'Jesus is the Messiah.' There was a Pharisee standing in the back and he shouted, 'No! That is not true! He is a false prophet!' Some left but most of the crowd stayed."

"A man came forward. He had injured his arm in a fall. He had no use of it for over a year. I reached out and touched his arm and said, 'In the name of Jesus of Nazareth, be healed.' I felt his arm grow warm and I watched him clench his fist and move his arm. He held it up to his face and his eyes grew wide. The crowd cheered."

"Another time we came across a man who could not speak. He simply touched his lips and extended his hand to us. Tershahn put his palm on the man's forehead and said, 'In the name of the Jesus the Messiah be loosed.' The man grunted a couple of times and said, 'I, I, I, praise be to Jehovah!'"

One day as a crowd gathered we were telling of the love of God and how he cared so deeply for everyone. He loves us more than the birds of the air and the beasts of the field. Tershahn looked at the crowd and saw an elderly man who was leaning on a crutch. Looking down, we noticed that he had a clubbed foot. We later learned that his foot had been injured as a baby when his nurse dropped him. His foot had been like that his entire life. Tershahn called him forward and the man hobbled up to us. Tershahn put his hand on his shoulder and said 'In the name of Jesus the Messiah be healed.' When the man reached out and grabbed Tershan's shoulder his crutch dropped to the ground. He extended his leg forward and we saw that it was no long bent. He slowly put his foot down and leaned on it. He picked his other foot up and stood on his healed leg. I heard the crowd gasp." Matthew looked at Levi and saw him smile broadly. Leaning toward Matthew he whispered, "Yes my friend! Yes!

"Tears streamed down the man's face and he could not stop grinning. He turned around a couple of times, faced the crowd and raised his hands over his head and shouted 'Jesus! The Messiah.' The crowd cheered back 'Jesus the Messiah!'"

"After two days we returned to Jesus. I am not certain our feet touched the ground as we traveled. Many others were gathered there. They were all talking so fast and with so much excitement. They had experiences just like Tershahn and myself. It was wonderful! Healing, teaching, casting out demons. I had never been so excited in my life."

No one under the tree moved. They were captivated by every word that came from the mouth of Demarcus. He smiled at the crowd, leaned forward and pointed a single finger upward. "My friends, Jesus told us all, 'It is wonderful what has been done. The kingdom of God is growing. The greatest word is not in the healing and teaching. The greatest word is that your names have been written in heaven.'" He stepped forward, grabbed the shoulders of a man up front, and gently shook him. "In heaven! My name is written in heaven!"

He stepped back again and looked up to the crowd. "There was so much joy, so much hope! But then everything changed. The religious leaders came and took the Master. Before we knew what had happened he was on the cross. I saw him myself." He paused and took a deep breath. "I watched as they took him from the cross and carried him away. Several followers were taken by the leaders and questioned. Some were beaten and told not to speak of him again." Levi gave a knowing nod. "We did not know what to do. How could this happen? All the teaching-the miracles-the prophesies-was it all for nothing? The city was in an uproar. Some were angry. Others were scared. There were some who held on to hope but most of us found places to hide."

"Tershahn and I found some others and hid ourselves in a small home in the city. We were all trying to figure everything out. A couple of days later some soldiers burst into the room and took the leaders. Some of us tried to defend them but only wound up with bruises and threats. I grabbed Tershahn and we escaped through a window. We left the city and stayed in the home of an old woman who lived nearby. We were so hurt, so confused. We were convinced that Jesus was the promised one. All the prophesies and signs pointed to him. We knew he was the deliverer. He was the one who would throw off the yolk of Roman rule and we would again live here in the promised land in peace. I cannot tell you of the hurt in my heart and soul. One day we were driving out demons and performing miracles in his name and the next day he was dead and we were hiding in a small room in an old widow's house."

"We made plans to go to the house of Tershahn's uncle. He lived about four miles from Jerusalem. We just needed to go to a place that was safe, where we could try and sort things out." Then he said the word that made Matthew's eyes light up. *Emmaus.* "So that's who this is!" Matthew whispered in amazement. It was all he could do to keep from shouting out the rest of the story. Once again Matthew was being ushered into the presence of a first-hand witness of the resurrected Savior!

Without pause, Demarcus continued. "I have never been so discouraged in all my days. With fear and confusion, we left early the next morning and began our walk west? When we were about couple of miles from Emmaus we came upon a man on the side of the road. He was sitting on a rock and looked like he was waiting for someone. When we reached him he stood and greeted us. He said, 'Friends, I too am going to Emmaus.' At the time we didn't wonder how he knew our destination. I guess we were too wrapped up in our own confused thoughts. He began to walk with us and asked us what we were discussing. It seemed so strange a question. Of course we were talking about what was on everyone's mind-the death of the prophet Jesus. He simply nodded. Then he began to speak and for the next couple of miles it was only his voice that we heard."

"As we walked on the road, his words walked us through the Holy Scriptures. He told us of the lives of Father Abraham, Isaac, and Jacob as if they were friends of his. He talked about the Egyptian enslavement and deliverance of our people like he was there. He told us about the very night the Exodus began as if it were yesterday. Prophesy, sin, forgiveness, and the love of God were subjects he seemed to dance through and explain with such clarity and authority."

Demarcus stopped as if to re-load. He had a look on his face of a man confused and hurt. Matthew did his best to stifle a chuckle. An older man pleaded with Demarcus, "Go on my friend." Demarcus smiled slightly and nodded. "We arrived at the home and were welcomed in. The stranger agreed to join us. His Aunt brought out some wine, fish, and bread. We talked for a few moments and then the stranger moved to his knees. He took the bread in one hand and the cup in the other and held it up. He broke the bread into several pieces and handed it to each of us. No one spoke. The wind pushed the door open and all of us turned toward it. When we looked back he was gone!"

Demarcus spread his arms wide with his palms up. "I cannot explain what happened next. It was if we had been under a blanket in a room full of light. Suddenly the blanket came off and we could see. But the light was not just around us. The light was inside of us! At the same time Tershahn and I yelled, 'The Master!'" Demarcus clenched his fists, bent his elbows and yelled, "It was him! It was really him! The other two were silent and confused. We both knew we had to get back to the others still hiding in Jerusalem. He had said that he would rise in three days and he did! We saw him! We were with the Savior!"

Matthew wrestled with the emotions of excitement and jealousy. To see Jesus face to face! Incredible! Demarcus' story continued. "We walked and trotted back to Jerusalem. As soon as we arrived we found several of the others gathered in a room above the home of one of his followers. It was the place the Master had shared the Passover with the inner twelve. We couldn't wait to tell them. We came into the room and said, 'We saw him! We saw the Master!' Peter said, 'Yes, we saw him as well. He was here!'"

"We learned that he had also appeared to some women at the tomb. We spent the entire night talking endlessly of his appearances, prophesy and all the Messiah had taught us. Without question it was the richest night of our lives."

Levi grinned and stood to his feet. Tears were seen in his eyes and he could not keep the smile from his face. Matthew's hand was over his mouth but he couldn't hide the smile he was wearing. He slowly shook his head from side to side in utter wonder. The rest of the day was spent with the people of the town asking the visitor questions. Many came to trust the Savior for forgiveness and vowed to be faithful followers. By mid-day the stranger had moved on.

The next day word came to Levi that several members of *the way* had been taken to the synagogue and held there for questioning. When he told this to Matthew he simply said, "I know." Levi gave him a quizzical look but Matthew covered himself by saying, "I mean, I figured there would be some opposition."

# Chapter 12
# Power

At mid-morning, Levi and Matthew sat at a corner table not far from the square. They were enjoying light conversation when a leader of the synagogue entered and sat at the table next to them. Levi recognized him and greeted him with a smile-less nod. The two sat in silence until Levi gave a heavy sigh signaling that he was intending on engaging the official. Matthew put his hand on Levi's forearm and tilted his head to the side as if to say, "Be careful!"

Levi turned his chair toward the official. The man immediately looked at Levi. Levi leaned in, "Is it permitted that I may ask you a question?" "It is so" the man said. "I would like to know about the people who were taken to the synagogue last night. Why were they taken and why have they not been released?" The official leaned toward Levi and interlaced his fingers while resting them on the table. "Our leaders are trying to find a way to stop this religious fanaticism about a dead teacher."

"A dead teacher?" Levi asked. His name is Jesus and he is more than just a dead teacher. Have you heard of the miracles and signs he performed?"

The official became somewhat disturbed. "Miracles? Those were tricks shown before some ignorant people who believed simply because they wanted to." Matthew slid his chair up next to Levi. These comments were more than he could stand and his training lurched forth. He asked, "But what about the empty grave?"

"The grave was empty because the followers of this man took his body and hid it while the guards slept."

Matthew did not try to hide his irritation. "How do you know they took the body?"

"The guards told us."

"But if they were asleep, how did they know the disciples stole the body?"

"We know what we know."

"I'm sure that answer makes sense to you."

Levi was surprised at the boldness of Matthew but made no effort to slow him down.

"How do you explain all the people who saw Jesus after the crucifixion? How do you reconcile the boldness his followers displayed when earlier they were too afraid to be identified with him? Why is it that so many of the disciples were persecuted?" Matthew realized he had crossed the line historically but he wasn't sure he cared.

"These people are seeking to persuade others away from our religion and they must be stopped at all costs."

Matthew didn't want to let that last comment slide. "And what was so wrong with what this man said that he should die?"

The official began to get demonstrative and stood up. "It is not just what he said, but what he did. If there were miracles many of them were done on the Sabbath, a violation of the law. I am told that often he did not wash before a meal. He edited the Holy Scriptures. He forgave sinners of their sins and only Jehovah, and he alone can do that. He spent his time among the lawless ones. Worst of all, many came to worship him as the Messiah and he did nothing to stop them. That is nothing short of blasphemy!" At that last comment he pounded the table with the palm of his hand.

Both Matthew and Levi wanted to respond but the man held up his finger in front of their faces. "Our religion is what has held us together for centuries. The law must be honored and the temple must be revered. If this man continued, his followers would have grown and the Romans would have felt threatened and stepped in and taken away our place-our authority. The people would be without leadership and be unrestrained." It was obvious that the man had lost control of his emotions and he shouted at the two. "I will speak no more of this Galilean Blasphemer" and he stood up and turned away making three spitting sounds as he walked.

Levi and Matthew sat at the table somewhat surprised. "A man's motivation always moves him" Levi said pointing his finger in the air. "We are moved to serve the master, and he is moved to serve the men." Matthew felt the makings of a sermon. He wanted to comment, but both men knew they too must leave. Matthew dropped two coins on the table. Without discussion they got up quickly and made for the door.

As they got ready to turn the corner, Matthew looked back. He saw the synagogue official working his way through the busy square accompanied by another official and two soldiers. He didn't have to ask where they were going or what their plans were. They picked up their pace and headed home.

In the early morning the two men were once again walking toward the Holy City. When they came to a divided road Levi commented that it would be wise to visit a small town close by. The name of the town was Bethany. From his studies Matthew immediately was familiar with the goings on in this location.

Levi felt the need to fill Matthew in on a significant episode he had heard happened here. "In this town there are two sisters. One is called Mary. The other sister I do not know. Perhaps her name is Rachel, but I am not sure." Matthew stifled himself from blurting out the name Martha and nodded at his friend. Levi continued. "They have a brother whose name is Lazarus. If possible we will speak to them about what I heard the Master did here."

The men immediately walked to the center of town and located the well. They sat on the edge of the stones and Levi drew the large bucket up. He drank deeply and handed the bucket to his friend. While Matthew was drinking he saw movement from his right. Letting the bucket drop down he saw a woman approaching with a bucket of her own. The men stood and she nodded to them without speaking. Levi's question broke the silence. "Shalom." The woman quietly said, "Shalom." "Good woman, we wish to find the home of Mary and her sister. Their brother is the one called Lazarus." At first the woman didn't speak. She worked the bucket back up with the rope and while reaching for the handle said, "I know of them. They are good people. They live all the way at the end of this street. Their house is the one next to the large tree." The men smiled at each other with Levi adding, "You are very kind. Peace be to you." The woman smiled and the men turned down the street.

When they came to the end of the street they found two trees in front of the row of houses. This gave them four options. They spent little time discussing which house to try first and approached the one agreed upon. They knocked and a door opened almost immediately. A short man stood in the doorway.

"Shalom" Levi said.

"Shalom" the man returned without much emphasis.

"We wish to be at the home of Lazarus."

The man used his thumb to point to the house next door.

The men bowed and moved away hearing the door close behind them.

They knocked on the door and waited. Soon the door opened and a full-figured middle aged woman stood before them.

Both men bowed and Levi said, "Shalom."

The woman returned the bow, "Shalom."

Levi continued, "We are followers of Jesus the Messiah on our way to the Holy City. We have heard about what the Master did for Lazarus and wish to see him if possible."

The woman opened the door. "I am Martha and my sister is Mary. Lazarus is at the market, but will be home soon. Will you come in?"

They stepped inside. Matthew looked around. Their home looked similar to all the other homes he had been in. But somehow it "felt" different. It may have been because Matthew was familiar with some of the stories connected with the three of them and Jesus. He could see Jesus in the room being waited on by Martha and listened to by Mary. In his mind he heard the voice of the teacher as he shared with a room full of followers.

Martha called for her sister. "Mary, we have guests."

In a moment Mary appeared from a side room. She was wearing a brown dress with a white sash. She had a slim build and delicate features with dark eyes. Levi and Matthew bowed to her and she returned one of her own.

Martha turned to the men and said, "These men have come to talk to Lazarus. They are followers of the Christ." "Of course" Mary said. We have had so many come to see our brother. He has become very popular and does not go without enjoying the attention. Will you care to sit for awhile?"

The men sat on the floor and leaned on the short table. Mary knelt by the men while Martha retreated to the kitchen to get some water for the travelers.

"Just like I imagined" Matthew said. Martha is busy serving and

Mary is with people. "Our brother will be back shortly. He has gone to the market to pick up a few things" Mary offered.

"We have heard that you were close to the Master" Levi said.

"Oh, yes" Mary said smiling. "Jesus came here often. He became like another brother to us. He would often stop by on his way to or from Jerusalem. Several times he spent the night with us. More than once the temple officials came looking for him but he was never here."

Matthew had a question he had always wanted to ask someone who would know. Up until this time it was only subjected to speculation but now in the presence of someone who knew Jesus so well, he knew the answered could be had. The question carried little significance but still it nagged him. "Did Jesus ever laugh?"

Mary laughed. "Of course he laughed! He was just like anyone else and had a very good sense of humor."

Martha entered the room with some bread and cups of water. She placed them down on the table and the thirsty men slipped them to their lips. Martha knelt next to her sister and joined in the conversation. "The Master smiled a lot. And he indeed had a wonderful smile. But he did enjoy laughing. Many times he laughed at the expression of someone who was healed and sometimes at the looks on people's faces when they witnessed one who was healed." Mary broke in, "I remember one time when Jesus and some of his followers were here. One of the men made a comment about a Pharisee that was talking to Jesus. The religious leader was talking to him, and in some sense lecturing him about the importance of being clean. He stressed ceremonial washing and the importance of physical purity. When the man turned to leave you could see a large stain on the back of his robe.

The disciple asked Jesus if he saw the man's robe and Jesus started laughing. The whole room joined in when Jesus said, 'I was wondering if anyone else had seen that. Not everything gets ceremonially clean!'

Martha spoke up again. "Then there was the time when one of the disciples slipped while getting into a boat. He stumbled and began to fall off the dock. He jumped into the boat and fell out the other side. He was unhurt but gave them great opportunity for laughter at his expense. Jesus was laughing so hard he said his sides were hurting." All Matthew could do by way of reaction was smile.

Mary began to get excited. She leaned forward on the table, chuckled and said, "One time when several men were here with Jesus, one of the disciples was talking about Jesus healing a man's son. The man was filled with joy. As they walked away, he leaped in the air and stumbled to the ground. The man looked back to see if anyone had noticed. The disciple mentioned to Jesus that he might have to heal the man's leg, and Jesus said, 'or his dignity' and the whole room began laughing.

It seemed to be Martha's turn so she spoke up, "One day Jesus was called to go to a home where a little girl was sick. On the way he was told that she had died. The Master said, 'she is not dead, but only sleeping. Several in the crowd laughed quietly at him. I even saw one person shake his head and say, *mashugana*." Matthew knew that was the ancient Hebrew word for crazy. "I was outside the family's home when Jesus went in. A few minutes later Jesus came out holding the little girl. She was very much alive and was smiling ear to ear. The crowd was silent for a moment then everyone including me and the disciples broke out in cheers. That night, as we all sat around a fire one of the disciples said, 'Master, you turned sorrow into laughter when you turned death into life. Who's the crazy one now?' We all laughed at that one."

Martha wasn't finished. "Not all the humor was intended for all of us to enjoy. There were many things that happened that had to be explained to us later. "Mary, do you remember the time Jesus was with so many here in this room. You came out with a small purse and offered it to the Master." Mary nodded and said, "I remember that!" She looked at the the two men and said, "As you can see, we don't have very much, but we wanted to give what we had to the Jesus." Martha continued. "Yes. But the Master did not take it. He said, 'You are very kind, but our Father has ways to meet our needs beyond what one would expect. In fact, he can supply in some of the most unusual ways.' Jesus looked around the room. For a moment, no one spoke, then all of a sudden everyone began laughing. We were laughing too but did not know why. Later, we asked one of the disciple about the point of humor and he told us something about finding a coin in a fish's mouth."

Mary jumped in. "So, to answer your question, yes, the Master did laugh. As you can understand, he had his serious moments, but he did have a wonderful sense of humor, and it was so much fun to see him and those who followed him enjoy times of laughter."

Matthew's mind flashed back to a drawing his mother had given him a few months before she went to be with the object of the drawing. It was called "The Delightful Christ." It showed the face of Jesus recovering from a deep bout of laughter. Some say it was the way Jesus looked after the resurrection as he reflected on the ultimate "Practical Joke" that was played on the devil. He kept the framed drawing in his office to remind him of the importance of humor in a person's life, especially in the life of a Pastor.

With all that the ladies had shared with them, he couldn't help but recall a Bible verse that now had new meaning to him. He remembered that Hebrews 4:15, said that Jesus was tempted in all ways just like we are but did not sin. That verse pointed strongly to Jesus' humanity. The way the ladies talked about him pointed to it as well. It hit home with him and helped him see Jesus in a new and refreshing way.

While he was chasing those thoughts, the door opened and in walked a man who had to be Lazarus. He looked to be about forty-years-old. He was taller than Matthew had expected and bore a longer beard marked with small streaks of gray. He carried a good sized sack made of burlap with apples, olives, cheese, and corn. His other hand held a container of goat's milk. Both the men and women stood up when he came in. Martha took the sack and brought it to the kitchen while Mary introduced him to the visitors.

"Lazarus! This is Levi and Matthew. They are followers of Jesus and have come to visit."

The men said "Shalom" in unison.

Lazarus crossed the small room in three steps. "Shalom and welcome. Please sit."

The men joined Lazarus around the low table. Levi said, "We are on or way to Jerusalem," Matthew noticed Levi's slight head bob. "We had heard of you." "Read of you" Matthew thought. "And we were thinking that since we were so close to your city, we might by chance meet you and hear your story of how Jesus raised you from the dead."

"Let Jehovah be praised" Lazarus countered.

Martha spoke up. "Many have asked him about it. It is a story that Mary and I have heard and told a hundred times, but somehow it never gets old."

"Yes" Lazarus said smiling, "From my perspective there is really not much to tell. I died and Jesus raised me from the dead. The end." Lazarus leaned to one side and waited in silence for a reaction. The room was somewhat tense with the men not knowing how to respond. Then

Mary said, "He's is joking!" Then putting an arm around his shoulder she said, "Lazarus, tell the story! Lazarus grinned. "Yes, yes, I will."

"I had been out tending our small garden. It was very warm and I was sweating strongly. I went to stand up and all of a sudden felt very weak and dizzy. I went down to one knee. Martha saw me and came out."

"I thought he had hurt his back. He looked like he was in a lot of pain" Martha offered.

"I was" Lazarus said pointing his finger in the air for emphasis. "My head began to throb. Martha brought me into the house and I lay down. Mary brought me a cup of water and a cool towel for my head."

Mary patted his shoulder and said, "I thought he had been in the sun too long. He has a habit of overdoing it"

Lazarus continued, "I fell asleep almost immediately."

"He slept for over two hours. We were so worried." Martha added.

"When I awoke I tried to get up but my head was aching terribly and I was very dizzy. I laid back down to rest some more."

Mary shook her head. "We knew something was very very wrong. Lazarus was in a deep sleep but was breathing very rapidly. Martha sent me to find Jesus. We had heard that he was in Qumran so I collected some food and water and left right away. On my way out of the city I passed a friend sitting outside of his home. He must have seen the worry on my face and asked me about it. I told him what had happened and that I was going to find Jesus. He called his son and told him to go with me. The two of us moved quickly and by the time the sun was at its peak we came to Qumran."

Mary took a deep breath and plunged ahead. "It was not hard to find Jesus. He was sitting in the middle of a crowd teaching something about the kingdom of God. I did not want to interrupt him so I waited a moment. Jesus saw me and motioned for me to come to him. I told him what had happened and he said that all would be well and that he would becoming to Bethany shortly. I thought that he meant very shortly as in that day so I left and returned home."

Martha picked up the story, "When Mary came home we were not here. Lazarus had died shortly after Mary had left. I sent someone to bring Mary back but they said they couldn't find her. We felt sure that Jesus would be coming soon and we kept looking for him but he didn't come. We needed Lazarus! We needed Jesus! We felt empty and hopeless. We could not believe that our brother was gone! We had the funeral and buried Lazarus in a tomb on the edge of town. Our hearts were as dark as our clothing."

"Two days later I saw Jesus coming down the road. I ran to him crying as I went. I told him about Lazarus but he seemed unmoved. He said Lazarus would live again. I didn't understand. I knew he would live again in heaven but it was not until later I realized he was talking about him living now."

Mary joined in again, "Martha sent for me. I was in the house with some of the mourners. I ran to Jesus. Through my sobs I told him about Lazarus. Then I saw something I had never seen before. Jesus began to cry. This made us all cry."

Martha said, "It was at that moment that we knew there was no hope. I felt so empty when Lazarus died, but to see Jesus weep made me feel even worse. His heart had joined our hearts and he truly felt our pain."

"Jesus walked to the burial ground and never said a word. No one spoke. We just walked behind him. We did not tell him where the grave was but he went directly to it. He stood in front of the tomb and told us to move the stone. I told him that we had prepared the body but that it had been four days and by now his body was decaying."

Mary pulled herself to her knees, "Jesus was not stern but he was direct. He told us only to believe and we would see the glory of God. There was a group of men with us and we asked them to move the stone. They gave us a strange look but did what we asked." Levi and Matthew knew the ending to the story but sat there motionless with their mouths open.

"Then Jesus yelled at the tomb." Mary raised her arms. In as deep a voice as she could, she called out, 'Lazarus, Lazarus, Lazarus! Come forth!'"

Lazarus joined in. "As for me, I had no idea what was happening. Everything happened so fast. It was so strange. I remember laying down and going to sleep. Then as I slept I heard the voice of the Master from far off-like it was outside in the street. At first I couldn't understand what he was saying but then I heard my name, loud and distinctly."

"But his voice was somehow different" Martha added. Normally his voice was strong but quiet. The was a voice that I had never heard before. It was loud and deeper. He sounded angry."

Lazarus spoke up. "When I heard his voice, I wanted to answer but somehow I couldn't. I opened my eyes but the room was fairly dark and I had a cloth over my face. I thought it was the covers. I tried to move them but I couldn't. Then I heard his voice again. This time it was thunderous. He said 'Lazarus come forth.' I sat up. Through the cloth I could see daylight. Finally, the cloth fell off my face. I stood up but I found that I couldn't walk. My arms and legs had been bound. Since I couldn't walk, I shuffled toward the light. I struggled and finally made my way to the doorway. I bent down and could see all the people outside. I was so confused."

"We couldn't believe it!" Martha said. "Lazarus was standing in the doorway of the tomb! We knew it was him and we knew that he was alive again. No one moved. No one made a sound."

"Then the Master spoke" Mary added, "He said in a voice we were used to, 'Unbind him and set him free.' No one had to be told a second time. Two men ran to Lazarus and had the grave clothes off in seconds. Our brother who was dead was now alive."

Matthew's mind wandered to a sermon he had preached years ago on this story. He remembered telling his people that when God saves a person he is given new life. Then it is the job of the church to unwrap him so that he is free to walk with the Savior. Some people are wrapped in addictions like alcohol, drugs, or pornography. The *grave clothes* on others are anger, hatred, vengeance, bigotry or other sins that are not easily seen. The church must step in and through the love of Christ remove whatever binds that person and free them to walk with him.

Matthew's thoughts were broken when Mary said, "We looked at Lazarus' face. He wasn't smiling but his face was bright. It is hard to explain. He looked dazed and confused but at peace if that makes sense." Both Levi and Matthew nodded.

"I was still confused" Lazarus said. "I have been told that I had been dead but to this day I still struggle to believe that. For me I had only taken been a long nap. I didn't dream. I didn't go in and out of sleep. I fell asleep and then a couple of hours later I woke up feeling well." "A couple of hours and four days later" Martha added smiling.

Mary spoke again, "People gasped but no one said a word. We all rushed forward to Lazarus. We just wanted to see him up close, to touch him, to talk to him. The grave clothes were off and our brother was alive and free! Then everyone cheered. When I looked at Jesus he was just standing there with his face looking slightly upward and smiling."

Lazarus held his hand up as if he needed to gain the group's attention. "After a few minutes I looked at Jesus. He stepped toward me and I quickly moved toward him. His eyes were shimmering like on the edge of tears. I embraced my Savior and my friend!"

"It was a day none of us will ever forget," Martha said. Our brother was dead and the Master brought him back to life!" "But" Mary added, "Since then it has not all be easy. There are some who would have preferred Lazarus to stay in the grave."

"Yes" Lazarus said, "We have had our struggles. For some reason, the Pharisees and other religious leaders have become very angry…at Jesus and at me!" Lazarus smiled. "What did I do? My part in this whole story was that I died, and I didn't try to do that!" Martha rolled her eyes at her brother's stab at humor.

"The religious leaders were afraid" Lazarus continued. "They were afraid that Jesus was becoming too popular. They thought that news of Jesus raising a man from the dead would spread quickly and would cause too many to follow Jesus instead of them."

Mary leaned in, "That's one of the reasons they sought to destroy Jesus."

"And Lazarus" Martha added. "That's right, Lazarus too" Mary said putting her arm on her brother's hand and nodding without smiling.

"Are they still giving you a hard time?" Levi asked.

"Not too bad" Lazarus replied. "At first they asked a lot of questions. It was pretty informal, just a couple of synagogue officials sitting down with me here at the house and asking me about it. They just wanted to know what happened. Then they brought me to the synagogue. They sat me down in the middle of a circle of several of the officials and some Pharisees and Sadducees. They pressed me pretty hard and in the end suggested that 'For the good of our people' Lazarus gave a knowing smile, 'I should tell the people that I had not died, but was only asleep.'"

"For four days" Martha said with a slight chuckle.

Lazarus shrugged his shoulders and tilted his head slightly to one side, "I was to tell the people that I was in a deep sleep and Jesus used some medicine to wake me up."

"When I kept telling the truth to those who asked me, they brought me in and told me as directly as they could that I was not to speak of it again. I was told that if I did not obey there would be consequences, very serious consequences."

"But how do you not speak of something so wonderful? When a miracle happens to you, how do you not tell somebody, anybody about what happened? Everywhere I went it seemed like someone wanted to hear my story. I felt like the Prophet Jerimiah. It was as if I had fire shut up in my bones. If someone asks, I'm going to tell them. I have nothing to hide!"

Matthew found himself pondering this without saying anything. He had often wondered and even preached about a person experiencing salvation and not sharing their story with someone. He struggled with those who claimed to have the Spirit of God in them but never said a word about what happened. If salvation is the greatest gift a person could ever receive why would anyone not want someone else to have it? He just couldn't understand it. He had often shared that faith in Christ was the *cure* for the cancer of sin. If you have the cure, why keep it to yourself? Lazarus' voice brought him back to the current conversation.

"One time, several of them came here to our home." Lazarus said. "This made me angry!" Martha added as she shook her head and frowned. Lazarus patted her hand and continued. "Two Pharisees with three soldiers came pounding on our door. It was an early morning and I had just gotten up. I opened the door and they said, 'Lazarus?' I said 'Yes?' They said, 'We have questions for you. You are to come with us!' I knew what they wanted but I said, 'What is this about?' They said, 'You will see. Come!' The two soldiers grabbed my arms and pulled me out of the house." Martha rose to her knees. Levi and Matthew both noticed how agitated she was becoming. She tried to remain calm but her voice began to rise. "They came to *our* house and grabbed *our* brother! As if he was some criminal! It is true there were criminals involved, but it wasn't us!" Lazarus looked at Levi and Matthew and smiled. He rubbed Martha's forearm a couple of times and patted her hand again. He said, "It is fortunate for them they did not take my sister! Who knows what she would have done to them."

"They brought me to the synagogue and questioned me again. I told them that they already knew what had happened and that I had nothing more to add. They wanted to know where Jesus was and I told them I didn't know. They pressed me on this but I really didn't know. I had not seen him since the day after he healed me. They accused me of lying and threatened to have me flogged. Flogged! For what?"

"For being raised from the dead" Mary said with a smirk. You are the object of a miracle and they threaten to punish you for it!" The men smiled in understanding.

Lazarus went on, "One of the Pharisees thumped my chest with his fist and told me 'No more! No more are you to speak of this event. You are to act as if it never happened.' I was not expecting that and did not know what to say. The other Pharisee grabbed my face and came down close to me. He snarled at me and said, 'If we here again of you telling people of this, you will be put out of the synagogue and we will destroy you! Do you understand?' I said 'Yes' but as you have noticed, I have not and I will not stop telling people the truth of what happened to me or who Jesus is." He ended that comment with a smile.

"Even if our lives are in danger" Martha commented.

"Yes" Lazarus said. "Even if our lives are in danger. Once when Mary and I were in the market two men came up and stood between us. I didn't pay them much attention but all of a sudden I looked and Mary was bent over. One of the men had her by the back of the head and was holding her down on a cart. Before I knew it, the other man had hit me in the belly and held my face down on the cart as well. I tried to move but he was holding the back of my head. He leaned down toward me and said one word; 'Silence.' Then they let us go and when we looked up, they were gone."

It was ovious that Martha was fighting for a chance to speak. "That's not all they did to silence us. One morning I went to the back of the house to find our goat dead. They had killed our little goat. These are terrible people!"

"Yes" said Lazarus nodding, "But we serve a great God. Our neighbors got together and replaced our little friend. And even now she is getting ready to have a little one of her own."

"I have heard on more than one occasion that the religious officials had made plans to end my life. Two times I have heard of the details of their plans for me. I have been followed in the market and back to our home. I am fairly safe here in Bethany, but I do not dare go outside of town by myself. I must still tell of the Master but I know that I must be careful as well."

"Yes" Levi said, "How can you stop telling everyone who Jesus is and what he has done for you? We all have a choice between the approval of men or the approval of God." He looked at Matthew who returned a knowing nod.

"But Mary has a story to tell you as well" Lazarus said nodding to his sister. Mary nodded rising to her knees. "Yes! I have a story as well. And I will not stop sharing it no matter what they tell me!"

Matthew knew what she was going to share but kept quiet. He was still struggling with the idea of being in the presence of those so close to Jesus. It was all he could do to keep from *filling in the blanks* or running ahead in the stories he was hearing.

"Well" Mary began. After the crucifixion of the Master" she paused for a moment and they could tell that she was holding her emotions in control. "After that horrible day there was so much chaos in Jerusalem." Matthew bent his head to the side in surprise as he saw her dip her head in respect for the city. "People were angry. People were in shock. People were afraid. A few of his followers had been taken, but most of us were hiding in different places in the city. None of us understood what was going on and we were all so surprised at how fast everything had happened. It seemed like one moment Jesus was in our home or in the temple or on a hillside, and the next moment he was on the cross. It was horrible!"

"I had never seen a crucifixion before. Of course, I had heard about them, but I had never seen one. It is so cruel! It is so painful. My stomach hurts even now, just thinking about it. I did not want to be there, but I could not stay away. This was the Messiah our people were waiting for. And our people were in favor of putting him to death. None of it made any sense."

"The Sabbath was nearly upon us so Joseph and some others took his body down. We had little time to prepare it. I went with the men to the tomb. Outside the tomb we quickly washed his body and wrapped him in grave clothes. There was no time for me to go to the market so we had no spices or leaves to put in the wrappings. None of us were expecting this! There just wasn't much time!" Mary's voice went down to a whisper.

Matthew noticed a tear fall from Martha's face. He struggled to keep control of his own tears. He crossed his arms and put a hand to his mouth. Involuntarily, he slowly shook his head.

"When we left the tomb we all went into hiding. I went to the home of my cousin who lived just outside the city. I think I cried all night and the next day. I felt so helpless, so lost. Over and over I asked myself, 'How could this have happened?' I was certain he was the Messiah. All the prophesies and the signs pointed to him. All his teachings and all the time we spent with him…" "And all the miracles" Lazarus added patting his own chest. "Yes" Mary said. "The miracles. He raised others from the dead as well. Everything pointed to him being the deliverer we had looked for, for generations. But in an instant it was all gone. We had nothing. Nothing! My heart hurt. My head hurt. And my face was never dry of tears."

"The day after the Sabbath, early in the morning, I gathered up some spices and made my way back toward the city. I did not care if anyone tried to stop me. I was going to the tomb and I was going to take care of the Master's body in the way we have always honored those who have died."

"When I got close to the city and turned on the road leading to the places of burial I came upon two of the other women who were followers of Jesus. They had the same idea and were on their way to the grave. We walked together and fought tears the entire time. When we got close we started talking about how we would open the grave. We hoped the temple guards would help us."

Matthew knew the story. He even knew about their conversation and what was to happen next. "This is like reading tomorrow's newspaper" he thought but kept everything to himself.

"It was still slightly dark when we arrived at the grave. We could see the two guards and noticed they were asleep. Then I saw that the stone was no longer over the tomb. One of the ladies raised her lantern over the opening and I looked in. I couldn't believe it! I stepped inside and looked all around. He was gone!" She put her hand on Levi's arm and asked, "Who could have taken him? I fell to my knees and began to cry all over again. To take the body of the Master, who would do such a thing? One of the women, I don't know which one, helped me up and we stepped out of the tomb. I looked up and to our left there was a man standing there. I thought he was the caretaker of the burial grounds. I don't know why but I ran to him and fell at his feet. I cried, 'Please sir! Please tell me where they have taken Jesus. Please tell us and we will go to him!' The man lifted me by my arms, I can still feel his hands on me. He lifted me to my feet and said, 'Mary.'" Mary looked around the room in excitement. Her faced beamed.

"He said my name, that was all. And I knew it was Jesus! He was alive! I fell to my knees again and hugged and kissed his feet. The other two did the same. He stepped away from us and pulled us up. He told us to go to the disciples and tell them that he is alive and will meet them in Galilee. We did not want to let go of him but he looked at each of us and gently said, 'All is well. Go.'" Mary took a couple of deep breaths. No one around the table spoke.

"We raced back into the city. We laughed and cried the whole way. We didn't know where all of disciples were so we made our way back to the last place we had seen them. We banged on the door but no one came. The other two women began calling out and soon the door opened. It was Peter. I said, 'Peter! Oh Peter! He's alive! The Master is alive. We saw him! We really saw him!' He told us to be quiet and pulled us into the room. There were several other followers there. We told them, 'The tomb is empty. He's alive. We saw him.' Peter asked us, 'Are you sure? Are you sure it was him?' 'Yes! Yes!' We kept saying. 'He's alive! He's really alive!' Then Peter and John ran out of the room. We knew they were going to the tomb and we knew they would find the tomb empty!

"Incredible!" Matthew thought. "To be there that morning...How could anything be more amazing that that? How could anyone keep this a secret?" He found himself fighting tears of his own.

The room again was silent. After a long time with no one speaking, Lazarus said just above a whisper, "My friends, He lives! He really lives!" "Yes" said Levi, "He lives!" "Yes he lives!" the other three said loudly. "He lives!" all five shouted as they stood to their feet.

Levi turned his palms up and said, "You have been so gracious to us. We thank you our brother and our sisters in Christ for your kindness. And we ask that in the name of the risen Christ, peace be upon this house."

"Yes peace to all of you" Matthew added.

"And may the Lord's peace be upon you as well," Lazarus said.

With that the two men left the house. Their spirits raised and their hearts encouraged.

# Chapter 13
# Worship

The next forty-five minutes were spent walking and talking as the men leisurely made their way to the city. They marveled about all they had heard and talked in great detail about the resurrection of Lazarus and Mary's account of meeting Jesus at the empty tomb. Both men admitted to sparks of jealousy over not personally witnessing either event. At one point Matthew asked Levi, "How will we know where the meeting in the city is?" For a moment Levi didn't answer but then he said, "The Spirit of God will lead us. We must be careful to pay attention."

When they arrived at the city they were once again met with the stares of the men in the gate. Matthew was a little less intimidated and thought, "Don't these guys have anything else to do?"

They worked their way through the crowd and found seats at an outdoor café. While waiting for assistance, they continued their conversation about the teachings of Jesus. Matthew was careful to begin his comments with, "I heard" or "I understand" which helped him avoid questions about himself.

Shortly, a woman came to their table to serve them. They placed their order and continued their conversation. Soon she returned and brought them water, cheese, bread and apples. When she placed the food in front of Levi she tapped the edge of his plate three times with her index finger. Matthew noticed it and looked at Levi. He raised his eyebrows and grinned. When she walked away he leaned forward and whispered, "Meeting tonight" and he placed two fingers on his lips signaling silence.

Soon the woman returned to retrieve their tray. When she picked it up they found a small piece of paper under it. Levi leaned forward and put his hand on the paper. He looked at Matthew and nodded. Leaning back, he slowly slid the paper to his lap and closed his hand around it while casually looking around. When they left the table they found a secluded place where Levi felt safe to open his hand. The note he held simply said, "Just before sundown at Jacob the Tanner's." He folded the note, tore it in four pieces, and dropped it on a nearby burn pile. Levi said, "I know this man. He is a good man and I know that he is a believer. It is a short walk south of the city. We must be there just after the sun sets." Matthew nodded in understanding.

The men found their way to Levi's brother's home only to find that he and his wife were away visiting her family. They spent the next few hours wandering the streets of Jerusalem. They engaged a few people in light conversation and eventually found themselves sitting on the edge of one of the wells. They raised the bucket and helped each other by pouring water into their cupped hands. They had not been there long when a woman with a clay jar approached. She was slender and had long wavy hair partly covered by a scarf. The men stood and stepped aside. Without comment, Matthew took the jar from her and held it under the raised bucket and filled it. He turned and handed the jar to her. She placed it on her shoulder, smiled, nodded, and said, "Peace to you." "And also to you," Matthew said.

As she turned to walk away, Levi said quietly, "He lives." The woman stopped but did not turn around. It seemed as if she was considering a response. Eventually, she turned and quietly said, "Come" and walked away. The men looked at one another and Levi nodded. The men left the well and followed the woman at a distance. A couple of times they saw her look back to see if they were still following. She rounded a corner and stood outside a home. When the men approached she stepped inside and they did the same.

Inside she put the jar down and said, "Welcome. My name is Rebeccah. I am of the tribe of Naphtali. My husband and I lived here for several years before he died. He was a very good man and earned a good living as a merchant." She paused a moment to gather her thoughts. "What is it that you meant when you said, 'He lives?'"

Levi felt comfortable in taking a chance. "We are followers of Jesus. It is he who we spoke about." The woman's face glowed and she gave a sigh of relief. "I too am a follower. Please sit." The men found places around the short table and she returned with cups of water and sat down at the table with them.

Levi asked, "How is it that you became one of his followers?"

Rebeccah gave a slight grin as if to say, "I was hoping you would ask." She cleared her throat and began. "I have always been a good Jew. I gave to the poor, went to the temple on the designated days, obeyed the commandments and avoided the Gentiles. I had heard many things about Jesus and even saw him once when he was here in the city. He sat at the same well where you were sitting and spoke to those around him. I listened the entire time. Never before had I heard someone speak such truth with so much authority. I had heard that he was not trained by any of the Rabbis but he spoke about the Scriptures like no one I had ever heard."

"Many talked about the signs and miracles he had done. They told stories of him turning water into wine, giving blind men their sight, and casting out demons. I even heard about him raising a little boy from the dead."

"One day while my I was visiting my sister in Bethany, a crowd had gathered right next door. The Master was inside teaching. The room was crowded but I was able to go inside and stand against the wall by the door. Jesus was explaining the commandments and teaching about the love of Jehovah. He was so kind and gracious. He spoke so clearly and taught many things that I had heard my entire life but did not understand. A few questions were asked but for the most part Jesus was speaking and all those in the room were listening."

"Jesus had his back to me but the room was so quiet I could hear every word he said. As I watched and listened I noticed the back of his head. His hair was long and brown and carried a slight wave. I imagined all the miles he had walked and all the places he had been. Somehow while I was thinking these thoughts I knew what I was to do."

"I worked my way through the people and out the door. I came to my sister's home and got a vile of perfume given to me by my mother shortly before she died. She told me that I would know the proper way to use it. Several times I have brought it to the temple and placed a drop on the altar. The priest always thanked me and told me that Jehovah was pleased with me."

"I brought the alabaster back to the house and managed to squeeze myself back to where I was standing. I stood there for a few moments listening. Jesus was talking about the love and forgiveness of sins that God had made available to all of us. I am not certain what came over me. Somehow understanding the love of God and the possibility of being forgiven without going to the priest, without bringing a sacrifice to the temple, without giving money, all became so real to me and I was overwhelmed. I tried to hold it in but the tears began to flow from my eyes. I don't think anybody noticed at first, but my heart was broken. I was filled with thankfulness and began to sob."

"I looked up and through my tears I saw the back of his head again. This was a man who shared the love of God with so many. These feet would go where Jehovah directed and no where else! His words would bring hope and healing, love, peace, and truth to those who would listen." She moved herself to her knees and paused. "In front of me was the long awaited Messiah! I was listening to the very voice of God!"

"Something very strange happened inside of me that day. As he continued to speak I stepped behind him. I don't know if anyone noticed and I really didn't care. My first thought was to pour a couple of drops on the back of his head and return to the wall."

Both men nodded. Levi's nod meant, "Continue your story." Matthew's nod however, meant, "I know where this is going."

Rebeccah continued, "I opened the bottle and as I was getting ready to put a couple of drops on the back of his head something inside of me said, *all of it*! I had to pour the entire bottle on the Master's head. I hesitated for a moment, but then I poured all of it on the top of his head. The room was filled with the aroma of the perfume. It flowed from his hair and down his back. A sense of peace and joy overwhelmed my soul. I had always honored Jehovah but this was a level of worship that I had never experienced. To me, this was the essence of true worship."

While she talked Matthew reflected on the idea of worship. He knew so many had interpreted worship in different ways and had witnessed people worshipping using various methods. Many of the forms of worship he saw were self-directed instead of having God at the center. Matthew knew that true worship was to bow. It meant to bow in body and in soul. From what Rebeccah was describing she was bent down with both her body and he spirit. She was experiencing worship in spirit and in truth.

But there was more! Matthew knew that one of the Greek words for worship meant *a kiss toward God*. It meant that your emotions would be engaged as you *romanced* the God of the ages! There was no doubt in his mind that this woman had experienced the very definition of worship. His mind returned again to Rebeccah's voice.

"When I stood up I felt clean and whole. In all my years of worshipping Jehovah I had never felt like that before. I heard some of the men around me whisper criticism. I heard words like *waste, money*, and *foolish*. Then the Master turned to me and smiled. I will never forget his words. He said, 'Woman, you have done well! May the peace of God be upon you.' And that peace of God had come upon me and it has never left. Even after the Messiah was crucified, murdered, I knew that it was not over. When I heard from so many that he had risen and that they had seen him, the faith I had only grew stronger. Unlike others, I have not seen him. But one day, I know that I will see him again. It is with that faith that I live."

Both men gave an agreeing nod.

So you see, I am a follower of Jesus as well. And yes, he lives!" "He lives" the men repeated.

The men invited Rebeccah to the meeting that night and she agreed to attend. They thanked her and left her home. When they stepped outside the sun was setting. They left the city and began the short walk South toward the location of the meeting.

It didn't take long for the men to arrive at the Tanner's home. It was a modest home like most of them, and like at the other meetings the entire front room had been cleared for guests. Three lanterns gave the room light and a slight breeze came in from two open windows. Several people had already arrived when the men walked in. They were greeted warmly by those around and found a place on one side of the room to be seated. Minutes later the house was packed with over seventy people. Most sat on the floor but some stood along the walls and a couple sat on the window ledges. There were mostly men but several women and even a few children pressed in to the room which was buzzing with conversation.

Soon a man stood up on one end of the room and addressed the crowd. It was Jacob the Tanner. "Welcome my brothers and sisters!" he said almost shouting. I am happy to have you here! We are blessed tonight to have an inner disciple of Jesus' here. His name is Peter and he spent three years walking with the Master.

Peter stood up and the room fell into silence. Matthew wondered at the absence of applause but then remembered about how important it was to avoid attention from the street. Peter was about average height and somewhat stocky. His head was uncovered and showed him to be slightly balding. His beard was fairly short. Matthew thought he looked a lot like the drawings he had seen of him and it made him grin.

Matthew sat in wonder. He was in a room just outside of Jerusalem filled with first century believers. Some were eyewitnesses of Jesus. He was about to hear from Peter, one of the apostles. He tried to avoid wondering how this could be happening and tried to focus on what the man was about to say.

"My friends, I am Peter. I spent my entire life fishing on the Sea of Galilee. Fishing was all I knew and I spent my days catching fish and my nights planning my next day of fishing."

"One day the Master came. He said, 'Deny yourself, take up your cross and follow me.' I had to make a choice. Fishing was all I knew. It was my life. I had to decide to give up the life I knew for a life of uncertainty. But there was something about Jesus that drew me. The way he spoke, the look in his eyes, the opportunity he offered. That day, I exchanged my nets for a chance to be with the Messiah and my life has never been the same. From the very first day I knew I was headed for a great adventure. The way he spoke, how he explained the holy book, his complete faith and trust in Jehovah. And the miracles! The miracles he did! Never in all my days had I seen anything like it. People were healed, demons were cast out, the day we fed over five thousand from such a small amount I will never forget."

"Always I will remember the day myself and the others were told by the Master to go ahead of him in the boat we often used. We were to go to the other side of the sea and he was to meet us there later."

"We had rowed for quite some time and then saw the sky darken. Storms on the lake can come quite suddenly and this proved to be the case. The wind increased and the waves grew. Before we knew it we were in the midst of a great storm. We rowed harder and harder but could make no progress. Our boat was tossed and turned as the waves grew. The rain pounded us and in moments all of us were drenched. We were at the mercy of the great storm. Several of the men, even those familiar with the sea, reached the point of panic."

"Then one of the men, I think it was Andrew cried out, 'Look!' I looked at him and he was pointing out into the middle of the storm." Peter lifted his arm and his head and pointed them to the far end of the room. The heads of many in the room followed him. "About fifty feet away we could see something. It would disappear behind each wave but we could tell it was getting closer and closer. Still, it was too dark to clearly see what it was."

"One of the men shouted, 'A ghost' and a few others said the same. But as it approached we could see that it was a man. When he was about thirty feet away he shouted to us, 'My friends do not be afraid, it is I.' At that point we thought it was Jesus." Peter brought one leg forward and leaned into the crowd. He raised his finger for emphasis. "Jesus was walking on the water. We were in the midst of a storm and there he was, walking on top of the water!" Peter paused as if to let his words sink in.

"None of us knew what to do. Our eyes had never seen anything like this. I don't know why but I shouted to the Master, 'Jesus, if it is you, call to me and draw me to you.' He simply said, 'It is I. Come!'"

"At first I did nothing. Then in a flash, my mind reflected on all the things I had seen Jesus do, all the miracles. He told me to come so that is what I was going to do. I put my leg over the edge of the boat. One of the men grabbed my arm and said, 'Peter, no!' Another man said, 'Peter, be careful!' When my foot touched the water it was such a strange feeling. It felt warm beneath my foot. The water seemed like it was jelly. As I slid over the side I put my weight on my leg and the water beneath it became hard. I didn't understand it but I kept going. The rain continued to pour and the waves were still big. I had a hard time keeping my balance. Jesus was close enough that I could see his face the whole time but the rest of his body would disappear each time the waves rose up. His arms were raised toward me." Peter held up both arms with his palms up. "My friends, I stood on top of the water! I began to walk toward Jesus. The wind was strong and the spray was hitting my face. I kept wiping my face and walking toward Jesus. A couple of times I almost fell over but I kept staggering toward him."

"Then all of a sudden, and I don't know why, I began to think about what I was doing. This was impossible! To walk on water? I saw the waves and felt the wind. I kept wiping the water from my face and fighting to see Jesus. But then I looked away. I looked back at the boat. It was about ten feet from me. The thought went through my mind that it was close enough that I could swim to it. At that moment, at that very moment I began to sink. I felt the water around my legs and then in an instant I plunged beneath the waves. I went deep under the water. It was so dark and cold! I fought for the surface. And came up. I could hardly see the boat. Then I looked up and saw him. It was Jesus. He reached down for me and I grabbed his hand. Immediately I came up and stood on the waves. Seconds later we were in the boat and the wind and waves had stopped. I sat down and Jesus sat next to me. No one said a word. I looked at him and he put his hand on my shoulder and smiled."

The room was silent. Several people grinned and a few shook their heads in amazement. Then one person broke the silence with the phrase, "Jehovah be praised!" Several others followed with "Jesus, the Messiah!" and "Glory to Jesus!"

Matthew looked over by the front door and noticed that Rebeccah had slid in and he used his elbow to get Levi's attention. He pointed his face toward the door and simply said, "Rebeccah." Levi noticed and smiled.

Peter raised his hands and the room grew quiet. "Equally strong in my mind is the memory of the night he was taken." Peter looked down. He placed his forehead in his hand and continued to talk. "We had celebrated the Passover and went with Jesus into the garden." He dropped his hand, took a deep breath and continued. "We often went there for special lessons and to pray. The face of Jesus looked troubled. He looked like a man carrying the weight of the world on his shoulders. He mentioned that his soul was grieved and told us that we must pray. He took James, John, and myself and we went away from the others. He told us to stay together and pray and then he went off by himself."

"The day had been long and it was getting late. We were exhausted. We knelt in prayer. I fought to stay awake but soon fell asleep. I later learned that the others had fallen asleep as well. Jesus came and woke us up. He told us that it was very important for us to stay awake and pray. He left us again and we went back to praying. But before long, we fell asleep again and soon Jesus stirred us awake."

Then the others came and joined us. Jesus told us all that the time had come. We didn't understand this and were about to ask him about it when through the trees we could see torches. A group of men were approaching. We stood there in the dark and waited. It was several men from the temple. They brought soldiers with them and surrounded us. Then Judas stepped forward." Peter shook his head and clenched his teeth. "Judas. He was one of us! He was with us from the beginning.

He was the one we trusted the most. He held the purse and looked after all that was given to us. He stepped forward and kissed the cheek of the Master."

Then the soldiers stepped forward. The high priest reached for Jesus. Everything happened so fast. I grabbed a sword from one of the soldiers. Without thinking I struck a young man next to the high priest. He grabbed the side of his head and screamed. The group stepped back. I thought that it was time for us to fight. I waited for the others to respond but no one moved. The Master held his hand up and everyone stopped. He told me to drop the sword. I didn't want to but I obeyed. Then he knelt down and picked up the young man's ear. He touched it to the side of his head and the young man was healed. He turned to all of us and said, 'Peace.'"

"No one spoke for a moment. Then I heard the high priest shout, 'Take them!' I thought we would fight them but everyone panicked and began running in all directions. I saw them grab Jesus right away. He didn't move. I don't know what happened next because I was running away with the others.

I learned later that Jesus had been taken to the home of the high priest. At first I looked for a place to hide but not knowing what was happening was too much for me to bear. I tried to sleep but couldn't. I left and wandered through the streets of the city. I was trying to figure everything out. Later that night, I went to the house. A good sized crowd had gathered outside. There were religious leaders, soldiers, and even citizens gathered in groups all around the outside of the house. I walked around listening to their conversations. Everyone seemed to have a different opinion of Jesus and different ideas on what should be done."

"The night grew cold. There were several fires with many people standing around them. I stood by one and a soldier pointed at me. He must have been one who was in the garden. He said, 'Were you one of those with Jesus in the garden?' I looked at him and didn't know what to say. Before I knew it I said, 'No. I was not in the garden. Then I moved away. I thought about leaving but couldn't. I moved to another fire and as soon as I stepped into the circle of people a man looked at me and asked, 'Didn't I see you with Jesus in the temple?' I said no, you are mistaken. I have not been to the temple and I have not been with this man. A few seconds later I found myself at another fire. A small servant girl came by the fire bringing wood. She brushed against me and looked up. She put the wood down and said, 'Are you not also one of his followers? I saw you with the man called Jesus.' I shook my head but she spoke louder. She said, 'I saw you with Jesus by the well in the square. You are a follower of his also!' I pushed passed the girl and said, 'No! You are mistaken! By the foundation of the temple I tell you I do not know this man!'"

"The moment my words ended I heard the cock crow. It was then that I remembered the words of the Master earlier that evening. I had been so bold when we were together. We had finished the Passover meal and Jesus said that soon we would all be scattered and would no longer follow him. I stood up and told him that I would follow him no matter where he went and no matter what happened. He looked at me and said, 'Peter. Oh Peter. It is certain that before the cock crows you will deny me.' I said no! I will never deny you! But he said, 'Yes Peter. In fact, you will deny me not once, but three times.'"

Matthew thought about the times he had denied the Lord. He never stated outright that he didn't know him, but there were a number of times that he remained silent when someone criticized Christ or made him the point of humor or used his name as a curse. He felt bad but could not imagine the heartache that Peter felt.

It seemed like Peter was staring right at Matthew when he continued. "My heart sank! I had betrayed the Messiah. How could I do that? We were so close. He was like a brother to me! I promised him I would never deny him but that is precisely what I did. And not just once but three times!"

Peter shook his head slowly. He looked like a man who was reliving a terrible memory. "I didn't know what to do. I had to get away. I ran from there and into the darkness. I left the city and went back to the garden. I fell to the ground and beat my chest and cried. I don't know how long I stayed there but the sun was strong in the sky when I left. I wandered back to the city and looked for the others. I found some of them and we stayed together trying to understand what was going on."

"The next thing I knew they were crucifying the Master. I tried to get to him but I was not allowed. I wanted to tell him I was sorry. I was so hurt and confused. I wanted to die with him." Every face in the room showed pain. Peter looked like he was about to cry.

"The religious leaders were looking for those who followed Jesus.

We heard that they had brought several people in for questioning. The whole city was in confusion. We spent the next two days in hiding."

"On the first day of the week several of us were in the room where we had celebrated the Passover with the Master. Very early in the morning there was a pounding on the door. We thought it was either the Romans or the religious leaders. No one answered. No one opened the door."

"Then we heard the voice of the women. They were calling our names. We couldn't understand what they were saying so we opened the door. They rushed in and kept telling us 'He's risen! The tomb is open! He's gone! He's alive!' "

"It was too much to believe! The women were so excited. They kept telling us about the Master being alive over and over again. Mary said that he had asked for me. He said my name! The Master said my name! I just had to see for myself. John and I ran out of the room and did not stop until we reached the grave. It was open and it was empty! We ran back to the city and told the others. Everyone was laughing and cheering."

"Now everything was different. We still had to avoid the authorities but we had such joy, such hope. We immediately left for Galilee. When we arrived, we met together in a room. We were talking about all that had taken place. And then we saw him." Peter paused as his mind reflected on that moment. "We had just finished eating. I was about to get up from the table when I looked at John's face. His mouth was open and he was looking over my head and staring. I turned and there by the door stood the Christ! Nobody moved. He just stood there by himself and smiled. Then he said, 'Shalom.'" Peter paused again. Tears had gathered in the rims of his eyes. Several others in the room were crying as well. These were tears of joy, tears of victory.

"The strongest men could not hold me back. I ran across the room and fell at the Master's feet. I clung to him and cried. He raised me to my feet and simply said, 'Peter.' I was afraid to look at his face. I thought he would be angry. I looked into his eyes and I saw only love and forgiveness. My heart was filled with joy! I began to laugh and I couldn't stop smiling. I have never rejoiced so much in my life. He was alive and I was forgiven."

The room erupted in applause. Several men stood up and hugged Peter. Matthew wanted to hug him too but the crowd around him continued to grow. Matthew looked over at Levi. He was grinning and wiping tears from his eyes. It was a great moment of celebration.

Peter sat down and Jacob the Tanner stood up. The room grew quiet once again. Jacob said, "Thank you Peter. The peace of the Lord be upon you." Several in the crowd repeated, "The peace of the Lord." Then Jacob said, "My friends, we have heard a great testimony to our great God." This was followed by several statements of "Amen" and "Praise be to God." Jacob continued, "The hour is late and it is now time for us to go. We will meet here again in four days after the sun has set. Let us go with the song 'I will lift up my eyes to the mountains' on our lips."

With that, Jacob began to sing and was immediately joined by the rest of the crowd. The tune had a distinct Hebrew flavor to it. Matthew had never heard the tune before which was not surprising. What was surprising to him was that he was somewhat familiar with the words. Somehow he recognized the words from a section of the book of Psalms. They came from a particular group of Psalms. He knew that as the Hebrews ascended the hill toward Jerusalem, they would sing these Psalms. These became categorized into the section called *The songs of ascent*. He couldn't join in the song but he closed his eyes and listened to the words enjoying the moment.

> *"I will lift up my eyes to the mountains;*
> *From where shall my help come?*
> *My help come from the Lord,*
> *Who made heaven and earth.*
> *He will not allow your foot to slip;*
> *He who keeps you will not slumber.*
> *Behold, He who keeps Israel*
> *Will neither slumber nor sleep.*
> *The Lord is your keeper;*
> *The Lord is your shade on your right hand.*
> *The sun will not smite you by day,*
> *Nor the moon by night.*
> *The Lord will protect you from all evil;*
> *He will keep your soul.*
> *The Lord will guard your going out and your coming in*
> *From this time forth and forever."*

After the song Jacob said, "And now my friends, let us all go with the blessing of our risen King." He held his hands up over the crowd and repeated words that Matthew was very familiar with. In fact, he had used these same words in benedictions at several weddings and funerals. They came from the book of Numbers.

> *"The Lord bless you and keep you;*
> *The Lord make His face shine on you,*
> *And be gracious to you;*
> *The Lord lift up His countenance on you,*
> *And give you peace."*

Then Jacob said the words that Matthew knew were common among believers, "He lives!" "He lives" The crowd repeated.

Jacob's words were followed by people exchanging hugs and well wishes. Matthew noticed that men were stationed at the front and back doors. As people prepared the leave they would look out the door and make sure it was safe to go. They also were careful not to let too many people exit at one time.

It was late when Levi and Matthew left. Their plan was to spend the night at Isaac and Miriam's house even though they were away. They walked in the darkness talking the entire way. The lights from the city guided them back but the light from the meeting energized them.

# Chapter 14
# Nicodemus

On his bed that night, Matthew's thoughts bounced from home and his wife and friends, to this other life and all the things he was experiencing. His heart still ached to see Melissa and their daughter. The faces of his friends still came to his mind. He wondered if this was now where he would be forever and concluded that he just didn't know. It was with these wonderings that he drifted off to sleep with a strange feeling of peace washing over his heart and mind.

The men slept later than usual. They didn't realize how exhausting their activities had been. For some time, they sat on the edge of their beds reflecting on the meeting the night before and talking about their love for the Savior. They made plans to go back to Levi's house and return to the city in a few days with his wife and son. Levi wrote a short note to his bother and Miriam and after helping themselves to some bread and fruit they moved toward Levi's house.

At home everything was as they left it. They spent the next couple of days tending the garden and visiting with friends. Levi went to the edge of town and sold two small blankets Hannah had made. When the day came for them to leave they gathered some food and began their journey to the *holy city*.

That afternoon found them in the home of Isaac and Miriam. Benjamin loved his Aunt and Uncle and did not hesitate to show his affection. After a meal he spent his time leaning on his uncle while the group sat around the table exchanging stories and enjoying light conversation. For Matthew the day crept along. He was anxiously waiting for that night's meeting.

Finally, it was time to begin the walk to Jacob the Tanner's house. Once again the group divided with Levi, Hannah, and Matthew leaving through one gate and the other three leaving through another.

A good size crowd had already gathered when they arrived at Jacob's. Matthew was surprised to find that he recognized some of the people from the last meeting. He was also certain that there were many newcomers. Before long the room was filled beyond capacity and every room was packed with people. Several stood in the back yard and listened through the windows.

Like before, Jacob stood and greeted everyone. He shouted, "Shalom" and the group shouted "Shalom" back to him.

"My brothers and sisters" he said, "This evening we have one who is well known to so many of you. He has come to tell of his time with the Master. He is a teacher of the law and a follower of the Christ. He desires to share with you where his walk of faith has taken him. Please extend the greeting of peace to Nicodemus.

A man who was seated near the front of the room stood up. He was above middle age and wore a white robe with a blue band of silk around the bottom. He had a gold sash and wore a matching head covering. His beard was gray with several streaks of black. He stood up and said, "Shalom, my friends." The crowd responded with "Shalom" and Matthew noticed that many bowed their head in respect. "This is Nicodemus" Matthew thought. "Amazing!"

Matthew reflected on all that he knew about this man. He had preached a sermon many years before about Jesus' conversation with him and in a tongue-in-cheek sort of way had labeled it *Nick at night*. He knew that the most popular Bible verse ever recorded, John 3:16, was spoken to this man and he couldn't wait to hear what he had to say.

Nicodemus began, "My friends, it is good to be with you! I would like to share with you my story. Many of you know that I was a Pharisee. I was a very devout and respected leader at the school of Pharisees where I had many teachers under my direction. I was an expert in the law and was deeply devoted to the religious ways of our people."

"One day while I was in the temple with a group of Pharisees, a young man approached us and announced that Jesus had entered the temple area. I had heard so much about him, the miracles, the teachings, even the love he showed to all those he met. Secretly I was very anxious to meet this man. Those with me wanted to meet him as well but for very different reasons."

"As soon as we began walking toward where we heard he was, a great commotion took place. Men and women were screaming and I heard men shouting. Then I heard his voice above them all. I did not hear all of it but I did hear him use the phrase, 'Den of thieves.' When we reached the outer court we saw men running in every direction to pick up coins and tables. Many animals brought for sacrifice were scattered throughout the temple area."

"We found Jesus standing in the middle of the crowd breathing heavily. He had a sash in his hand. Johannas, who was serving as one of the chief priests walked up to him demanding an answer. I remember him raising his fist at Jesus and saying, 'Where do you get the authority to do this?'"

"Jesus looked right back at him and told him, 'Destroy this temple and I will raise it up in the three days'. We all thought he meant the *Holy temple*. Many scoffed at him and a few used the word blasphemer. It was only after his death and resurrection that some of us came to know he was speaking of his own body, his own temple." The room was shrouded in silence as Nicodemus paused.

"Then Jesus looked directly at me. His dark eyes that were filled with such anger softened and I saw intense compassion like never before. He walked through our midst, brushed by me and stopped behind me. He turned slightly toward me and whispered, *tonight*. It was so strange but I knew that I was to meet him later that evening."

"I could not wait for the evening to come. I sent a page to find him and let me know where he was. He was in a home not far from the temple. When I knocked, the door opened and three men who I had seen him with earlier exited. The door was left open and I entered."

"Jesus was alone and waved me in. He offered me a cup of juice and we sat down together. As we sipped it he asked me what it was that I wanted to know. I told him that the miracles he had done were a testimony to who he was. I told him that I believed that he came from God."

Matthew knew what Jesus' response was and covered his mouth to keep from blurting it out. "Jesus said to me that unless a person is born again he cannot see the kingdom of God. This was very confusing to me because I had experienced all the born again stages a good Pharisee goes through. I had been circumcised, received my bar-mitzvah, married, trained in the school of the Pharisees, all of them. I could only think that he was speaking of physical re-birth. I brought this to his attention and learned that the re-birth he was speaking of is of the

Spirit."

"Then he told me something that I had never heard. He told me that Yahweh loved everyone in the world so much that he sent Jesus to be the ultimate sacrifice for us all. He said that whoever believed in him, he would not experience eternal death but would have the life that only Yahweh could offer."

"We spoke for over an hour and he told me so many things. When I left, so much was spinning in my head. I was not yet ready to become a follower of Jesus but I knew that I had somehow been in the very presence of God. Though many days went by I never forgot my time with him. I saw him several times since then-walking in the streets, talking to the crowds, hugging and blessing the children. Once, I saw him on the steps of the temple. He looked up at me and smiled."

"One evening I was summoned to meet with the other Pharisees, elders and religious leaders. We met in the courtyard of men in the temple and were to find Jesus. We knew he was somewhere just outside the city walls. I was not sure of the plan but I knew in my heart that it was not good. As we walked through the temple I lagged behind and eventually stepped to the side and let the other leaders go on."

Nicodemus pause so that the group could grasp what he was saying. No one in the room made a sound. They all sat transfixed on every word he had to say. He held his hands out with the palms up. "Everything happened so fast. It was like a whirlwind! Before I knew it Jesus had been beaten and the crowd was calling for him to be crucified. Just days before he had entered the city on a donkey to the cheers of the crowd. Now this same crowd was calling for his life. I must confess that although I wasn't part of it, I did nothing to sop it. I am guilty by self-exclusion and inaction."

"But I *was* there the morning the guards from the grave came in. They rushed into the room where one of the chief priests and several of us had gathered. They announced that the stone covering the tomb had been pushed aside. They said the ground shook and the stone came off the entrance. When they looked up there was an angel sitting on the stone and they were paralyzed with fright. When they gathered themselves and looked into the tomb it was somehow filled with light but nothing else. The body of Jesus was gone!"

Silence enveloped the room. Tears from many flowed freely. A number of men and women had wide grins on their faces and several looked upward and shook their heads in wonder.

Nicodemus continued. "I knew what had happened. I knew he had risen! With tears filling my eyes I slowly backed out of the room and went home to my wife and children. As I was leaving I heard the Chief Priest say, 'We must not let the people know this. The people must not believe that he has risen from the grave'" Nicodemus paused as several men stood up and hugged him. Several shouted "Hallel!" Many began talking among themselves and the excitement and the noise in the room began to grow.

After a few moments Nicodemus raised his hands and the noise drew down. "My brothers and sisters, there is more. I must tell you this. About a week after we heard about the empty tomb my wife and I were at the market. As usual it was very crowded and people jostled us from all sides. My wife was putting some vegetables in the basket I was holding when I looked up and saw him. I saw Jesus on the other side of the square! He was just standing there looking at me. When I saw him my heart leaped. He smiled at me and nodded. I looked toward my wife and I saw her smiling and staring at him. She saw him too! When I looked back he was gone! I pushed myself through the crowd to where he was but he was not to be found. My wife and I laughed and cried at the same time. We had seen the risen Lord!"

No one moved. Nicodemus took a deep breath and looked down at the ground smiling. He lifted his face and scanned the crowd. Faces all over the house were smiling. A few seconds later one man stood and shouted "Hallel!" Then another rose to his feet and yelled, "He is alive!" Soon everyone was standing and shouts came from all over the house, "He is the Lord!" He has risen!" "In him is salvation!" "Amen!" "I believe!"

As Nicodemus turned to slide into the crowd a lone voice began singing. Then several voices joined in. In moments the entire houses was filled with their voices loudly singing:

> "The Christ has come,
> The Christ has come,
> His name is Jesus,
> His name is Jesus.
> He is the Savior,
> He is the Lord,

*The Christ has come,*
*And he lives today!"*

The song was sung several times and when it ended it was replaced with applause and cheers which continued for several minutes. No one seemed to be concerned about the noise which must have been heard outside in the street.

When the noise died down and the people were seated once again, Peter stood up and the room was once again silent. He thanked Nicodemus for his words and then addressed the crowd. "The Spirit of the Christ is among us. To become a follower of his you must believe that he is the Christ and that he has come for your salvation. He is the spotless lamb of God given to us for the covering of our sins. Repent and confess." Heads all around the room nodded.

Peter continued, "Are there those among us who have a need?" His eyes drifted slowly around the room. Shortly a young man who looked to be about seventeen stood up. He spoke very quietly and seemed embarrassed. "My name is Titus and I am from the tribe of Judah." A man near him shouted, "Bless the tribe of Judah!" The boy smiled slightly. "Some of you know that my father died last month. Our family has had very little and now we have less than very little. We are in need of food" He paused and started to speak again but then stopped and began to sit down. Behind Levi and Matthew, a voice cried out, "I can help." Then another said, "I as well!" Then three or four spoke up offering to contribute with the others.

Peter grinned. "Are there others who have needs?" In the back of the room a man stood up. He looked to be about fifty years old. He pointed to the woman seated at his feet and said, "I am Hezekiah and my wife is Naomi. We have heard of Jesus and have traveled to find out more. We have no place to stay and no money for an Inn. We have been trusting Jehovah to provide." As he sat down two men spoke up at the same tine, "I have a place for you." "I have room!" The two men looked at each other and smiled as laughter filled the room.

Peter said, "Jehovah Jireh! Please see one of the men when we dismiss. Anyone else?" The room became quiet once again.

Then a stocky middle aged man struggled to his feet. He had his right arm in a sling and a bandage covering his wrist and hand. His voice was just loud enough for everyone in the room to hear. "My name is Reuben from he tribe of Levi" Matthew looked over at Levi and smiled. Levi shrugged his shoulders and smiled back.

"Some of you know me. By trade I am a worker in iron and I am a follower of Jesus the Messiah." This was met by nods and several *Amens!* "A couple of weeks ago my hand was badly burned while I was working with a large piece of metal. I took care of it even seeing a physician. I have seen the priest in the temple and have been assured that it is not leprosy. Each day the pain grows and the infection spreads. The pain is now up to my elbow."

Before the man continued Peter waved him forward with the word, "Come!" The man moved carefully through the crowd seated around him. He came to Peter and held out his arm. As Peter began to removed the bandages and let them fall to the floor, the man winced. Reuben stood still while the last bandage fell. The wound was open, red and puffy. Some who were up close turned their heads away or looked down. Reuben held his elbow with his left hand and looked down at it. He turned his face toward Peter when he began to speak.

Peter looked skyward and said in a loud voice, "It is the Spirit of Christ who heals you! Be free! Be whole! Be healed!"

Reuben closed his eyes and breathed out one one quiet word, "Yes!" He quickly opened his eyes and when he looked at his hand his face lit up. He removed his elbow from the sling and straightened it. There was no pain! He looked down at the back of his hand and saw that it was clean. It wasn't even scarred. He opened and closed his hand several times. Then he hugged Peter and said, "Thank you! Oh, thank you!"

Peter held him by the shoulders and looked into his eyes and said loudly, "All praise and glory to God Almighty! Praise the risen Savior!" The man turned toward the crowd and lifted up his hand. He turned it in several directions and yelled, "Yes! Praise Jesus the Christ!" The room erupted in applause and shouts of praise. Everyone stood and cheered.

While they were standing and cheering a man entered the room and weaved his way through the crowd. He came directly to Peter and said something to him. Peter motioned for the crowd to be quiet and instantly there was silence.

Peter called to them. "My brothers and sisters, it is time for us to dismiss. Temple soldiers will soon be here. Please go quickly and quietly. And may the peace of our risen savior be with you." Several shouted "Halle!" "Peace be with you" and "Jesus Christ is Lord!"

Within minutes the entire house was empty. In the rush Matthew got separated rom the others. He knew the way to Isaac and Miriam's so he saw no need to panic.

When he turned the corner he was met by a dozen soldiers moving fairly quickly. He immediately stepped out of the way and for some reason decided to look away, hiding his face. He knew where they were headed. He smiled slightly and thought, "That was close!" Then he breathed a quick prayer of protection for Jacob, the owner of the house.

# Chapter 15
# Desperation

Shortly after leaving the house and working his way in the direction of the city Matthew found himself walking with a man and his wife. He recognized them from the meeting. They both looked to be about twenty-five-years-old. The man spoke first, "My name is Josephus and this is my wife Kareesh." Matthew shared with them his name and the men shook hands.

Matthew explained that he had lost his friend Levi and was heading toward the city. The man said, "I do not know this man Levi, but if you need a place to stay for the night, you are welcome to come with us. We live in Bataan but we are staying with my aunt just outside the city. I'm sure she will have room for you." Matthew thanked them and explained that he had a place to stay in the city.

"Then will you please come and have something to eat with us?" Josephus asked. "My aunt's home is on the way to the city. Matthew saw no reason not to accept and agreed to join the two. Josephus smiled, "It is not far and my aunt will be happy to meet you."

The three of them talked the entire way to the aunt's home. It wasn't long before Matthew found himself being greeted by Josephus' aunt. Her name was Sarai. She looked to be about forty-five-years of age. She was fairly tall and very thin with an obvious sunny disposition.

"I am so glad to have you as my guest" she said, "I do not get many visitors since my husband passed away." She invited them all in and retreated to the kitchen. The three of them sat down and she returned shortly with a tray holding biscuits, cheese, and cups of water. She placed it on the table and sat down to join the three of them.

It was then that Matthew realized he hadn't eaten in several hours. He did his best to slow himself down to avoid being rude. As they ate they talked about the meeting of *the called out* ones as so many had begun to refer to their gatherings.

When they mentioned the healing of Reuben's hand, Sarai's eyes lit up. "I know Reuben! He is a man who works in iron. He is a strong man but very kind." They explained how he stood up and Peter brought him forward and cried out for his healing. Sarai said, "Jehovah is known as *El Rapha* and it is so refreshing to see his name in action." She glanced at Josephus and Kereesh and they smiled back at her. She gave a wry smile and tried to hide it behind a biscuit. Matthew felt left out and pressed for more information. "Is there something more you wanted to tell me?"

Sarai moved to her knees and returned the biscuit to the tray. "Well" she said, "Since you have pressed me so hard I will tell you." Kareesh giggled, "Oh, here we go" she said. "You can tell it took a lot of prying to force her to share."

Sarai began, "A couple of yers ago my husband Daniel and I were visiting his brother in Tiberius. We had stayed for two days and prepared to leave. I was riding our donkey and Daniel was walking beside us. Up ahead we saw men and women hurrying toward the lake. A man going past us told us that Jesus was by the shore. When we got close we saw him. He was walking through the crowd of people. Several times he stopped to hug children and to say something to a man or a woman. I saw Jairus, one of the synagogue officials approach him. I do not know what was said but I saw him pat Jairus on the shoulder and begin to walk with him."

"I had heard many things about Jesus. Some called him Rabbi and others called him teacher. He was called prophet by many. But there was one name I heard him called that spoke to my heart-to my very soul. It was the name, *healer.*

"You see, I was very sick and getting worse. I had an issue of blood that could not be stopped." When she mentioned that Matthew knew exactly who she was and what was to happen. He fought to keep a smile from his face as she continued. "I had been to many physicians and healers who promised to make me well but I only got worse. As I'm sure you can imagine, it affected me deeply. I always felt so weak. I could not take care of my husband. I was without children. I was labeled unclean and could not go to the temple or synagogue. Some even called me demon possessed and urged me to confess my sin and be healed."

"For twelve long years I struggled. My husband Daniel was such a good man! He encouraged me and took me to whoever we thought could help. But day after day, and treatment after treatment" she leaned forward and lowered her voice "and dollar after dollar...nothing!"

"So when we came across the healer, my heart skipped a beat. Jesus and the crowd were coming right toward us. I got off our donkey and my husband knew exactly what I was thinking. We started to walk toward the Master but were separated by the crowd. Jesus was surrounded mostly by men and me being a woman was easily brushed aside. I tried to hold my ground but was too weak to resist the crowd that was pressing to get next to Jesus."

"I wanted to speak to him, to tell him my story but I couldn't get close enough for him to hear me above the noise of all the people. I looked for my husband but there were too many people in the way. Two times I was almost knocked to the ground. Jesus was now even with me and about to pass me. I just wanted to be close to him and to touch me and if possible, take away my sickness. I leaned into the crowd, and pushed my hand between two men. When I reached forward I was knocked to the ground. As I fell to my knees my hand caught the very bottom of his robe. Without knowing it I held on and pulled him backward. I let go immediately but the crowd stopped. I heard his voice but didn't know what he said. When I looked up the crowd had parted and Jesus was looking directly into my eyes."

"I felt something go through my body. It felt like a chill but much more intense. I shook for just a moment and then looked back at Jesus. At first I was frightened. I didn't know what had happened. I thought perhaps he would be angry. But those eyes, those eyes! They looked so kind and loving. I lost sight of everything and everyone. I felt like Jesus and I were the only two people in the world. He took my hand and pulled me to my feet. And then he spoke to me. I can still hear his words! He called me daughter. He said, 'Daughter your faith has made you well. Go in peace and be healed.'"

Matthew sat there motionless. After a short time Kareesh broke the silence, "I never get tired of hearing that story." Matthew thought, but dared not speak, "And I never get tired of reading it."

Sarai continued, "I did go in peace. And the peace that I left with has never left me. He is my Savior in so many ways. He cleansed my body as well as my soul!"

The small circle of believers was bathed in joy. Soon it was time for

Matthew to work is way back to the city and Isaac's house. He left with some fruit, and the blessings of his new brother and sisters in Christ. An hour later he entered Jerusalem and stood in front of Isaac's home. He was greeted by everyone with hugs and pats on the back. They were genuinely glad to see him.

That night as he began to drift off to sleep he reflected on all that he saw and experienced earlier that night. He missed Melissa and his home deeply, but in a very strange way felt that he was home. His last thought was, "This is not a dream that I'm having. I'm here for good. I need to get a job…"

The next morning brought the usual bright sunshine on the city of Jerusalem. He joined Isaac and Levi in some chores behind their home and then sat down to a large breakfast. Before long he found himself on the road with Levi and his family.

He spent a great part of the trip filling the others in on his experience with Josephus, Kareesh, and Sarai.

They arrived back home late in the day and found their home and the town exactly how they left it. They sat down to dinner and Matthew shared with them his desire to get a job and settle down in the area. "Then you will be able to bring your wife with you?" Levi asked. "Definitely" Matthew answered desiring that more than they could imagine. They agreed and promised to keep watch for opportunities.

Two days later Levi told Matthew, "We have friends in Capernaum and their son is to be honored with his bar-mitzvah. We are all going to the celebration. It is a three day trip and we will be leaving tomorrow. Will you join us?" Refusal did not enter Matthew's mind so he agreed and looked forward to the trip and time of celebration.

The next morning found Hannah in the kitchen baking bread as a gift and biscuits for breakfast. By the time Matthew descended the stairs there was fruit on the table and Levi was pouring what came close to being what he considered coffee.

He really didn't understand it but Matthew realized that although Levi brought home very little money, the family always had enough to eat and even had enough to share with him and others who needed it. Matthew thought, "When I get a job, I will be eager to share with them." Then he thought, "But what can I do?" Those thoughts and others tumbled around in his head as he sat down and enjoyed yet another good meal in the home of these kind people.

The three men worked in the garden for a short time. Matthew volunteered to empty the bucket of rocks even though it was only half full. What he really wanted to do was meet up with young Simeon. He had no agenda. He just felt like speaking to him again, maybe asking him a few more questions about Jesus.

Levi didn't question him and Matthew headed off down the street toward the town rock pile.

Matthew looked around but saw no sign of Simeon. He dumped the bucket and stood near the pile for a while. He was about to leave when he saw a man approaching carrying his own bucket. He looked to be over seventy. He had a long white beard and a robe with several bands around the bottom. He walked slowly and by the way he swung the bucket Matthew could tell it was empty.

When he reached the pile Matthew greeted him, "Shalom"

The man put his bucket down and looked at the pile of rocks. "Shalom" was the only reply.

"I could have saved you a trip and brought you the ones I just dumped." Matthew was alone in seeing the humor in it.

"Yes" was all the man said. Then he asked, "I do not know you. Are you from the village?"

"No" Matthew answered. "My name is Matthew and I am staying with my friend Levi."

"Ah, Levi! He is a very good man, and a man I hold in great admiration, even though we see things differently."

This piqued Matthew's interest. "Differently?"

"Yes. He is a follower of the teacher Jesus. And I am not."

"What do you think about Jesus?" Matthew asked.

The old man hesitated. It seemed as if he didn't not want to get into a discussion and certainly not an argument. "Jesus said some good things. I am told that he healed some people and showed several signs. But he was not the Messiah we were waiting for. His death proved that."

"But what about the resurrection?"

"What resurrection do you speak of?"

Matthew could tell the man knew what he meant "On the third day, just as Jesus had predicted, prophesied, he rose from the grave."

The man shook his head slowly as he crouched down and began to place some stones in his bucket. "This is something that simply did not happen."

Matthew turned his bucket over and sat on it. "But what about the empty tomb?"

The man looked up and paused, "Ah, the empty tomb. There are many who have used that as proof that this teacher is alive. However, an empty tomb is evidence of an empty tomb. It is not evidence that a person rose from the grave."

Matthew was doing his best to remain calm, "Then what do you believe happened to the body of Jesus?"

Without looking up he said, "Our Rabbis have given correct explanation to this. They have told us that during the night, the disciples or other followers of Jesus came and took the body. Then they hid or buried the body in some other location. It is not a hard thing to do."

"But why would they do that? And how did they do this without the guards stopping them?" Matthew almost used an argument he had used before, "But the disciples suffered horrible deaths..." But he knew that had not happened yet.

The man continued to gather rocks. "They did this to hold on to something they held dear, to keep this teacher alive in the minds of his followers. It is not difficult to understand."

Matthew felt the need to get to the heart of the matter, "What if I gave you evidence that he is alive? What if you saw him? What would you say to that?"

The man looked up again, "My friend, our people are the chosen ones. We have been blessed by the hand of Yahweh for centuries. We have the temple, the Torah, and the prophesies of protection and provision. We do not need a story of a man claiming to be the Messiah nor do we need stories of a man rising from the grave."

Matthew tried to control his voice. He saw that this man's disbelief was seated in the will, not the intellect. He knew that if a man refused to believe what he saw that it was a matter of the will, not the mind. Still he felt compelled to continue the discussion, "But what about all the people who have testified, many of them under a vow that they saw Jesus?"

Standing up he said, "This is something we do not have an answer for. Perhaps they saw someone who looked like this man. Perhaps they saw what their heart desired their eyes to see. The mind is a very powerful thing. Shalom." And he slowly turned with his bucket and began to walk away.

"Shalom" was all that Matthew could manage. He thought, "Maybe someday he will come to believe. Maybe someday." And he gave a heavy sigh, picked up his bucket and headed back toward the house.

At the house, preparations were completed for the group's trip to Capernaum. Levi had borrowed his neighbor's wagon and donkey. The few things they would be bringing were already on board. Hannah and Benjamin would ride in the wagon while Levi and Matthew walked alongside. Levi was excited to see his friend Jeriah and the rest of his family.

# Chapter 16
# Capernaum

The trip to Capernaum was uneventful. One night they stayed at an inn, and the next night they stayed with relatives of Hannah's. On the road they passed many going in the opposite direction and each was greeted by a "Shalom my friend." From Levi. Matthew smiled slightly and thought, "This man has precious little and might be the happiest man I've ever met...the difference salvation in Christ can make."

Levi shared that his family and Jeriah's family would get together about twice a year. He explained that he met ¬¬¬¬¬¬¬¬¬Jeriah a few years ago and the two had become close friends. Through a misfortune of Levi's their two paths crossed and somehow developed a bond that made them seem like long-time friends.

Levi was riding the wagon from his cousin's home up in Cana. He noticed that one of the wheels in the front was making a good bit of noise. He ignored it planning on giving it some attention when he arrived home. The grinding increased until the entire wheel fell off hurling him from the wagon. He landed in some scrub bushes and except for a bruised ego was unhurt. His biggest concern was the condition of his neighbor's wagon.

"I never saw him approach but as I sat on the side of the road trying to decide what to do Jeriah and his son came up behind me. He put his hand on my shoulder and said, 'Friend, are you hurt?' I told him I was unhurt but the wagon was injured. He laughed and said, 'Wood and metal are not difficult to fix.' Then he helped me to my feet and told me his name.

The wheel was only missing a pin and he sent his son to find one in the village. Jeriah shared some fruit with me and while we waited for the boy, we talked the entire time. Mostly we talked about the Master. He shared with me how he met Jesus and what he had taught. A couple of hours later I was on the road home with a repaired wheel and a new friend in my heart.

Matthew smiled broadly, "Friendship! So precious, so necessary." He reflected on several of the friends he had. The statistics indicated that most men over thirty did not have three close friends with which to share their most intimate thoughts and feelings. He also knew that for Pastors, it was even lower. Matthew knew he was blessed. He had several men he felt very close to. He was intentional about his relationships and he had built several close buddies both in the ministry and among the laity. He deliberately built time into his busy schedule to be with his friends and was so thankful that he had. They were *there* for him and he was *there* for them.

When Matthew's father died, he walked down the aisle with his family and was surprised to see no less that four of his close friends in the pew. They drove over six hours to be with him and to comfort him. On more than one occasion he had stated that "A true friend is someone who comes in when the rest of the world is going out."

Matthew's mind wandered back to a time when he hit a piece of metal with his lawn mower. He never saw it but he certainly felt it. The metal had embedded itself in his leg requiring surgical removal. When he was in recovery, three of his friends and their wives were there. Matthew felt a richness come over him as these men came to mind.

Levi explained, "Jeriah and Judith and their son Malchi are followers of Jesus, but have not let go of so many of the Hebrew ways. When you have done so many things for so many years it is not easy to turn it off like a lamp."

Matthew knew that all too well. He had come to repentance and faith in Jesus Christ when he was twenty-one. He had finished his junior year in college and was home working a summer job pulling orders in a warehouse. It was there that he met Tommy. Tommy was a year younger than Matthew. He went to a different college and Matthew couldn't help notice that he had biceps to spare. He often spoke about his faith in Christ. Besides his biceps, Matthew noticed two things about Tommy. He was always patient, never pushy. And he didn't just talk about his faith, he lived it. Matthew went to church a few times with Tommy and enjoyed it for the most part. But his conversations with Tommy and the things he heard at church raised more questions than answers, questions that had never entered his mind before.

Many times, during their breaks they had deep conversations about the Bible, eternity, heaven and hell. Finally, almost in exasperation Matthew blurted out, "Okay, I understand! I admit I'm a sinner and need forgiveness. Now how does that happen?"

"Not this way Tommy said flexing his right bicep indicating it wasn't something you worked for. He went on to explain the need to ask for forgiveness and the give Christ the *deed* to your life.

That night as he lay in bed, Matthew asked Christ for forgiveness and to be Lord of his life. The bear hug he got from Tommy the next day told the story of Tommy's excitement for him.

Two weeks later Matthew was back at school and during the first weekend he was out with some buddies *getting their buzz on*. The next night it was more of the same.

When Sunday came he awoke too late to attend church. That afternoon was the first time that he came to the conclusion that he had *blown it*. He contacted Tommy explaining everything and Tommy walked him through the concept of repentance and renewed commitment.

So in part Matthew understood how tradition and old habits die hard. He realized the struggle there must be when a tradition is so deeply imbedded in a culture, especially a culture as old as the Hebrew one was.

His thoughts were broken as Levi said, "Well, there's Jeriah's house. Thank you Lord for safe travel." The house sat by itself on top of a small knoll. It was a good bit different than the houses Matthew had been to. Most of the homes he had been to were white and had flat roofs. This one had a thatched roof that had a pitch to it. The walls were more tan than white and the windows had flower boxes below them.

As the wagon came to a stop in front of the house the door opened and Jeriah stepped out. He was taller than average with a close cropped beard and a ready smile. "Ah, Levi my friend! I am so glad you are here." The men embraced then Levi turned to help Hannah off of the wagon. Levi turned again and put his arm around Jeriah's shoulder. "This is my friend Matthew. Matthew this is Jeriah, the finest man you will ever know. Jeriah laughed. "Levi, you are as kind as you are ignorant." He gave a hug to Matthew and said, "Welcome friend!" Then turning to Hannah he said, "And Hannah, the best part of your marriage!" He hugged Hannah then leaned over to Benjamin. "Benjamin, a fine boy! Soon you will be taller than your father." Standing again he said, "Today we eat together but tonight we feast together." Smiles were seen all around.

The group went into the house and were met by Jeriah's wife Judith. She was a somewhat heavy woman with a round face and rosy cheeks. She laughed as she hugged everyone and said, "Come in! Come in! Leave the dust of the road outside and come in!" She was introduced to Matthew and put her hands on her hips and said, "Welcome to our home! It is so good to see you!" Turning to Benjamin she said, "Benjamin, you are more handsome than ever!" and she cradled his face and kissed him on the top of his head. Benjamin looked down and tried to hide a smile.

Levi extended the package of bread to Judith and she said, "Thank you my friend. I will put it in the kitchen. It will not last long in this house." Levi turned and waved his hand at their son Malchi. "Malchi! The man of the day! So good to see you!"

Malchi was a slender boy with dark curly hair. He smiled and said, "Thank you!"

"Come sit down" Jeriah said to his guests as he directed them to the short table in the middle of the living room.

"We're going outside" Malchi announced as he motioned for Benjamin to join him. The two boys disappeared almost instantly.

The conversation was lively as the five adults sat around the table. Without effort Matthew saw how easy it was to enjoy the company of Jeriah and Judith. They were fun and friendly while at the same time being gracious and kind. It reminded Matthew of several couples he knew in what was quickly becoming another world.

One such couple was Randy and Michelle. They were dear friends of Matthew's and Melissa's. The two couples had shared so many ups and downs of life together. There were meals, parties, double dates, graduations, weddings, and Bible studies. They shared both laughter and tears as they walked through life together. This was the very definition of friendship.

Later that day the house was filled with activity. Everyone was busy preparing for the ceremony at the synagogue and the celebration here in the home. While Malchi busied himself reciting the Torah, Hannah and Judith were putting the finishing touches on the food. Benjamin and the men were loading the wagon with supplies to be used in the synagogue during the ceremony and the party afterward.

Moments later the entire group was on their way to the center of the village to participate in Machi's bar-mitzvah. Matthew was particularly excited. He had read about the ceremony but had never attended one. When they arrived at the synagogue, each person took off their shoes and washed their hands in a large basin of water. Both the men and women donned head pieces and Malchi was given a special robe and a silk shawl to wear. Benjamin and Malchi were escorted to a special room where they participated in ceremonial washing.

Before long the synagogue was packed with people. The ceremony lasted about an hour. It began with the congregation singing together. Naturally Matthew didn't know the words so he did his best to fake it. Two Rabbis came to the front with one leading them in prayer. Malchi was summoned. Matthew found himself pulling for his new young friend. He was brought up to the small stage and asked several questions which he answered quietly and correctly. He recited a large section of the Torah perfectly and ended by singing part of the Scripture. A prayer of blessing was said over him and he was given a copy of the Torah. His shawl was removed from his shoulders and replaced with another that was to be his for the rest of his life.

Malchi knelt before the crowd. One of the Rabbi's stood behind him. He raised both his hands and looking upward he prayed, "Jehovah, our great God and king. We place before you this young man who is worthy to be called your child. Bless him and bless your people through him. Amen"

The Rabbi then addressed the crowd, "And now children of Israel, I present to you Malchi, a son of the covenant!" Malchi rose to his feet and the entire room erupted in cheers and applause. It reminded Matthew of an athletic event. He had often lamented that he wished people would get as excited about their faith as they did about their favorite team.

The crowd poured through the doors into the adjoining room. Music, singing, and dancing went on for hours. Malchi was never without someone hugging him, kissing him, giving him a gift, and welcoming him into this step of manhood.

Matthew mused over all that was going on. "In American society the closest thing we have to announcing a person's entry into adulthood is the day the have a *sweet sixteen* party or get their driver's license."

Later that evening, a large number of people gathered back at Jiri-ah's home. They ate, sang songs, and told stories until late that night. Finally, the last guest left and the rest of the exhausted people retired to bed.

As Matthew lay on a cot that night he reviewed all that had taken place over the last few days. He faded into sleep with the thought, "It is so strange to encounter so many who all have the goal of getting close to a God they've never seen. Jesus walked among them and so many of them missed him."

The next morning Matthew awoke to the aroma wafting its way down the short hall to his room. He lay there for a few minutes thinking about the kind of food being prepared: Biscuits, hummus, and fish. He was sure there would be fruit although he couldn't smell it. He retrieved his robe which he had washed and hung in the window to dry and moments later found himself at the table with the rest of the guests and family. Breakfast was followed by the loading of the wagon for the long ride home.

On the other side of the road they saw a Roman cart being pulled by a horse. There were three men riding in it and one man in a cage with a face covered in blood. Matthew asked quietly, "What's that all about?" Levi shrugged his shoulders, "With the Romans, who knows? It could be anything from speaking against pilot to murder." They saw the wagon stop and one of the soldiers dismount. They thought it best to be moving on.

Just before they pulled away they heard a man call out. "You there! Stop! Do not proceed!" Everyone turned to see one of the soldiers quickly walking toward them. The group froze. As the soldier crossed the street he removed his helmet. He looked to be about middle aged and Matthew had a sense that he was in command of the other two.

"Claudius my friend!" Jeriah said quietly. The two men stood facing each other. Jeriah turned toward the others. "This is Levi and Hannah. And this is their son Benjamin. They have come to celebrate Malchi's bar-mitzvah last night. They are believers." They smiled and nodded a hello. "And this is my Levi's wife Hannah and their son Benjamin." Then extending his hand toward Matthew he said, "And this is our friend Matthew. He has been staying with them in Gaphna for several days." He too is a follower of the Messiah. Matthew went to shake his hand a received and handshake that confused him a bit. Instead of grasping his hand, Claudius held him around the wrist. Matthew realized immediately that this was the Roman way.

One of the other soldiers left the wagon and approached them. Claudius gave him instructions. "I need to speak to these men. Stay by the wagon and watch the prisoner." The man put his fist to his chest in a salute and moved back to the wagon with the other soldier.

Jeriah spoke to Benjamin and Malchi. "Stay with your mothers. We won't be long." He gave them a wink and directed Claudius and the two other men around the corner of the house. A few feet off the main road Claudius put his hand on Jeriah's shoulder. "Are you well?" Jeriah smiled. "I am well and greatly blessed. And you?" The Roman returned the smile, "I am well. My faith in Christ grows as the days go by." Matthew couldn't believe it. A Roman…A Roman soldier who has come to faith in Christ! How cold this have happened?

Without prompting Claudius continued, I can not talk long my friends. It is very dangerous for me to spend much time with you. It is enough for me to know that you all are well. When I am free from dispatch which is not very often these days, I am blessed to meet with Samuel. Do you know him?"

"I do not" Jeriah said. "He is a believer?"

"Oh, yes! And very strong in the faith. He has taught me so much."

Before he realized it Matthew blurted out, "But how did you come to faith in Christ?"

Claudius chuckled. He glanced back toward the wagon. The men were still in their places. In a strong but low voice Claudius began. "About two years ago, I was serving under the hand of Marcos in Tiberias. He is a good man but very strong and decisive. He was very popular both among the Romans as well as the Hebrews. He had risen among the ranks and was charged with leading one hundred men."

"Marcos had a servant named Alexander. He had been with Marcos for over seven years and was in charge of his entire household. Marcos holds loyalty in high regard and if you are loyal to him, he is loyal to you. He treated Alexander more like a son than a slave."

Matthew found himself smiling slightly. He knew this story but only by the label, *The Centurion's Slave*. He was amazed to hear the story first-hand and to get the details by someone who was involved.

"One day, Alexander grew sick. Several Physicians had been to see him but his condition only worsened. I was with Marcos when he was summoned to his home. He was told that there was nothing more that could be done for his servant. I watched Marcos' face grow sad and knew how much he cared for Alexander. He spent the rest of the day and all that night by the bed of his servant."

"One of the Hebrew Physicians came by to check on the boy. His face told Marcos that it would not be long before the servant would expire. The man was about to leave when he turned to Marcos and told him about a healer named Jesus who was not far away. He said that perhaps he could do something."

"We had heard about Jesus and knew several things about him. We had several reports of miracles he had done. We knew he had a large following and that he was not far away in Capernaum. Marcos ordered me and three others to go with two of the Hebrew leaders to speak to Jesus."

"A few hours later we came upon a large crowd gathered by the sea in Capernaum. The Jewish men spoke to Jesus on behalf of Marcos. They explained to him about Alexander and told Jesus what a good man Marcos was. They even told him of the help he had been in the building of the synagogue. I saw Jesus smile and heard him say, 'We must go to Tiberias.' The crowd moved with him and myself and the three others moved quickly ahead. We arrived back in Tiberias an hour before sunset and told Marcos that Jesus agreed to come and would be arrive shortly. This seemed to give him hope and he went inside to sit with Alexander."

"A little while later I saw a large crowd coming over the far hill and I knew it was Jesus. I told Marcos and he came outside and stood on the porch watching the crowd approach. He told me to go to Jesus. He understood the Hebrew ways and knew that for a Jew to enter the home of a Gentile meant defilement. He told me to tell Jesus that they were both men of authority and that he need not come further. He said that he believed that Jesus could heal his servant with words alone and without the touch of a hand."

"I ran to Jesus and told him what Marcos said. He turned to his followers and spoke of Marcos' faith. He called it greater than the faith of the Hebrews and told me to return in peace. I ran back to Marcos. He was still on the porch when I arrived. I told him what the Master had said and while I was speaking I saw Alexander come out and stand behind Marcos. He looked so strong and healthy. He said, 'Master, what is it that you are looking for?' Marcos turned around and was surprised to see him standing there and hugged him. Marcos said, 'Jesus has healed you! It is Jesus who has done this! He is the promised Messiah!'"

"It was on that day that I began this journey of faith that I am on. I believe Jesus is the Christ, the promised Messiah."

The three men smiled. Jeriah stepped forward to hug him but Claudius held him back with a hand on his shoulder. He turned and looked toward the wagon. The men had not moved but were watching in eagerness. He wished the men well and turned and walked quickly to the wagon. Moments later the four of them were on their way back home and Levi was sharing the conversation with the Hannah and Benjamin.

At one of the inns that night, Matthew lay awake on his bed. So many thoughts were rumbling through his head. Everything seemed so surreal. This wasn't a dream! It lasted so long. He hungered, thirsted, and got tired. This couldn't be a dream! But it didn't seem real either. In some strange way he felt like he had fallen somewhere in between. He fell asleep with the words on his lips, "Lord, what are you trying to show me?"

Two days later they arrived back in Gophna, tired but fulfilled from their long trip.

Matthew spent the rest of that week gardening and working on clothing for the market. At the end of the week Matthew was approached by a wealthy man named Gaddiel. He met him a few times before and knew him to be a believer. He had seen Gaddiel at a meeting of *the way* in Jerusalem. Gaddiel had gotten word that Matthew was looking for employment and he explained to him that he had an undershepherd who would soon be moving away to be with his ailing father. He wanted to know if Matthew would be interested in taking the man's place and looking after part of his flock. The job would require him to be in charge of about fifty sheep. This was no small task!

The idea intrigued Matthew. He knew little about shepherding sheep. His experience was in shepherding people. He thought of the similarities. They both needed protection and nourishment. They both needed to feel safe and secure. They needed a place to rest and be refreshed. He had done all of those things as a pastor/shepherd at church. He wondered, "What would it be like to be a shepherd like

David?"

He thought a great deal about the twenty-third Psalm. It was his favorite. He often referred to it as *The song of the Shepherd* and he had memorized it, preached on it, and used it numerous times in funerals. He often pointed out that the six verses could be seen in two parts. Many times he shared the idea, "When things are good (verses 1-3), you talk *about* the shepherd. When things are bad (verses 4-6), you talk *to* the shepherd. Particularly at funerals he emphasized that for the believer death is but a shadow. "Shadows frighten us because they keep us from seeing things clearly. They hide things and make us feel like we're in danger. But shadows can do us no harm." Matthew smiled as he reflected on those words and more and more he thought about what it would be like to go beyond talking about shepherding and actually be a shepherd.

At the end of the week the family would be heading back to Jerusalem for a gathering of *The Way*. They had learned that Peter would be preaching and Matthew couldn't wait for the week to pass.

# Chapter 17
# Gratitude

One afternoon Levi and Matthew went to a small café near the square. As they talked Levi kept looking around for a familiar face. The woman who had previously waited on them was not there. They knew when the meeting would take place and who would be speaking, but they did not know where it was to be held. Several times they lowered their voices as they spoke. Certain words and phrases like Messiah, Jesus, resurrection, and King of Kings called for caution. They were careful, guarded, and discreet.

A waiter came by their table and asked if the men were in need of anything else. Levi had recognized him as one who was at a meeting of *The Called Out Ones*. The man crossed his arms and both men saw him use his index finger to tap his upper arm three times. Levi moved his hand to his face and used his finger to tap his cheek three times as well. The man smiled and said very quietly. "Phillip the tanner." Levi smiled and nodded. He knew who Phillip was and was sure that he would be able to tell them where the meeting in Jerusalem was to be held. They left the café and walked a few blocks in search of Phillip.

They got to Phillip's place of business and found the door open. A fairly tall man had his back to them. When they entered the man turned around. He was wearing an apron and gloves and held a short knife that he had been using to scrape a hide that was stretched over a wooden frame. He smiled revealing the loss of a front tooth and a scar down the entire left sided of his face. He placed his hands on his hips but did not let go of the knife. "Shalom! May I help you men?" Levi bowed slightly at the waist. "Shalom. I am Levi and this is my friend Matthew."

Phillip bowed in return. "I am Phillip." He smiled and waved his hand across the shop. "I am a tanner."

Levi's eyes followed his hand, "We were told to seek for you to find the location of the meeting in Jerusalem." As always Levi gave a slight bow of his head.

"What meeting is it that you seek?" Phillip asked leaning to the side and looking at the doorway.

"A meeting of *the way*. We are believers in the risen Lord Jesus."

"Yes *the way* Phillip responded. "And who is it that told you that I am the one to direct you?"

Matthew spoke up, "We were at the café just off the square. Our waiter told us that you are the one to ask."

"And what is it that you seek there?"

Levi smiled, "We seek the fellowship of other believers and to learn more about the King of Kings."

Phillip seemed to loosen up. "By the altar of the temple, tell me the truth, are you officials of the temple or synagogue?"

"By the altar of the temple, we are not" Levi said. "As I said, we are only men who are are followers of Jesus and seek the fellowship of other believers."

This comment made Phillip relax. He put the knife on the counter and pulled off his gloves. "I too am a follower of Jesus. Forgive me for my words but I must be very careful as you can imagine." He used two fingers to run them along the scar on his face. "A gift from the Romans."

The men nodded in understanding.

"As you know, since the resurrection those who believe, have been under pressure from the Romans as well as our own people. It has not been easy and many have paid a price to name the name of Jesus."

Matthew said, "We understand."

Phillip didn't speak. He looked down for a few moments. Lifting his head, he said, "Well, if you do not understand I believe that one day you will. Jesus told us that he recognized that there were many who hated him and that we should not be surprised if men hate us." He cocked his head to one side, raised his eyebrows and tapped his scar.

The men nodded in recognition.

Phillip continued, "The Master told us that the price we may have to pay here on earth will be well worth it for the glories we will experience in heaven. No matter the price, we should be willing to pay it to spend eternity with Jehovah."

Matthew thought about so many who had suffered for the sake of the Gospel. He had read about them, talked about them, and even met many who had lost so much to carry the name of Jesus. So many times he felt the pangs of guilt when he complained about being *inconvenienced* for the sake of the Gospel. He had often been reminded of a phrase he learned in college, "I complained of having no shoes, until I met a man with no feet" and understood how that applied so well when he was tempted to feel sorry for himself. The phrase fit appropriately as he stood in front of Phillip.

Phillip continued, "The swords of the soldiers are sharp and the hands of our religious leaders are strong. These times call both for caution and wisdom. Please forgive me for being guarded" The men nodded showing both their forgiveness and agreement.

"Please sit" Phillip said, coming from behind the counter and ushering them to a table full of tools. "I will tell you of the night that strengthened my faith in the Christ so greatly."

The three men sat down. Phillip took a deep breath. "A couple of months after the resurrection I was at a meeting of *the called out ones*. We were meeting in a room over the house of Mary, the mother of John, who had become a believer. We were all afraid because Stephen was stoned by our people and James was taken to Herod who had him killed. We had been praying and sharing stories of Jesus and even quietly singing. Without warning, the door burst open and several soldiers came into the room. Everyone froze. They called for Peter but no one answered. One of them grabbed a woman close at hand and held a knife to her throat. Peter stepped up and was thrown to the floor. I grabbed the arm of one of them and he turned with his sword and cut me across the face. He turned me around and pushed me against the wall." He opened his mouth and tapped the place where his tooth had been. Phillip paused to let the incident marinate in their minds.

"In seconds Peter and the soldiers were gone. We knew that it would be the last time we would see Peter on earth. Many left the room but several of us stayed to pray. We were praying for Peter but deep in our hearts we felt that he would be killed as well. Our prayers were mixed with tears and fear. We had no idea what would happen next." Matthew knew but like other times he dared not speak up.

"I stayed in the room with the others and we prayed. We all fell asleep, but about midnight one of the servant girls woke us up. She was very excited and said that Peter was at the door. We told her it could not be Peter and told her not to open the door but find out who it is. She kept telling us it was Peter and I remember one of the men suggesting that perhaps Peter had been killed already and that his spirit had come to be with us. I got up and opened the door. It was Peter!" he said using his index finger to make a point.

"We could not believe it! Everyone embraced him. Everyone shook his hand. A large woman hugged him so strongly he looked like he was in pain. The room was filled with laughter and praise to Jesus the Messiah".

"Peter told us how he had been delivered. He had been chained between two soldiers and was asleep. Peter said he was dreaming of Jacob wrestling with an angel of the Lord all night. When the angel touched Jacob's hip and put it out of place, Peter said he felt pressure on his own hip. He woke up and the room was full of light. He struggled to see and soon he could tell that an angel stood before him. He looked at his hands and saw that the chains were off. The angel told him to get up and leave the cell. When he stood up the gate opened. He walked out of the room with the guards never waking up. As he walked to the end of the hall, that gate opened as well. He walked from the prison and found us in the room where he had left us a few hours earlier."

"I was a believer but that night my faith was solidified. I knew, I just knew that everything I had heard and seen concerning Jesus was true. Since then I have heard so many stories of the miracles of Jesus as well as those of the disciples." Phillip leaned in, "He is the Lord. He is the Messiah. He lives." Without prompting the two men said, "Yes! He lives."

Phillip explained, "The meeting will take place in the courtyard of a man called Zelek. Just before you get to the main gate of the holy city there will be a road that crosses your path. Go to the left and you will come to a well. About five hundred yards passed the well you will see a large house on the right. A purple sash will hang from the handle on the door. It is there that we will meet in two days.

The next two days could not pass quickly enough for the men. They busied themselves with chores and visited with friends to pass the time. When the day came for them to make the long trek to the city Matthew joined Levi and his family and they began their journey.

The directions Phillip gave were correct. They found the road, the well, and the purple sash just as he had explained it. The home of Zelek was larger than most homes. Matthew reasoned, "Zelek must be doing alright for himself to afford a place like this." When they got to the door and knocked, they found the door slightly opened. A servant boy stood and looked at the four of them without speaking.

Levi spoke up, "Shalom. We are believers who are here for the meeting of *the called out ones.* The servant gave a slight smile and opened the door. When they entered they were surprised that very few were in the front room. Moments later they understood why. They were escorted to the courtyard where hundreds had gathered. The atmosphere was noisy and festive. The energy and excitement of the gathering was tangible.

Very soon everyone sat down. The sun had set and a welcomed breeze was blowing. A man stood up at one end of the courtyard. He was elderly but looked strong. He had a long gray beard and wore a dark blue and white headpiece and leaned on a cane. The crowd immediately fell silent when he spoke.

"Welcome my friends! The peace of the Lord to you! I am Zelek from the tribe of Ephraim. I am a man who has been deeply blessed by Jehovah." No one spoke but as heads nodded, Matthew could feel the sentiment of the room, "That is for sure!"

"I am a follower of the risen Lord Jesus Christ." This was followed by several saying, "Amen, Praise Jesus," and "Glory to the Lord!"

"I welcome you in the name of Jesus and am excited to host this meeting. Tonight we are blessed to have with us, Peter, who spent three years with the Master."

Peter stood up and the courtyard broke out in applause. He held his hands out for the accolades to stop and in a few moments the area was quiet again.

For the next hour Peter told those gathered about his relationship with Jesus and the things that Jesus talked about. He told them about God's love and forgiveness, reconciliation, what loving your neighbor looks like, and the parable of the king who forgave a man who owed so much. Matthew's heart skipped a beat when Peter began to speak about the time he, James, and John were called aside to join Jesus on top of a mountain.

"We did not know what to expect, but we joined Jesus and climbed the mountain. As we walked Jesus said very little. Jesus told us to stand in a particular spot and he moved ahead a few feet."

Peter moved one leg forward and leaned on it with one hand. He pointed the index finger of his other hand toward the crowd. "Then something miraculous happened. The wind began to blow. It blew harder and harder and we struggled to keep our balance. And just as suddenly it stopped and all was calm. When we looked at Jesus we saw a great light around him and his clothes were white as snow. His face was glowing as if a light was shining from it. The light was so bright that we had trouble looking at him and we kept blinking our eyes. Then we each felt something. It was like a surge of power that went right through us. A bolt of energy hit us and great strength came upon us. Joy overwhelmed our very souls."

"Then we looked and saw Moses and Elijah standing with Jesus." "A representation of the law and the prophets" Matthew thought. Peter turned both of his palms up and stood erect. "They never looked at us, only at Jesus. It was as if we weren't there. We could not hear what they were saying but they placed their hands on him and stood very close to him as they spoke with him. Somehow I thought how wonderful it would be if we had a place for each of them where we could come and speak with them when we desired. Before I knew it I called out to the Lord and said, 'Lord this is a good thing for you to be here. If you desire, we will make a tabernacle here for each of you!' As soon as I said this I realized how foolish that sounded."

"Then something happened that brought fear to each of our hearts." "The voice of God" Matthew thought though he was careful not to even let his lips move. Peter continued, "The sky was clear but suddenly we saw a cloud appear. It was black as coal but had a wide golden band around the edges. We tried to look at it but the brightness of the edges hurt our eyes. All of a sudden a booming voice like thunder came from the cloud. Fear gripped our hearts and we fell to the ground" Peter put his face in his hands. "We hid our faces and heard the voice, and it was the very voice of Yahweh, "This is the son of mine who I love deeply. He greatly pleases me. Listen to him and obey!'

No one moved. Everyone was locked onto every word that Peter spoke. He said, "We serve a mighty God." Numerous heads nodded. "The same God who brought judgment on Egypt, parted the Sea of Reeds, fed our fathers in the desert, went before our people to fight against our enemies is the one who raised Jesus from the dead." Several voices shouted words of praise.

"The power that he showed in pushing back the Jordan river and bringing water from a rock is the power that he shows us today. Do we have any here who want to testify to the power of Jehovah?"

For several minutes, no one spoke. People looked around to see if any would volunteer. Then a man stood up by the far wall. He didn't move toward Peter but stood where he was. He seemed to be about forty-years old and looked nervous in the middle of such a crowd. "I am Sacar from the tribe of Benjamin" he began. "For many years I lived as a leper. When I was a young man, I was visiting the temple with my family. As we were preparing to leave the court of the women, we heard a woman scream. When I turned to her I saw that she was pointing at me. At first, I didn't understand. Then a priest came over to me. He put his hands on my shoulders and looked at me. His next words changed my life. I will never forget them! 'Unclean! You must go!' I was confused. I didn't know what to do. But then the priest and several others used rods to push me from the temple area. The whole time they were yelling, 'Unclean! Unclean!' My mother and father tried to step in but they were pushed away. After I was forced from the temple area others forced me from the city with rocks. Before I knew it I was outside the city and all alone."

Sadness swept across the faces of everyone and many shook their heads in dismay. "I soon joined the commune south of here called, Elahn. There were about forty of us there. In the first year I lost my left ear, my cheek, and three fingers. Pain breeds pain and comfort is found in similar pain. I never really found comfort but had plenty of pain. The next year I lost all my toes of my left foot and the rest of my fingers on my right hand. My nose was gone and I limped on an infected left foot. Seldom did we have contact with anyone outside of our camp. Sometimes we would find food and clothing left near the road not far from our camp." Matthew's mind wandered a bit, "Sounds similar to how some people in church treat others who are hurting. Give enough to feel good but don't get too close!"

"My parents would come to check on me a few times a year but they would have to stand on the hill and speak to me." Several in the crowd had their hand over their mouths as Sacar continued. "I spent a great deal of my time in self-pity. I kept thinking 'Why me? What did I do that was so wrong that this happened to me?'"

"Somehow, and I'm not sure how we heard of *the Healer*. We didn't know his name but we got word that he was soon coming to Jerusalem. Some scoffed and chose to live in hopelessness. Some couldn't walk, but ten of us decided to try to see him." A flash of familiarity came across Matthew's face. "I know where this is going" he thought.

"Early one morning, we gathered a little food and headed in the direction of the city. Some of us struggled to walk so it took a good measure of time for us to reach the city. We stood away from the side of the road not far from the central gate. A few people tossed us some coins as they passed, but most of the time we sat along the road wondering whether or not we had misheard and were wasting our time. By mid-day there was still no sign of the healer. We began talking about going home."

"Then we saw a group of people coming over the hill and heading our way. There were about twenty of them and we were sure that it must be the man who had healed so many others. We knew we were to call out *unclean!* but we were afraid we would miss our chance at meeting the one who might heal us. So we stood up, hobbled to the road, and waited."

"As they came closer we heard whispers from the group. They said words like *lepers, Not too close, Unclean,* and *dirty*. Soon, they were right in front of us and didn't move. The two groups stood staring at one another. Finally, the Master stepped toward us."

The courtyard was cloaked in silence. No one moved and many faces displayed feelings of pity, wonder, and awe. "The healer, Jesus moved his hand to brush the crowd aside. He walked right up to us. He put his hands on several shoulders." Sacar looked down in sadness. "None of us had been touched by a *clean* person in years. He gave us no instructions. In fact, he spoke little. He looked at all of us and just said, 'Be healed! Be whole!' "

"I felt my body grow very warm, as if I was getting a fever. Then I began to tingle all over. It started in my feet and worked its way up to the top of my head. I didn't know what was happening and I felt dizzy. Then my friend Ezra looked at me and said, 'Sacar! Your ear!' I reached up to touch my ear and saw my hand." He held up his hand in front of the crowd. "My fingers had grown back! My ear, my nose, and my feet were all healed!" Sacar began to talk faster and faster and with more excitement. "We looked at each other and looked at ourselves. We couldn't believe it! The group began clapping and laughing at us.

Right there in the road we all began rejoicing."

"Jesus told us to go to the temple and show ourselves to the priest. The temple! The priest! None of us had been inside the city, much less the temple for a long time. But we were to go that day!"

"We all began walking and running toward the gate of the city. We moved through quickly rejoicing. We passed many people who looked at us and stared. We wore the clothes of lepers but we were whole. It felt so good not to shout *unclean* and to pass people who did not hold rocks in their hands."

"When we reached the temple steps Ezra turned back. I asked him where he was going and he told me, 'To find the healer. I must thank him!' The rest of us moved up the steps in search of one of the priests. We found one and he examined each of us and pronounced us *clean*. We *were* clean! We *were* healed! We *were* whole!"

"I spent more than half an hour at the altar. How good it felt to be in the temple! I laughed and I cried. When I got up to leave I decided to go back and see the healer. I wanted to thank him and to be around him. I wanted to follow him. I moved quickly out of the city but couldn't find him. I wandered around the city but never came across him or any of his followers. So I went home to be reunited with my family. The look on my parent's faces is a sight I will never forget. That night a great celebration was had in our home. It was the greatest day of my life and I will always be thankful!" Then Sacar raised his hands and looked up. His voice grew loud as he shouted, "Jesus is the Messiah and I am a follower of his!"

The entire assembly rose to its feet and gave a deafening applause. Many who were near Sacar hugged him and patted him on the back. This went on for an extended period of time. Then Peter rose and held up his hands for silence. Once again the crowd grew quiet and before long everyone was seated again. Peter said, "Jesus is Jehovah Raphe! He is our God and our healer!" Again the crowd began to cheer, and again, Peter raised his hands for silence. Then he said, "Are there any among us tonight who need a touch of the hand of the Almighty? Does anyone have a need we must pray for?"

Several raised their hands and Peter called them up and directed them to corners where several men stood waiting. They were surrounded and had hands laid on them in prayer. After a few minutes Peter raised his hands to pray and all grew quiet. "Our Heavenly Almighty Father, let it be according to your great will. Amen!"

The moment he said *Amen* the crowd began to clap. A man stood and shouted out, "Peter, my nephew!" He reached down and pulled a young boy up to his side. The boy looked to be about twelve years old and stood with a crutch under his arm. Everyone grew quiet as the man loudly said, "He fell from a tree and damaged his leg. He has not been able to straighten it for several weeks!" Peter held out his hand with his palm up and simply said, "Come." The boy and his uncle slowly worked their way to where Peter was standing.

Peter asked, "Do you confess Jesus as the Christ?" The young man looked at Peter and said clearly, "I do!" Then Peter looked upward and loudly said, "It is by the power of the Lord Jesus Christ that you are healed." Peter reached down and gently removed the crutch from under the boy's arm. The young man slowly straightened his leg out. He gently put his foot down and shifted his weight onto it. Several in the crowd gasped. The boy's arms came up and so did the noise of the crowd. Shouts of "Praise Jesus!" and "He is the Messiah" and "The glory is to God" were heard throughout those gathered.

While all that was happening, a woman was led through the crowd and up to Peter. She was tall, thin, and elderly. When she stood before Peter he said, "What is it that you want the Lord to do for you?" No one in the crowd sat down and those near the back craned their necks to see what was happening. No one made a sound.

The woman said, "I want to see again. I have been blind for over twenty years." Peter nodded in understanding. Then he placed his hands on her shoulders and said loudly, "It is the Lord Jesus Christ who heals you." Peter placed one hand behind her head and the other over both her eyes. He looked up and said, "Blessed be the name of the Lord Jesus Christ our maker and our healer. Be opened!"

The woman blinked and her eyes fluttered. She moved her head back and forth as she continued to blink. Then a wide smile broke across her face. "My eyes! I see! I see! I can see!" The crowd erupted in applause. Matthew was close enough to hear her even above the roar of the crowd. "Thank you! Oh, thank you!' She made a move to kneel at Peter's feet but he caught her hands and pulled her upright and very loudly said, "You are healed by the name and power of the Lord Jesus the Christ! Give thanks and praise to him only!"

Peter again faced the people with his hands raised for silence. They remained standing while they grew quiet. "My friends, the call of the Master is for forgiveness. Repent of your sins and you will be forgiven and be a child of Abba Father. Then you must forgive others as he has forgiven you and lead them to faith in Jesus the Christ."

Peter began to sing and the crowd joined in. As much as he wanted to join in, Matthew did not know the words. But he lifted his face, smiled, closed his eyes and joined them with his heart.

> *"He is Lord! He is Lord!*
> *He has conquered sin and death,*
> *And he is Lord…*
> *He is King! He is King!*
> *He rules and reigns my life,*
> *And he is King…*
> *He is Savior, He is Savior!*
> *He has forgiven me of my sins,*
> *And he is Savior…*
> *He is Master! He is Master!*
> *He lives inside my soul,*
> *And he is Master."*

While the crowd applauded a man stepped up to Peter and spoke into his ear. Peter held up his hand and turned to the crowd who became silent. "Brothers and Sisters. The time has come for us to depart. Go quickly to your homes. Be at peace with all you meet and walk in the light and love of our Savior Jesus the Christ!"

The crowd dispersed orderly with surprising speed. Moments later the courtyard was empty. Levi and Matthew were some of the last to leave. When they reached the front door they understood the reason for the rapid departure. They met several temple officials and a dozen Roman soldiers heading into the house. Levi and Matthew were pushed aside and the men entered the house without waiting for permission. Levi looked at Matthew and silently communicated to him his desire to see what was going to happen. Matthew just nodded and followed him back into the house. Levi sent his wife and son back with Isaac and Miriam.

When they got inside they found a place in the shadows where they were close enough to see and hear what was about to happen. The soldiers were led to the courtyard where Peter was standing with Zelek and two other men. They heard the others coming but did not run and hide which surprised Matthew and Levi. The two men hiding couldn't hear everything being said and their view was partially blocked by the bodies surrounding the Peter and the others, but they saw and heard enough to understand what was happening.

Zelek spoke up. "Why is it that you have entered my house? What is it that you want?"

A soldier stepped toward Zelek. With one hand resting on the hilt of his sword and the other a fist in Zelek's face he yelled, "Silence!"

The synagogue official faced Peter and asked him what they were doing here tonight.

"Nothing but worshipping the Lord" Peter said.

The official knew where this was going and knew what to ask.

"And who is this Lord you are worshipping?"

He turned to the official and without hesitation said, "Jesus, the one whom you crucified."

"No" the official shouted. "He is not the Lord! You speak blasphemy!"

Peter squared himself to the official, took a deep breath and said, "I speak what I know is true."

The official raised his voice again, "You do not know what is true! There is only one God, and it is Jehovah!"

"Yes" Peter countered, "And he has come in the flesh!"

"Blasphemy! You speak nothing but blasphemy!" he said as he shook his fist at Peter.

Peter raised his voice to match that of the official's. "I speak what I have seen and heard." The Scriptures point to one coming to save his people. His name is Jesus. He has come and you have killed him."

"No!" the official screamed, "No! He is not the one who was to bring deliverance! He was but a teacher who gathered people to himself. He spoke lies and blasphemy as well!"

"He spoke the truth. You do not want to hear the truth because worship would go to him and not to you! That is the truth!"

The official pushed Peter and he moved backward a step.

"You speak nothing but blasphemy against Jehovah and our people. You will not be allowed to enter the synagogue or temple. Nothing you bring for sacrifice will be accepted!"

Peter gave a slight smile. "I have no need of the temple or the synagogue. Jesus is my sacrifice! He is the Lamb of God who takes away the sins of the world."

Matthew and Levi heard a distinct slap. "You will speak no more of this dead teacher!"

Peter interrupted him. "He is alive. The tomb is empty and he is alive!" the official stepped back as Peter continued, "I have seen him. I have touched him! You destroyed his body but he rose from the dead and he is alive!"

"Enough!" The official screamed. "You will speak no more of him! You will not tell others about him. You have been warned!"

Those from the temple stepped back and the soldiers stepped in. They completely blocked the view Matthew and Levi had. But they heard everything that followed. They wanted to step in but knew it would be useless. Peter and the others were in the hands of the Romans. Only God could intervene.

Matthew and Levi heard the blows and the grunts from the center of the circle. The officials and a few of the the Romans walked away and left the beating up to the soldiers. Moments later the soldiers marched out of the house leaving Peter and the others on the floor.

Matthew and Levi came out of hiding. They rushed to the place where the men lay on the floor. Their faces were already swollen and they each held their sides as they lay on the floor. Peters lip was bleeding and he had a cut over his left eye. One of the men cradled his arm commenting that it might be broken. With the help of Matthew and Levi, the four of them sat up groaning.

Peter spoke first. "It is certain that we should not invite any of them to our next meeting." The three other men smiled and one of them said, "It hurts to laugh."

Another said, "I think I hurt one of them with my face" which brought more chuckles from the group.

There was a short moment of silence broken by Peter who struggled to his feet. "May our Heavenly Father forgive them!" "Yes" the others said rubbing their faces and arms. Levi and Matthew just shook their heads in admiration.

Matthew thought back to his own life and ministry. He had never been physically assaulted but had his share of verbal attacks. One time in particular a man who had lived in Frayton his entire life, stopped by

Matthew's office. He was a big man both financially and physically. He had visited the church several times but was not a member. Matthew knew about him but didn't really know him. They talked for awhile and then the man made a proposal.

The man's daughter had been dating one of the young men who was a member of Fortress Baptist Church. They dated for over a year and became engaged. After a couple of months, the young man decided to break off the marriage plans and dissolve their relationship. The young girl was devastated. The man suggested that Matthew discipline the young man and no longer let him attend the church. Matthew balked at the idea and told him he had no intention of doing so. The man threatened in no uncertain terms to make things tough on him and the church in Frayton.

Over the next couple of months, he spread rumors about Matthew. Everything was brought up. His sermons were taken out of context and questions regarding finances were brought up. Finally, a rumor was spread that Matthew was having an affair with one of the members. Several families left the church preferring to be in an environment that was less controversial. At one point he considered asking the young man to seek another church. He knew this was not right, but saw it as a possible solution. Matthew was being bullied like a young school boy. The leaders of the church rallied around their Pastor. They encouraged him to seek legal counsel who sent word to the wealthy man of legal action regarding slander and defamation of character. Shortly all the rumors died down and he was able to resume his normal activities.

Matthew thought about the amount of sleep he'd lost and how deeply it affected him. In the present context he felt like a coward and was somewhat ashamed. Here he was in the presence of men whose very lives were threatened and they didn't back down an inch.

After he and Levi were assured that the men were okay, they left and began their walk to Isaac's house. There was no end to their conversation along the way. Before they knew it they were back at Isaac and Miriam's house and were telling the others what they had experienced. A good while later they readied themselves for a much needed night's sleep.

A day later found Matthew with Levi and his family back in their town. Matthew spent the next day with Gaddiel, the owner of the sheep. He was introduced to Abida, an older man whose position

Matthew would be taking. The man had been with the owner for over twelve years and it was clear they had a healthy relationship.

# Chapter 18
# A Shepherd's Life

Early the following day Matthew met Abida on the edge of town. He asked Matthew where he was from and Matthew explained that he was from a very small town called Frayton, "A good way from from here." Before Abida could ask another question, Matthew offered, "But I am staying with Levi and Hannah here." This seemed to satisfy him and he smiled and nodded in approval.

Abida knew that Matthew had no experience in shepherding sheep and led him out to the pasture to introduce him to his *family*. When they reached the corral Abida stood on the hill overlooking the sheep in the pen. Stretching both his arms out he said, "Behold, my children!" Matthew smiled with appreciation over the obvious care this man had for his charges.

For the next two days Abida instructed Matthew in the care of sheep. Matthew was amazed at how much this man knew about these animals. Each of them had a name connected to their personalities. There was lily. She was a small lamb who overflowed with affection for Abida as well as the other sheep. Bull was a goat who pushed his way to the front of the group and was always first at the feeding trough. Matthew looked down to see Momma. She was the protector of the others, particularly the smaller ones. Matthew noticed how different sheep would lift their heads when Abida called their names. Even the sheep knew their names!

The shepherd opened the gate and made a sound with his mouth. "It is the command to follow" he said. The sheep filed out of the pen as Matthew gave a poor attempt at imitating the sound. He felt slightly embarrassed. Abida smiled, "It will come. Be patient."

The Shepherd tapped his staff and walked. The sheep dutifully followed. They walked along a hillside with Abida giving instructions along the way. He told Matthew that trust is the key to good shepherding. If the sheep know you care for them and will protect them and lead them well they will follow the tapping of the staff even while eating. He explained how easily frightened they become when loud noises are heard and how they will often rush to the side of their protector.

At length they came to a large field. Matthew saw another shepherd with his sheep on the other side and noticed that Abida and the other shepherd each raised their staff toward one another in an honorable greeting.

Abida pointed with his chin across the field. "That is Mosha. He is young and has much to learn but he has a good heart and cares very much for his sheep. Matthew nodded but said nothing. Abida continued, "Some shepherds, because they are not owners of the sheep, leave them when trouble comes. But a good shepherd always puts himself between the sheep and danger." Jesus words, "I am the good shepherd. The good shepherd lays down his life for the sheep," immediately came to Matthew's mind.

"I am told that one time Mosha fought off three or four wolves who attacked his little flock. If you ever get close to him, you will see a large scar on his upper arm. He did not get away without injury, but the wolves did not get away with a lamb."

"Sometimes ministering to sheep can be painful" Matthew said nodding and thinking about the life of a Pastor. "Yes" Abida said, "The hills and valleys are full of trouble and you must be alert at all times. Come, we must stay ahead of the sheep and look over their afternoon table." "Table?" Matthew questioned. "Yes" Abida said, "Often a large field is called a table. It is a wonderful place for the sheep to graze and we can sit and rest while we watch them. But we must look it over before the sheep wander too far into it. Like other places it carries some dangers we must protect them from."

"What kind of dangers" Matthew asked.

"There are thorns and thistles, but they usually are not a problem. The sheep will avoid them. They might bump their noses against them but we will take care of that at the pen. What we must look out for is an enemy that often lives in the field."

"What enemy?"

Leading Matthew into the field Abida said, "The brown adder. It is a snake. It is not poisonous but does not hesitate to bite the nose and faces of the ones who get too close. Often a sheep will become infected from the bite. Come we must look things over."

Matthew followed and soon Abida stopped and drew his attention to the ground. "Here is a hole probably with an adder inside. We will prepare the hole."

Kneeling down by the hole, Abida drew his pouch of oil from his side. He tipped the pouch allowing a small stream of oil to cover the rim of the hole. "Adders do not like the smell and this will keep them in their hole for the day." Matthew nodded. "He prepares a table before me in the presence of my enemies" leapt to his mind and he turned his head slightly to hide his smile.

They allowed the sheep to graze for a couple of hours and then Abida stood signaling that it was time to move on. "The sheep will need water soon and there is a stream not far from here. We will lead them to it." He made a noise with his voice and pounded his staff. The sheep began moving as they looked up. Matthew continued to be impressed by it all.

By mid-day they had reached a small stream. The stream flowed gently but not gently enough for Abida's *family*. "We must build a pool" he said removing his sandals. He reached between his feet and grabbed the back of his robe. He pulled it forward and tucked it in the sash around his waist. His robe was transformed into long shorts. Matthew followed his lead acting as if it was not a new move for him. They spent an hour building a dam on the edge of the stream. Several sheep stood by watching the men work. The sheep seemed to know what their care-takers were doing and they waited patiently for them to finish. When the task was completed a pool of standing water was created and the sheep moved to the edge of the pool and leisurely drank.

Abida explained that sheep are not wise animals but they are smart enough to know that a moving stream is very dangerous. "Sheep do not swim well and the weight of their wool soaked with water will pull them under." This made sense to Matthew and he nodded in understanding and thought, "Quiet waters."

By the end of the day they had traveled several miles and came to a sheepfold. Abida explained that it was understood that the shepherd who arrived first had claim to the pen for the night. "First come, first served" Matthew thought.

A few rocks needed replacing on the top of the wall and the men went to work right away. They placed branches with thorns on the top discouraging intruders from making any attempt to get at the sheep. In less than half an hour the men completed their task.

Abida made a strange noise getting the sheep's attention. Matthew made a poor attempt at imitating it making Abida chuckle. Most of the sheep looked in Abida's direction. He tapped his staff three times and made another noise. The sheep all began to migrate his way.

As they reached the opening to the sheep pen, Abida knelt down and held his staff across the doorway. He greeted each of them by name and looked them over from nose to tail before lifting his staff for them to enter. As they moved passed him he also counted them. Several of them carried thorns on their coats that he removed quickly. There was no pain or danger involved but he didn't want to invite trouble. He placed a drop of oil on any sheep that had a scratch or scrape on its nose or head and rubbed it gently into the wound. "You anoint my head with oil," floated to the front of Matthew's mind.

A very young one nestled up next to the men. Matthew had noticed that it never went far from Abida and often came and rubbed against the shepherd in a sign of affection. She was appropriately named was *Ahava* the Hebrew word for love. Abida explained that her mother had died giving birth to her and that he had fed her with the milk from other sheep. He rubbed the underbelly of the little one and she rubbed her head against his knee. He had a special affection for her and she returned the love.

Matthew thought about the love he had for people. He remembered how his heart overflowed with love when he first became a believer. He was so excited about his salvation that his heart was filled with joy and appreciation.

One night, shortly after returning to campus for his junior year in college, he felt a need to be alone. He found himself alone at as small pond on the edge of campus. The night was cool but not cold and he lay on his back gazing at the crystal clear stars. Deep and serious prayer was new to him but somehow being alone on such a beautiful night, brought it to him without much effort. His commitment to God deepened and he decided to be *all in* with his relationship with the Lord.

Soon a meteoric time of growth began in his life. He joined a campus Bible study, became friends with a local Pastor who mentored him, and devoured his Bible. Matthew had often thought of his early days as a believer and was thankful for those the Lord brought his way to love him and nurture him in the faith.

When the last of the sheep were in the pen, Abida stood and smiled at Matthew. "All fifty are here. We have done well," and he patted the side of Matthews shoulder. "Now we must prepare for the night." He instructed Matthew to gather sticks and twigs for the fire they were about to build. The sun was setting rapidly and a fire would be needed for warmth and protection.

Matthew had been camping his entire life and felt comfortable in the elements. Within minutes he had gathered a couple of armfuls of *fuel* and brought them to the entrance of the pen. Abida had assembled some dry grass and had used his knife to split some small twigs for kindling. He struck his flint, blew on the spark and moments later they had a fire blazing before them.

"Besides Jehovah," Abida said, "This is our greatest friend. It will keep us warm, cook our food, and keep the beasts away."

"Beasts?" Matthew said more curious than alarmed.

"Yes" Abida said nodding. We do not have lions here although a saw one a few years ago. I drove him away with a stick from the fire. What we must look out for are wolves. There are many among the hills and they will come at night looking for a meal," he tilted his head in the direction of the pen.

"And now, dinner" Abida said sliding his pouch to his side. He unrolled his blanket and sat on it. Matthew did the same. They each pulled out some salted meat and poured water on it. Then with sticks they roasted the meat over the fire. In a few minutes they feasted on meat, cheese, and bread, washing it all down with cool water they had gathered from the stream earlier in the day. The men talked through several subjects lightly and ended with a conversation about Jesus. Abida was not a follower of Jesus but seemed to be open to learning more. With the sheep safe in the fold, and blankets and the fire to keep them warm, they rolled to their sides and slept soundly in the doorway of the sheepfold.

The sun poked over the hillside waking them up. A breakfast of a few dates, some bread and water took little time and moments later the sheep were turned loose for a morning grazing and a leisurely walk in the direction of the city. The routine of tending and protecting the sheep would be repeated throughout the day.

Matthew enjoyed every aspect of shepherding and seemed naturally suited for the job. He recognized the names of several of the sheep and called them out on occasion. The sheep seemed to recognized his care for them and were naturally attracted to him. It took no time for *Ahava* to be drawn to him and he returned the affection. He learned to make the various sounds with his voice directing the sheep and soon could repeat the rhythm of pounding the staff indicating his location and reassuring the sheep of his presence.

The day was filled with rescuing sheep, tending wounds, creating drinking pools, and leading the *family* to fields they had scoped out to be sure they were free of natural enemies.

After examining all the sheep, securing them in a sheepfold, building a fire, and eating a small meal, Matthew and Abida were ready for bed. Sleep came quickly and was deep and restful. In the morning Matthew would be going back to Levi's and would return the following week to assume the role of Shepherd by himself.

The bright sunshine woke both the men and the sheep and Matthew bid them all farewell and began his five mile walk over the hills toward town. He arrived in the village by mid-afternoon and was given a warm greeting by Levi and his family. The last couple of days had given him so much he wanted to share with them. The rest of the day was spent helping Levi put the finishing touches on some fabrics and loading the wagon for another trip to Jericho the next day.

# Chapter 19
# Discovery

The morning broke bright and clear and after a quick meal the men mounted the wagon and pointed it in the direction of the ancient city of Jericho. Later that day the city was in sight. The plan was to meet a merchant in Jericho, spend the night, and then head further north to meet another one Levi knew in Alexandrium.

For some reason, Matthew began to whistle a familiar tune. He smiled and almost let out a little chuckle when the children's song, "Joshua fought the battle of Jericho" came through his lips.

Levi turned to him and said, "That is a happy tune!"

"Yes" Matthew countered. I learned it as a boy in…" He almost said Sunday school, but managed to shift his words to, "My father's house."

"There are words to it as well. It's about Moses' servant, the great military leader Joshua. Would you like to hear it?"

"Of course!" Levi said slapping Matthew's leg.

"Alright" Matthew said raising his hands to demonstrate the motions to the song.

"Joshua fought the battle of Jericho,
Jericho, Jericho,
Joshua fought the battle of Jericho,
And the walls came tumbling down!"

"That is a wonderful song!" Levi exclaimed laughing and clapping his hands. He nodded toward Matthew and the two men began to sing.

Strange looks came from those on the road who heard them sing but this did nothing to silence the men. They sang the ditty several times through as they neared the city gate. They slowed the wagon down as they entered the gates and went through silently understanding that most people might not share their enthusiasm about the walls of their city collapsing.

They passed by several Roman soldiers without incident. Once inside, Levi shifted his weight, faced Matthew, and patted him on his knee. He raised his finger, smiled and quietly sang, "And the walls came tumbling down!" Matthew laughed out loud and shook his head.

Less than an hour later, they met the merchant and had exchanged some of the goods for money and were happy to relax over an evening meal at a local inn. They were to spend the night there and leave for Alexandrium early the next day.

During the meal, Matthew watched as an elderly man approached Levi. He called him by name and leaned into him whispering something in his ear. Then shook his hand and walked away. Matthew was sure he saw the man slip something in to Levi's hand and felt certain it was information regarding a meeting of *the way*. Levi smiled and nodded at Matthew.

"Such good news my friend!" Levi whispered. "Tonight we will meet other brothers and sisters and we will once again celebrate the risen Savior's life!" Matthew couldn't wait!

Later that evening Matthew and Levi rode to a large dwelling just outside the city walls and about a half-mile from the gates. Already the room was filing with people and the excitement was building. The windows were opened and a welcomed breeze was blowing in. Soon, the other rooms began to fill as well as the courtyard.

In a moment the place was bursting with people and the noise developed into a loud buzz. The atmosphere carried all the excitement of a major sporting event and Matthew was enjoying the liveliness and enthusiasm of the crowd. Some were sitting down front and many were perched on window sills but most were standing in anticipation of something special happening that night.

After what seemed like a long time a man stood up in the center of the room. Many people whispered and several times Matthew heard the name Mark. Matthew wondered, "Could this be the apostle Mark?" He knew he didn't need to ask because he was sure he would soon have his answer.

The man extended his right hand toward the crowd and the room immediately became silent. "My brothers and sisters, good evening!" The vast room responded with a resounding "Shalom!"

"I greet you in the name of the risen Lord Jesus Christ.

The room applauded.

"To travel with the Messiah for almost three years was a privilege and an honor. Sometimes I struggle to believe that it really happened. Many times I am tempted to ask 'Why me?' This is something I will not know until I see the Almighty in glory"

*Glory!* someone shouted drawing Matthew's head in his direction. Many others nodded in agreement.

Mark continued, "I have chosen not to question Jehovah about this but rather to focus on what I heard and saw as the Lord led us in and out of cities and villages."

"I want to share two things Jesus taught us and so many other followers during his time of ministry. First of all, Faith must be at the center of all we say and do. God will lead us but we must have the faith it takes to obey. Trusting in the Lord with everything is not an easy thing to do. There is a strong temptation to follow our own understanding and experience. But when we brush that aside and follow *his* leading he makes our way clear.

It was all Matthew could do to keep from shouting. Proverbs 3:5-6 were his favorite verses in the Bible. They were his *foundation verses.*

"Trust in the Lord with all your heart

and lean not on your own understanding.

In all your ways acknowledge him,

 and he will make your paths straight."

"Faith means going upstream from what my heart and mind are telling me to do" Mark explained. "It doesn't have to be popular, or convenient, or even make sense. It may be risky and often will take you in a direction you did not plan to go. But faith, real faith brings change. Sometimes faith changes circumstances and situations and may bring opportunities. But faith always changes us. When we act in faith the Lord rewards us with more faith and soon we are saying and doing things we never dreamed of."

"As we traveled with Jesus, we witnessed him do things beyond our imagination. We saw lepers and crippled ones healed. Through *his* faith we witnessed the wind become silent and the waves lay flat. The blind saw and the dead were raised." Almost all those present nodded their heads.

"One day Jesus commanded a large group of us to select a friend and go out from him. We were not to carry any provisions with us, only the staff we held in our hands."

"The sending of the seventy" Matthew thought. He knew that to finish the story would be inappropriate and he leaned forward to lock on to Mark's words.

"What happened when we left the Master is beyond my understanding. My friend Micah and I traveled west toward the sea. We had only walked a couple of miles when we came upon two men on the road. One of the men was blind. His friend told us that no one knows how it happened but gradually his eyes grew dim. One morning about three years ago, he awoke and could see nothing. He was completely blind from that day on."

Micah and I looked at each other. He smiled at me and I nodded to him and simply said the word, *faith*" Mark used his own hands to demonstrate. "Micah placed both his hands over the man's eyes. He said, 'In the name of Jesus the Nazarene receive your sight.' We had no need of asking questions. His face told us everything. He blinked a few times and then smiled. 'I can see' he said. 'I can really see!'"

"Both men kept thanking us over and over. The man who was healed knelt and tried to worship us. We stopped him and told him 'All glory must be given to Jesus the Messiah.' We spent the rest of the afternoon telling them of Jesus the Christ."

"Later that day, we met a woman by the side of the road. She carried a crutch and was begging for food and alms. We walked directly up to her and told her we were followers of Jesus the Christ. She told us she was born without the use of her left leg."

"We asked her if she wanted to be healed. She looked at us with great doubt on her face. Micah told her 'Do not doubt. Only believe!' I took her by the shoulders and said, 'In the name of Jesus the Christ be healed.' Her arm lifted from her crutch and she looked frightened as if she was afraid she would fall. But her leg held strong. She looked startled, then surprised, then giddy. She leaned from one leg to the other and back again. She kept saying 'Thank you! Thank you! Thank you!' We told her only to thank Jehovah. Then she turned her face to the sky and kept saying 'Thank you! Thank you! Thank you! We joined her in laughter and praise to Almighty God. It was a wonderful time!"

"The next day we returned to Jesus. The others had similar experiences. Blindness, leprosy, deafness, paralysis, and many other sicknesses were healed by the power of God and the name of Jesus. Some even cast out demons in his name. The look on the Master's face was wonderful!

He glowed with the joy of the experiences of those who followed him. He told us that the real fulfillment is found in having our names written in the lamb's book of life."

"So my friends, faith is the essential element to following the Lord. Faith and trust in Jehovah pleases the Heavenly Father. In fact, without faith we are unable to please him, because our very belief that he exists is founded on faith."

"But there is something else that is essential in the lives of every true disciple of the Christ. It is a very hard element but important just the same. It is the concept of genuine forgiveness."

"I will never forget his words. The Master told us that in the word of God it is written and we have heard, 'An eye for an eye and a foot for a foot.' We all understood that. We had heard that since we were children. But Jesus told us that this has become misapplied. He said that this was a judicial instruction that men have used in a social setting. It was meant to keep those enforcing the law from over-extending the punishment for violations. It was intended by God to be a restraint on the judicial system. Instead, men have used it to match social transgressions against them. If a man insults you, insult him back. If a woman gossips about you, find something harmful to say about her. He shared with us how easily things can get out of hand, and that this is not the desire of Jehovah."

"Jesus directed us to leave it where it falls. He said that instead of giving insult for insult, we must forgive. In fact, he said that if we are struck on our one cheek, we are to turn to that person the other cheek."

Matthew's mind wandered to something he had read about a Russian political leader. He said, "You Christians believe that when you are struck on one cheek you must turn to that person the other cheek. But when I am struck on one cheek, I strike back so hard that I will knock the other Man's head off." Matthew smirked and wished that man could be with him right now.

Mark continued, "Forgiveness is not an easy teaching to accept, but it is the way of the Master, and it must be the way of his followers. Remember that even from the cross, Jesus asked that those who were crucifying him be forgiven." The crowd nodded in unison and several shouted, "Praise be unto Jesus!" and "Yes, Lord!" Then the applause began. Mark raised his hand over everyone and the group settled down.

Mark extended his hand to his right, "One who has become a friend of mine has come to testify of the healing power of Jesus." He smiled and nodded toward a man who stood up. He had a nervous smile on his face as he made his way to the side of Mark. He wore a wide band around his forehead and a tan robe with a brown sash. He wove his way through the seated crowd and finally came to Mark who greeted him with a strong hug.

The man cleared his throat. His smile never left his face. "My name is Zeleh. I am the son of Timaeus but those close to me call me Bartimaeus." Matthew searched his memory, "Could this be?" "I was born blind." Matthew heard himself whisper, "I knew it!" Levi and several others close by gave him a look that he pretended not to see.

Bartimaeus nervously twisted the sash around his waist. "I am from this city and spent my days sitting by the gate begging alms from those passing by. Many felt that I was blind because of some sin I had committed. They equated health and riches with God's favor and poverty and ill health as some sort of lack of righteousness. But this is not so! Being blind since my birth was proof of that." He shrugged his shoulders and said, "Unless I had committed some sin in the womb of my mother." The crowd chuckled realizing the absurdity of the scenario.

"But such as things were, myself and many others were at the mercy of those who would pass by and share from the extra they had. I was sitting by the gate with my friend Beor. He was blind as well. We heard a crowd approaching the city and hoped that we might receive something. We called to them and a few coins fell our way but the crowd passed and entered the city. Being blind we often heard more than those with sight. We heard their conversation as they passed. We heard the name Jesus spoken several times and asked who he was. We learned that he was a teacher, prophet, *and* healer! A healer! We had just been passed by a man who could heal." Bartimaeus looked down and shook his head, "We were so discouraged. But this is the life that we lived. When things are a certain way one gets used to it and accepts it. You have no choice."

"Later that afternoon we heard a large crowd coming out of the city gates. Once again we hoped to receive something from them. Then we heard it! We heard the name. It was Jesus!" He clapped his hands as he said the name. "Jesus was coming through the city gate and walking right toward us. Above the noise of the crowd Beor shouted, 'Perhaps Jehovah will smile on us and this Jesus will bring healing to us.' The crowd moved slowly and soon we knew Jesus was close to us. We both stood up and shouted, 'Jesus, Jesus!' Several near us told us to be quiet. One man even pushed me knocking me down. But I would not keep silent. I yelled as loud as I could, 'Jesus, Son of David, have mercy on me!'

"Then the entire group grew quiet. I am told it was because Jesus raised his hand. At first I was frightened. Then I heard him speak. I will never forget his words. He said, 'Come here to me.' A man standing close by told us, 'Get up. The Master is calling for you.' I jumped to my feet and we felt our way through the crowd and came right up to Jesus. He said, 'What do you want me to do for you?' I knelt down. I felt Beor kneel beside me. I said, 'Rabbi, I want to receive my sight.' Then he said to me, I remember it like it was moments ago, he touched my shoulder and said, 'Go! Your faith has made you well.'" The crowd gasped. Many were wiping tears from their own eyes.

Barimaeus paused for a moment and took a deep breath. "I blinked a few times. My head began to hurt as light flooded my eyes. I put my hands over my face and kept blinking as water poured from my eyes. Moments later I was standing up and looking into the face of the Son of David! I turned to Beor and could tell that he too could see. The tears of pain and discomfort quickly turned to tears of joy! We could see! We really could see! We both shouted, 'We can see! We can see!' Then we turned to Jesus and kept repeating 'Bless you! Bless you Son of David!'"

The Master hugged us both and walked back into the crowd. But there was no way we were going leave him. We became followers of his and walked with him for several days. Our lives have never been the same physically or spiritually." He extended his arms from his sides and shouted, "All praise and glory to Jesus the Lord!" Mark stepped up to him and embraced him. The crowd exploded in cheers and applause.

This went on for quite a while until Mark once again raised his hand over the room. Quietness again came quickly. "My friends," he said, "We have one who comes tonight for healing." He motioned into the crowd for a man to come forward. Two men stood up and made their way to Mark's side.

One man was elderly and the other looked to be about twenty years old. Mark put his hand on the old man's shoulder. "This is Obadiah He cannot speak or hear." Stepping forward he pointed to the younger man, "And this is his Grandson, Simeon." Then facing the crowd Mark said, "Two years ago Obadiah became sick and lost his voice and his hearing. He no longer has the use of his left arm as well." "A Stroke?" Matthew wondered and thought about all the people he knew who struggled after having a stroke.

Then turning to face Simeon he asked, "Simeon, is Obadiah a believer in the Lord Jesus Christ?"

"Yes" Simeon said. "We both are!" Obadiah nodded as Simeon spoke.

Then Mark placed his left hand on Obadiah's shoulder and raised his right hand. Very loudly he said, "In the name of Jesus the Nazarene, be opened!"

Immediately the man moved his head from side to side. He placed a hand over each ear alternatively and smiled. Then tears rolled from his eyes. He cleared his throat a couple of times and then said, "I, I can hear!" Then his eyes grew wide in surprise and he said, "And speak! I can speak!" he opened and closed his left hand a coupe of times. Then he raised it up. "My hand!" he said grinning even wider and turning and hugging Mark. "Thank you! Oh, thank you my friend! Once again, the room exploded in cheers and applause. Only the ones up close could hear above the noise as Mark said loudly, "Praise the Lord God Almighty for *HIS* benevolent hand!"

Finally, when the noise of the room died down, Mark pointed to a man in a corner by a table. The man motioned to another and they carried the table over the heads of the seated people. The table was brought to the center and placed in front of Mark. Two other men stepped forward bringing a large loaf of bread wrapped in a towel and a large cup obviously filled with wine. The entire group was to participate in the Lord's supper!

Marks spoke loudly and forcibly. "On the night the Master was taken, we were in Jerusalem. We had gathered with him in a room above a home. I remember so strongly how Jesus the Messiah washed *our* feet. *He* washed *our* feet! The King of Kings stooped to take the place of a servant. He did this to show that we, his followers, should serve one another. My friends, one of the marks of a follower of the Christ is our willingness to serve. It is not always easy and not always received well but we must look for ways to serve one another as well as others we meet."

"Then the Master sat up before us at the table. His words will never be forgotten. He held up the bread and said, 'This represents my body' and he broke it in two. He said, 'My body is to be broken for you.' Next he held up the cup and said, 'The wine is a symbol of my blood, and it is to be shed for you.' He told us that as often as we eat of the bread and drink of the wine, we demonstrate that we remember what he has done for us."

"We didn't quite understand it all. Living in the moment does not carry with it the benefit of reflection. It was only after he died that we were able understand what his words meant at that moment."

Having said that Mark paused a moment. He looked upward and moved his lips without speaking. He held the loaf of bread over his head, broke it in two, and simply said, "His body." Then he held the cup above his head and said, "His blood."

Somehow all of this took on new and fresh meaning to Matthew. He had led and participated in *The Lord's Supper* countless times but this was different. This was special. It became real to him in a way he had never experienced before. He remembered a time when he dropped the tray of bread. He thought about the time he heard a child use the word, *snack* and he remembered getting into deep discussions with other Pastors over the use of grape juice verses wine. He saw more clearly than ever how they missed the point entirely.

Mark took a piece of bread, dipped it in the cup of wine and reverently placed it in his mouth. After swallowing it, he broke the bread into five or six pieces and handed them to the people sitting in front of him. Likewise, he poured the wine into six brass cups and handed them to those seated up front.

Mark stepped to the side of the table. He stretched his arms across the room and said, "This bread and this wine represent both the body and the blood of the Lord Jesus Christ. Take you all of it in memory of what the Lord has done for you." Then he nodded and sat down.

Matthew watched as the bread and wine were passed. He saw men and women, young and old, friends and strangers helping each other as one held the cup and the other dipped the bread. He heard parents explaining to their children what was happening all around them.

When the elements came to him, he broke off a small piece of bread. The cup came by and Levi held it as Matthew dipped his bread. Then he held the cup as Levi did the same and they placed it in their mouths together with joy. It felt warm and tasted sweet as it slid over Matthew's palate. "Now this, this is real communion" Matthew thought as he looked around the room. "So many different people from so many different places, living so many different lives. And yet here we are packed in this room, rejoicing over what the Savior has done for all of us."

When the bread and wine had been passed to everyone, a man from the other side of the room began to sing. He had a strong baritone voice and sang a tune that to Matthew's ear was very *Hebrewish*. He sang a few words and then was joined by those around him. The song swept across the room and soon the entire gathering was engaged in singing. It was sweet. It was loud. It was sincere.

> *"His body was given to all,*
> *His blood was shed for all.*
> *For all of our sins,*
> *For all of our shame,*
> *His body and blood he gave.*
>
> *His body was given for us,*
> *His blood was shed for us.*
> *For all of our sins,*
> *For all of our shame,*
> *His body and blood he gave.*
>
> *His body was given for me,*
> *His blood was shed for me.*
> *For all of my sin,*
> *For all of my shame,*
> *His body and blood he gave."*

As if it had been rehearsed, the entire assembly broke out in hugs and shouts of praise. The love and joy expressed were beyond anything Matthew had ever witnessed. After a few moments Mark stood and held out his hands for silence. The room grew still as Mark began to speak.

"And now children, let us all depart in peace. Look up and receive the blessing of Jehovah." He extended both arms over the room and began to pray. Before Mark finished the first line, Matthew knew the words. He had used them on several occasions himself. They were from Numbers 6:26-27 and were the words given by God to Moses for Aaron to share over the children of Israel.

> *"The Lord bless you and keep you;*
> *The Lord make His face shine on you,*
> *And be gracious to you;*
> *The Lord lift up His countenance on you,*
> *And give you peace."*

Several joined him in saying Amen. Mark closed by adding, "And now let us go, to share with others what the Lord has done for us. "Shalom!" A resounding "Shalom!' was returned.

It was almost two hours before the last person left. Levi and Matthew lingered long after most people departed. They just couldn't get enough of talking with fellow believers and hearing how they came to put their faith and trust in Jesus. When they finally left they talked all the way back to the inn and rested well that night.

# Chapter 20
# Alexandrium

In the morning the men found themselves at a table downstairs enjoying a leisurely breakfast. They place the remaining fabric in their wagon and began their trip north to Alexandrium. The city was almost twenty miles away and would take most of the day to cover the distance.

They arrived that evening and located the shop of the man who was to buy the fabric. The next morning, they would meet with him and complete the transaction. Alexandrium was much larger than Matthew had expected. It boasted of a large square with dozens of shops surrounding it. A good number of people walked about and many stood in groups of four or five talking and laughing together.

The men found an inn and made arrangements to spend the night. They went upstairs and dropped their bags in the room. Levi poured water from a pitcher into a basin and the two men washed their hands. They descended the stairs and left the inn walking a couple of blocks to a small cafe.

After a short wait they were seated at a table in the corner of a crowded dining area reviewing all they had seen and heard in Jericho, and making plans for the next day. They would finish their business in Alexandrium and then head home to Gophna arriving before nightfall.

While they talked, Levi kept looking at two men seated a couple of tables from them. Levi commented that he felt like he knew them but couldn't place where. They were dressed in the usual way and had no abnormal look about them. He also noticed a man sitting by himself three tables over in the other direction. He was sure he didn't know him but by his dress concluded that he was some sort of religious leader.

When Matthew and Levi finished their meal they got up to leave. Without warning, Levi approached the table where the two men sat. Matthew followed and stood behind him wondering what he was about to say. "I am sorry to intrude," he said, "But you men look familiar. Where is it that I would know you from?" The men looked surprised but not alarmed. Looking up and smiling one man said, "I am Tobiah, and this is my friend Thomas. We are not from here." "We also, are not from here" Levi said. "Perhaps we have met at a meeting," he added with a little caution. "We have been to many meetings," Tobiah said. "It is possible that we have seen you there." Motioning with his hand he said, "Please sit with us a moment."

Levi smiled and pulled the chair from the table and sat down. Matthew followed suit. Thomas spoke up. "We have been to several meetings to talk to people about the Messiah." Both Levi's and Matthew's faces lit up. "We have been to meetings for that purpose too!" Levi said. With no further hesitation Thomas asked, "Are you followers of Jesus the Christ?" Levi looked around and smiled. Leaning in he said, "Yes! Yes, we both have become followers of Jesus!" Both Thomas and Tobiah extended their hands and the four men traded handshakes.

Tobiah nodded toward Thomas. "Thomas walked with the Master," he said, trying not to sound too boastful. He can tell you things about Jesus that no one else can. Levi and Matthew looked at Thomas who only nodded. "Thomas the disciple?" Matthew thought. "Doubting Thomas?"

Levi slid his chair closer. "Please tell us what it was like to be with the Master." Taking the invitation, Thomas cleared his throat and spoke in a quiet but clear voice. "I walked with him for almost three years. I didn't intend to be with him that long but when you are in the presence of one like Jesus, you do not want to leave. It was not like being in any of the schools of the Rabbi's. There was no test, no fee, no requirements to follow him. You just went where he went and listened and learned! So many followed him as we traveled along from city to city and town to town."

"He healed many and each time my heart raced. He made the Scriptures so clear and to listen to him teach made you hunger for more. He was always teaching. He would point to a flower, the temple stones, birds, children, the sand, whatever was close by. There were lessons about Jehovah in everything. He would place a small seed in his hand and tell us about faith. He said that even a small amount of faith would bring great results. He held up a flower and told us to trust Yahweh to provide for us."

The volume of Thomas' voice began to increase as the excitement of his memories came to life. Looking around, Tobiah patted him on the forearm and Thomas nodded and lowered his voice once again. "And love! He talked about love all the time. The love of Jehovah, the love we should have for one another, even the love we should extend to our enemies. But he didn't just speak about it. He showed us what genuine love looked like!"

On the night that they took him, we were all in the garden with him. The temple leaders came with soldiers. There were so many of them and Judas was in the front. Judas was one of us! We trusted him!" Thomas gave a slight smile, "My friends, when you trust someone with your money, you really trust him. And Judas held our purse. The Master knew he was stealing. Nathaniel told him, but he still did nothing. He said, 'Nothing will go out that will not come back.'"

Thomas scowled, "Judas stepped up and called him Rabbi. Rabbi! With all the time we spent with him and all we saw him do, the only title Judas would give him was Rabbi?" Thomas did nothing to hide his anger. Matthew thought he would lean over and spit but he regained his composure and continued. "And then he kissed him. As soon as that happened, they put their hands on him. Peter pulled a sword out and struck a young boy standing by the priest." Thomas leaned further in and smiled. "I think he was aiming for the priest." The other three smiled as well.

"Then Jesus healed the boy. I saw it! The boy was screaming. Jesus stepped forward and grabbed the boys hand and moved it away from his head. His ear was completely gone. The Master picked it up and put it back in place and he was healed. I tell you it looked as if nothing had happened. Who does that? Only a man who teaches on love and demonstrates love with his life. Not just for his friends, but even for his enemies!"

"For just a moment, everyone stepped away from Jesus. No one spoke a word. Then the priest shouted, 'Take him!' and the soldiers stepped in a grabbed him. I didn't understand why he didn't resist. I had no sword but I wanted to fight. But there were too many of them."

"We didn't know it then, but it was all according to his plan. We thought they would bring him to the temple court, question him, scold him, maybe even beat him. But they would let him go and we would be back together soon. Myself and several others who stood close to

Jesus were grabbed by the soldiers as well. But the priest told them to let us go. Jesus was the one they were after. We all slipped away into the darkness."

Thomas was obviously choked up as he continued, "I remember that night as if it was a moment ago. I was with John and Bartholomew. We spent the night at John's friend's home in the city. Somehow a neighbor heard what was going on and told us that the priests planned on crucifying Jesus. All of us were angry, disheartened, and scared. There was nothing legal about it. We didn't know what to do. We left and went to the place where they held Jesus. We stayed close enough to see what was happening, but not so close as to get arrested as well. We couldn't believe it! How was this possible? Jesus had done nothing wrong! How could they do this thing? As you know, they beat him and crucified him just as they planned."

Thomas looked down. His face bore the look of a man ashamed. "Before we knew it Jesus was on the cross. I saw him from a distance and I watched him die. I saw them take his body down just before sundown, before the start of the Sabbath. I stood there is disbelief. I was so disappointed. I was devastated. Jesus was the deliverer we had heard about all our lives. He was going to give us the freedom we wanted from the Romans. Our people had always been oppressed and enslaved. The Philistines, Amorites, Egyptians, Assyrians, Babylonians, Persians, and now the Romans! Even during the time of the kings we only had freedom for short periods of time. Jesus was the answer. He was our promised deliverer!"

Thomas became exited again. "Think of the army we would have. He could give us food. He would heal the sick and injured. If a person died, he could raise them back to life! People were following the Lord by the scores! There were hundreds of thousands in the holy city when Jesus entered. They were all cheering for him and lifting him up in worship! We knew it was time for him to lead us to freedom!"

All four men glanced at the man sitting alone as he got up from his table. They couldn't help but notice the look of disgust on his face. He walked across the room and exited the dining area in haste. They turned their attention back to Thomas.

Matthew and Levi were glued to his words, Thomas looked down again and cleared his throat. Shaking his head slowly he said, "But all that changed that night when they took him in the garden. All our hopes and dreams died with him on the cross."

"For the most part many of us went our separate ways. The Romans and the temple officials were looking for those who were close to Jesus. We didn't know if they would just question us, beat us, or maybe crucify us as well so we did our best to keep to the shadows. A few of the others began staying in the home where we were with the Master last."

"I got word that many of the disciples had left for Galilee and early on the first day of the week, went to be with them. It took some time, but eventually I found where they were. When I knocked on the door, there was no answer. I said, 'It is Thomas. Please open!' The door opened quickly and Thaddeus pulled me in. Everyone was excited. 'He's alive! He's alive!' They kept repeating. I didn't understand at first but they explained to me how the Master had come and entered the room with all of them. I did not see how that was possible. I saw the blood. The sound of the nails was still ringing in my ears. I was there! I watched him die! I told them it was impossible but they kept telling me it was so. I refused to believe unless I saw him myself. I wanted to talk to him, to touch him, to feel the marks made by the nails in his hands and the cut in his side. I wanted to make sure that it was not just an illusion or even a ghost."

"The next day, I had to return home to my village to tend to my father who was not feeling well. I stayed there for two days and then went back to Galilee to meet with the others. We were in the room eating a light meal when I saw the face of Peter. He was looking at the wall behind me. He dropped the food from his hand and opened his mouth. I felt a strong breeze on the back of my neck. I turned around and right behind me was the Master." Both Levi and Matthew sat there motionless. Thomas made a fist with both hands and held them in front of his face. "I saw him! He was standing right behind me! He looked different but in so many ways the same. I can't explain it, but there was no doubt that it was Jesus!"

"I stood up and faced him. He put his arms out and spoke to me. He said, 'Thomas.' He called my name! He said, 'it is I. Touch my hands and side. Do not doubt. Only believe.' I fell at his feet. All I could say was, 'My Lord and my God!' Everyone gathered around him. They were hugging him and each other. For a long time, I just stood there in the middle of all of them and kept repeating, 'My Lord and my God.' My friends, he lives!" All three men repeated, "He lives!"

The four men talked a few minutes more then Matthew and Levi rose to leave. They exchanged blessings on one another and the two walked across the diner and exited. When they reached the corner, Matthew looked back. Pulling Levi's arm he said, "Levi, look!" Levi turned and looked in the direction of the diner. They saw the religious leader they had seen earlier leading another man and four Romans inside.

"Lord, please protect them" Levi said. Matthew followed it with an "Amen!" They knew there was nothing they could do and that it would be wise to make themselves scarce. With that they turned in the direction of the inn.

The next morning, they awoke early, had breakfast and then made their way to the shop. The shop owner's name was Elam and he and Levi seemed to be old friends. He invited them in and offered them some hot *tea*. The men drank their tea and talked of random issues in the city. Levi was grateful that Elam bought all the fabric and paid more than a fair price. They left the shop and walked back to the inn to buy some food for the trip home.

When they got back to where the the wagon was, four men stood by holding the reins and leaning against the wagon. Because of the way they were dressed Matthew immediately knew they were synagogue officials. He also noticed three Roman soldiers standing inside the shop. It took only seconds for him to realize that this was trouble.

One of the men let go of the reins and asked, "What are your names and what brings you to our city." Levi took the lead. "I am Levi and this is my friend Matthew. We are from Gophna and have come to trade with Elam." The man looked from Levi to Matthew. He paused a moment and said, "Come with us!"

Levi looked at Matthew and shrugged his shoulders. The men knew it would do no good to resist. They followed the others and saw the Romans leave the shop and trail behind with the donkey and wagon. They walked a couple of blocks and came to the synagogue. Matthew and Levi knew immediately what this was about.

They were brought inside the synagogue and escorted through the large lobby and placed in separate rooms. Matthew saw no reason to be overly alarmed at this point. He was instructed to sit down and was left in the room alone. He reasoned that Levi was in the same situation in the room across the foyer. Matthew looked around the room. It was fairly sparse with a couple of high tables lightly decorated with cups and plates. He figured it was used for small gatherings and possibly a classroom.

A few minutes later the door swung open and in walked four synagogue officials with a Roman. The soldier stood to the side looking bored. A short fat man with a medium length beard and a pointed hat, asked him, "What is your name?" He said, "Matthew" and resisted saying, "We already told your buddies that."

"From where do you come to our city?"

That was a difficult one. There was no way he could tell them exactly where he was from so he said, "We are from Gophna but were in Jericho last night."

"And what tribe are you from?" An even more difficult one. Since Jesus was from the tribe of Judah and Roans 8:17 instructed him that followers of Christ were *joint heirs* with Jesus he felt comfortable in saying "Judah."

The man leaned toward Matthew. "We have heard that you have been in discussion with some others about Jesus. Is that true?"

Matthew was now in a situation that he had often labeled, "Gut-check time." This was a time when those following Christ stood at the crossroads of *denial* leading to the town of *Comfort* and *truth* leading to the town of *Commitment*.

Matthew simply said, "It is so."

"And what is it that you have to say about this Jesus?" The man said, sneering when he used the Lord's name.

Matthew hesitated but only long enough to find the right words. "I am a follower of the risen Christ. He is the Messiah."

The next words from the man came as no surprise. "Blasphemy" he snarled. "You speak of this dead teacher as the Messiah."

Matthew shrugged his shoulders. "That is only because that is who he is."

"Silence! This is not so!"

"It is so!" Matthew countered matching the voice level of the man. "Jesus is the promised Messiah." He was about to continue but the man's backhanded slap cut him short. His face burned slightly from the blow.

"Jesus died and was buried. There is no more to the story than that."

Matthew felt that a reply was called for. "He rose from the grave on the third day just as he said he would. The empty tomb is proof!"

The man grabbed Matthew by the neck. "You speak lies. We know the disciples took his body and hid it. They continue to tell stories of seeing him but we know they are lies."

"Then don't worry about it" Matthew thought but dared not say. The man continued, "You will not bring these lies to our city. You will not tell these stories to others! Are you understanding this?"

Matthew started getting angry. He clenched his teeth which often happened when he became upset. He looked at the full bellied man and said, "I cannot change what has happened in my heart and soul." Then he paused to gather his next words. He knew they would be biting ones but he didn't care. "You are too steeped in your religion to understand that the Messiah has come and his name is Jesus. He…"

A blow to the back of the head knocked Matthew off his seat. He landed hard on the marble floor and immediately felt a welt rising on his forehead. Two sets of arms picked him up and he was set roughly back in his chair. He was alarmed and sent up a quick prayer.

The man grabbed Matthew's throat again. This time the pressure he gave began to choke him. He struggled to breath. "You will not speak of this man in our city again. Are you now understanding this?"

The hand released his throat and he was able to respond. "I understand your words" was all he said.

From his left side he received the blow of a fist that he never saw coming. This drove him to the floor once again and the room began to swim. He made no attempt to get up. His ears were ringing and his head was throbbing. Another set of arms pulled him from the floor. He was expecting to be sat down again but this time they only held him up.

The man stood in front of him. His face showed nothing but anger and hatred. "You will leave our city and not speak of this man again. If this is something you do not understand we will meet again and you will have a great desire that we had not."

With that, the two men holding him up dragged him to the door and across the lobby. They opened the door of the synagogue and pushed off the porch and down the steps. Matthew tumbles like a bag of laundry. He landed on the bottom and rolled to a stop at the wagon. He lay there not wishing to get up for a few moments. Several people passed by and a few gathered to stare.

After a short time two men stooped down to help Matthew up. He was slightly dizzy and stood still not daring to attempt to walk. One of the men asked him, "My friend, are you alright?"

"I will be" was all Matthew could say.

They heard the doors of the synagogue open and Matthew cringed as he saw Levi being tossed off the porch. He rolled down the steps and stopped right next to where Matthew was standing. With one hand on the wagon he reached down and helped the others assist Levi to his feet.

Levi's forehead was bleeding a little and his lip was swollen. He looked at Matthew and gave a slight grin as he nodded his head. Without being asked he said, "In time. In time I will be my friend. Now help me onto our wagon. The men who stood by were quick to help both men onto the wagon. One of them looked at the synagogue and said, "Not all the men in Alexandrium are like this my friends." Matthew nodded toward them, grabbed the reins and steered the wagon toward the city gates.

When they left the city Levi nudged Matthew and said, "The Lord is to be praised that we have been found worthy of being treated so harshly for his name." "Yes" was all Matthew said and the two men road for several miles in silence.

When they entered Levi's home Hannah and Benjamin rushed to their sides. Hannah cried, "Levi! What happened?" Before he could say a word she noticed Matthew's face as well, "Matthew, you too! What has happened to the two of you?" Levi gave a slight smile. "We are alright. We just made the acquaintance of some of the religious leaders in Alexandrium." He gave an unconvincing chuckle and added, "I don't believe they are as open to the message of the Messiah as we are."

Benjamin brought both the men a cup of water and they each downed it quickly. Matthew was surprised not to feel as bad as he was sure he looked. He still suffered from a dull headache and his cheek and side were very sore but other than that he didn't feel too bad. Levi seemed to have suffered worse and complained mostly of sore ribs and a swollen lip. A restful night's sleep would do both of them good. The next day Matthew was to start his new job as a shepherd. He knew he needed to be strong enough to travel and to look after the flock.

# Chapter 21
# Matthew, The Shepherd

Matthew was up with the sun. He was surprised to find himself less sore than he anticipated. His cheek hurt but only when he touched it. His head and the rest of him were not so bad. "Perhaps the adrenalin" he thought. Levi was in a good bit more pain than Matthew. He moved around slowly being careful not to agitate his wounds. The soon-to-be shepherd ate a small breakfast of fruit and bread and grabbed the sack of food Hannah had put aside for him. They asked the Lord's blessing on him as he left their home. He made his way out of the village and came to a very large and noisy pen holding most of the sheep belonging to Gaddiel. Abida had left him a note saying, "The blessings of Jehovah be upon you! Tend the *family* well my friend!"

Matthew would be taking fifty sheep and was instructed by the lead shepherd to head west for three days before returning the following week. Matthew gave the familiar but distinct call and was surprised at the immediate response of the sheep.

With his staff at the gate, the lead shepherd counted out the fifty and gave Matthew a go-ahead nod. Matthew began tapping his staff as he led the way and was dutifully followed by *the family*.

They meandered through the Judean hillside continuing on a slow but steady movement in a somewhat westerly direction. The air was fresh and clear and a slight breeze brought new smells of fresh foliage from the far hills. Matthew felt relaxed and fulfilled as he walked slowly along leading his charges and scanning the hills for dangers and fresh pasture.

They came upon a small stream and Matthew went right to work. Taking off his sandals and turning his robe into work pants, he waded into the stream. Several sheep watched him from a safe distance as he blocked the flow of water with rocks. Finally, the *still waters* were ready for the sheep and they began to gather in droves at the edge of the pond to slake their thirst in the hot Israel sun. They jostled each other and jockeyed for position as they lapped up the cool water from the pool. Matthew sat on a nearby rock constantly scanning the hills for danger.

The rest of the day was spent slowly leading the flock across the plains to an area he was told held a sheepfold to be used that night. The pen was on the other side of a ridge that offered a clear path but held a steep incline in many places. He would have to make several trips up and down the ridge helping and guiding some of the younger ones and encouraging the stragglers.

So many of the sheep needed direction. They often walked and ate as they went, not looking up or paying attention to what lay ahead. They needed encouragement to follow a path that was steep or narrow. They needed assurance that they were safe and that the shepherd cared for them and was always close by.

Matthew found his mind wandering over these things. He could easily see how his own life mirrored the lives of the sheep. So many times he needed direction, assurance and encouragement.

His mind bounced back to a time he received a text from his wife shortly after he arrived at the office. She told him she wasn't feeling well and didn't feel up to meeting him for lunch. The entire time they had been married she had never been sick except for an occasional head cold.

He told her to go back to bed and see if she felt better later on. Two hours later she called saying that she could not stop vomiting. Matthew knew he needed to return home so he grabbed his keys and phone and quickly headed for the car. Although the drive home was short, it felt like eternity. He did his best to avoid building the worse case scenario and found himself praying out loud as he pressed his way toward home.

He pulled into the driveway, clicked off the car and ran for the house not bothering to close the car door. He knew the house would be locked and he fumbled for his keys as he moved. He entered the house and headed straight for the bedroom. There he found his wife curled up on the floor with her hair matted against her face from the sweat that was pouring from her body.

"Melissa! Melissa!" He shouted as he knelt by her side. She opened one eye weakly and Matthew knew she was in deep trouble. Within seconds he had the 911 dispatcher on the phone and was assured that help was on the way. Minutes seemed like hours and Matthew found himself alternating between prayers to the Lord and comfort for his wife.

The rescue team arrived and assessed the situation. She was burning up and had great pain in her belly every times she moved. She was given fluids and morphine and was gently lifted to a gurney. When the pain medicine began to work, she managed a slight smile and kissed the back of Matthew's hand which was interlaced with hers.

Time seemed to slow down even more at the hospital. Matthew waited about an hour as the doctors, nurses, and technicians tended to his wife. He contacted their daughter who was on her way. In between his own prayers he made several calls and texts to friends telling them what was going on and asking them to pray. A few friends arrived just before the hospital spokesperson entered the waiting area and escorted Matthew to a consultation room.

In the side room he was told that Melissa had a burst appendix. She was in surgery at the moment and they were doing everything they could to help her. She was bleeding internally and was poisoned by the contents of her appendix. They would know the outcome soon. Matthew was speechless. He looked down not knowing what to ask or how to how to respond. His wife's life hung in the balance. He never saw it coming and was not mentally or emotionally prepared for this.

Back in the waiting room Matthew met with his friends. Four more had arrived as the word spread. He was given hugs and pats on the back. He told them what he had learned and was led by the group to another room for prayer. When the group began to pray, Matthew was overwhelmed by an unusual sense of peace and comfort. His good friend Cliff prayed as the entire group bowed and agreed. Part way through the prayer Matthew felt a warmth in his chest and legs begin to build. The warmth turned into a tingling sensation which spread over his entire body. In any other setting he would have been alarmed but here, with these friends in prayer, he knew that it was from the Spirit of God.

Tears came but they were not tears of fear or sadness. They were tears of thankful appreciation as God was assuring him of his control and sovereignty. He was in a very real way experiencing *the peace that passes all understanding.*

An hour and a half later the hospital spokesperson returned and without leading Matthew to another room shared that the surgery was over and that Melissa was doing well and was expected to recover fully. The tears that flowed from Matthew and the others were berthed in relief as well as thankfulness.

Matthew snapped back to his present life (or what it seemed to be) and realized he was smiling. Little Ahava was nuzzling against his leg and looking for some attention. The bleating of the sheep further brought him back to the task at hand.

He called to the flock several times and they responded in groups. They would walk up a steep incline to the top of the ridge. The path was narrow and at one point made a sharp turn. The trail fell off to the left sharply on the edge of a five- foot drop-off. Beyond the ledge, there was a much further drop. Matthew positioned himself at the turn and was able to guide the sheep in single file around the dangerous spot. As each group made their way to the top he worked his way back down and called to another group.

After two hours the entire flock was on the plane above and were milling about waiting on their shepherd. Matthew stood on the edge of the ridge scanning the field below for any strays. Seeing none, he surveyed the field ahead. A few hundred yards away was the paddock he was looking for. He worked his way through the flock tapping his staff as he went. The sheep responded predictably and followed their leader.

His timing was perfect! The sun would be setting in about two hours giving him just enough time to ready the pen, look over each sheep, and gather wood for the night. There was a large tree overlooking the sheepfold offering welcomed shade that would keep his charges cool. A few branches had fallen but were cleared away in minutes. Matthew stood on the side of the entrance and called the *family* in.

He leaned his staff across the entranceway blocking any sheep from bypassing his examination and count. Many of them had twigs and briars in their coat and he removed them easily. He rubbed each sheep's head and gave him a number out loud to keep track of the flock. A few had scratches on their noses or legs which Matthew took care of with an application of oil.

As he got to the last few he began to be concerned. It was becoming very apparent that not all of them were there. Tending to number forty-nine made this feeling a reality. He led all the sheep out of the pen and then back in, recounting in both directions. Now there was no doubt. One of his *children* was missing! "How is this possible?" he chided himself. "My first outing and I lose a sheep!

He closed the wooden gate and placed a branch against it locking the tribe in. He had to go back and find that missing one. Matthew's mind bounced from one possibility to another. A snake bite, a trapped leg, wild animals, lost. All held equal ground in his imagination. All the lambs were accounted for so he knew it was an adult.

Matthew trotted down the narrow path and across the meadow. Moments later he stood on the ridge scanning the field below. Night would arrive soon. He knew he must find that lost sheep! He called and listened, called and listened. Everything was quiet.

He quickly worked his way down the ridge using the large boulders to slow his decent. When he reached the bottom, he called out to the lost one again. He paused and listened but heard no reply. He knew there was one missing! He had counted and re-counted. He had to find her, even if it took all night!

He began to walk along the lower field scanning the edges as he went. Suddenly he heard the faint sound of a bleating sheep. His heart quickened as he stopped and held his breath trying to determine where it came from It was over the edge of the far end of the pasture. He was sure of it!

He called out again and again as his pace quickened. Every few yards he stopped to get a better reading on where the noise was coming from. When he got to the edge of the field he slowed his gait so his momentum would not carry him over the cliff. He leaned over the edge and about twelve feet below found the object of his search. She must have walked too close to the edge, lost her footing and tumbled over. Thankfully she was able to catch herself on the ledge to keep herself from falling to her death.

The lost one was standing on a narrow precipice helplessly looking up at her shepherd. Matthew was only equipped with a straight staff rather than one with a hook in it so pulling her up was not an option. He knew he had to work his way down to the helpless one and somehow lift it up to a stable place and bring it to safety.

There was an exposed root about half way down that he could grab and lower himself the rest of the way to the frightened animal. The dirt was loose and he would have to use extreme caution as he made his way to her. His plan was to begin a slow and controlled slide on his belly and grab the root when it was within reach. Then he hoped to swing his legs toward the ledge while continuing to hold on to the root. After he was on the ledge he would somehow lift the animal in stages to the top. His hope was that she would get a foothold and be able to get herself to the top.

At first, all went well as he slid headfirst, down the steep bank in a controlled sort of way. He grabbed the root and had a firm grip on it. He was about to swing his legs downward when somewhere far away, he heard a strange screech and a loud boom. This was followed by the snapping sound of the root. His right leg caught on something, another root or a rock, sending him headfirst toward the ledge and the sheep. Now he was no longer sliding but falling. He grasped at rocks, roots, dirt, anything he could get hold of, but there was nothing solid to grab. He had no control over what was to happen next. He was at the mercy of gravity and the laws of physics. Everything happened so fast!

He looked up just in time to catch a glimpse of the old bearded man he had seen the night of the accident. The man was standing on another ledge behind the sheep. He had his staff raised with the end pointed in Matthew's direction just like before. There was no time to wonder. There was no time to think. He was falling the last few feet toward the sheep and the ledge and didn't have time to raise his arms in protection. Thoughts of the pain he was about to feel shot through his mind. He fell directly onto the back of the sheep face first. He felt the softness of the wool touch his face as his head led the way for his body. His neck snapped back and he heard more loud noises all around him.

# Chapter 22
# The Return

He seemed to black out momentarily. He opened his eyes slowly and found himself sitting upright. He reached for the sheep but she was gone. It was completely dark and he sat still in shock and confusion. There was a curious sound all around him. After a short while he understood that he was hearing the pounding sound of rain. In the darkness, he reached forward and felt the steering wheel of his car. It was covered by the deflated air bag and he could smell the strange mixture of powder and oil. "What is happening?" he thought. It was all so strange and confusing.

He sat still without moving, trying to assess the situation and get a grip on what was going on. Moments later he heard several voices calling out. "Here he is! Are you okay? Sir, are you alright, are you okay, are you hurt?" He turned his head slowly in the direction of the voices and could make out the faces of two or three men staring at him through the broken window.

He was dazed and confused. He saw the outline of the car's hood crumpled and pushed up toward the broken windshield. The flashlights from those outside the car revealed a very large tree directly in front of his vehicle which was quickly being enveloped in steam.

He moved slowly and deliberately as he tried to put all the pieces together. Deftly, his right hand released the seat belt as his left hand lifted the door handle. To his surprise, the door opened and he was able to slide out in spite of the protests from the men outside.

He stood up slowly, cautiously. A few others joined those who arrived first and asked him, "Are you okay?" One man held an umbrella over his head as a young man said, "We've called the EMS, why don't you sit down?" Matthew only nodded. He stared straight ahead. After a brief pause he looked at the group and weakly said, "I think I'm okay."

Those gathered looked at each other and shrugged when he followed it by saying, "My Lord and my God. My Lord and my God, My Lord and my God." In the distance they could hear the sirens from the ambulance. Two men stood on each side of Matthew and guided him to a nearby log to sit down.

In short order the rescue workers arrived and Matthew was taken to a nearby hospital. His confusion went with him. Although they were constantly attending to him, he responded very little. He was stunned not so much from the accident, but from the strange events that had taken place. Just minutes ago, he was a shepherd in Israel trying to rescue a sheep. He *knew* he was there! He was tending sheep on the hillside outside of Gophna. He had friends in the towns and villages all around the area. He had been to Jerusalem. He had worshipped with other believers. He and Levi were beaten by the religious leaders. He was there for several days. He was really there!

Matthew was checked into the hospital. For observation purposes, he would spend the night. Melissa arrived as he was being wheeled from the x-ray area. She was relieved that he was uninjured. She held his hand and kissed him several times fighting tears the entire time.

The days passed slowly. He took a few days off from the church, not because his body needed it, but because his mind still could not grasp what he had experienced. He just knew it was as real as the current reality he was pressed back in to. He told Melissa in great detail all about what had happened to him. She listened patiently not venturing an explanation. She didn't understand what had happened any more than he did. All she knew was that the man she loved was safe and that he had experienced something very unusual.

His wife and church family saw the change in Matthew. It was easily noticeable. It affected everything in his life. He was always loving and caring but now his love for people inside and outside the church grew to a whole new level. His patience went beyond what was normally expected of a Pastor. His conversations were less about current affairs and more about Jesus and his love for everyone. The biggest impact however, was seen in his preaching. He preached like a man on fire. His enthusiasm for the word of God and the urgency with which he shared it were monumental. Whenever he began to preach he would start slow and deliberate. But then as he got further and further into the text and the message, it was like a different person came forward. He seemed like a man who not only talked about what he believed to be true, but one who was standing on a body of evidence that proved it to be so.

The church body caught on to his enthusiasm and began to reach out to the community like never before. New ministries were developed, volunteers came forward, money was given, and connections were made to other churches and community organizations. With his leading the church increased its giving to foreign and domestic missions. They even set aside finances to be given to other churches who were struggling to meet their budgets. The biggest change that Matthew noticed was that of the relationships between individual members. Long held grudges were resolved. Forgiveness was extended to offending people, sometimes without them seeking it. The young people began to reach out to older members and spend time with them and the Senior Adults began to get involved with the youth ministry.

In a very short time the church began to grow. They had been leveled out for several years and had just accepted that as normal. They were a comfortable group who were satisfied with *doing* church. But now they had a new hunger. Now they were concerned with *being* the church. Both the lost and the unchurched were sought out. Connections were made across racial barriers and several minority families began attending. People who had never spent time with others of a different skin color now sat with them and spent time with them outside of the worship service. In short, the church began being what the church was formed to be in the first place. It became an oasis of refreshment and encouragement. It became a place that was deeply concerned about those outside instead of just looking to the needs of those inside. Instead of being a house full of *perfect* people, it became a place where those with flaws could feel safe. Socially, people were accepted and spiritually they were challenged. It was almost as if a sign above the door that used to say *Clean up your life and come in* was taken down and in its place was a sign that read, *If you are hurting and need help, welcome!*

A few Saturdays following his release from the hospital, Matthew and Melissa ventured out to a local flea market. It was a very large venue and drew both buyers and sellers from a surprisingly long distance. They weren't looking for anything in particular. They just enjoyed walking around and talking to the various venders and other patrons. They usually ate lunch at one of the many booths and generally enjoyed a day away from their normal routine.

Matthew had slowly accepted the idea that between the time his car hit the tree and the time the air bag hit him, his mind had protected itself by giving him a dream of some measure. It felt so real but he knew it was impossible.

Nevertheless, because of what he went through, his faith in all that he believed regarding the Bible and Jesus Christ was stronger than it had ever been. In some strange sense his faith grew as his other experience began to fade. His doubts regarding the truthfulness of the Gospel steadily dropped away. The Gospel was as true and as real as the life he lived. His faith was as firm and steadfast as iron. Even Melissa noticed it and wondered. It was refreshing! It went beyond faith. His core beliefs about the Bible, the miracles of Jesus, the resurrection, and salvation, were more of a matter of fact than a matter of faith.

At one point in their outing a very strange thing happened. They were working their way to the food area. They held hands as the large crowd was gently pressing and jostling against him and Melissa. Matthew happened to look up and across the mass of people he saw a man facing away from him. He was about twenty yards away and somehow he seemed out of place. His clothes were different. He wore a long robe. Curiosity took hold of Matthew's mind. He stood on his toes and moved his head side to side trying to get a better look at the stranger. As if on cue, the man turned to face Matthew. It was him! The man from the street and the ledge! Matthew pulled on Melissa's arm "Look!" he shouted. Melissa stood on her toes as well. She yelled, "Where?" The crowd continue to move in every direction periodically blocking their view. Matthew pointed across the crowd. "That man over there in the robe. You see him? The one with the long beard!" For just an instant the crowd seemed to part giving Melissa a clear view. The man smiled slightly and lifted his staff pointing the end toward the two of them. "I see him!" Melissa exclaimed as the crowd filled in the voided space.

The two of them snaked their way through the crowd and came to the spot where he was standing. But he was gone! Matthew stood on his toes and looked in every direction. He even jumped up several times to see above the mass of people. There was no sign of the man. Melissa grabbed his arm and pulled herself toward him. "Who was that?" she asked. Matthew took a long breath. "He was the man I told you about. The one I saw on the road and the ledge!" Melissa stared for a moment letting it all sink in. She slowly nodded her head in acceptance of what he had been telling her. She didn't understand it but knew that what Matthew had told her was more than just a dream or hallucination. Tears filled Matthew's eyes and he let out an audible sigh. "I knew it was real! I *knew* it!"

He felt Melissa's arm slide into his and in an instant his heart was at peace and his mind was full of faith and assurance. He put his arm around his wife and pulled her close. They were no longer hungry so they eased their way back to the car. Matthew's thoughts were now trained on his relationship with the Lord and the years of great ministry that lay ahead of them. They drove home silently and at peace.

# About the Author

Dr. Jirgal is a 1980 graduate of Gettysburg College where he became a four-time conference champion, All-American, and inductee to the Middle Atlantic Conference *All Century Team* in the pole vault. He holds an undergraduate degree in health education and physical education. Following graduation, he taught on the high school and college level while coaching football and track in both venues. He holds masters degrees in health education, sports medicine, and divinity, as well as a doctorate in ministry.

He has been the director of Sports Medicine at Wingate University, area director for the Fellowship of Christian Athletes and has served on the staff of Hickory Grove Baptist Church in Charlotte, NC, as well as leading Lakeview Baptist Church, in Monroe, NC as the Senior Pastor. He has served on the local board of directors for the Fellowship of Christian Athletes, New Orleans Baptist Seminary and the ministerial board of Wingate University. He currently serves on the board of directors for The Carolina Study Center, and Fathers in Touch ministry.

Dr. Jirgal is the founder and director of *The Jirgal Leadership Institute* where he strives to equip people for success in leadership roles. He and his wife Pam have three children, Joshua, Caleb, and Sarah. They reside in Monroe, NC.

# OTHER BOOKS
# BY DR. STEVE JIRGAL

*The Path of a
Champion*

*Dying to Live*

*Life Points*

*Principles of
Wholeness*

*Mining the Mind
of King Solomon*

*Laws to Live By*

Questions regarding any of these titles can be
directed to Jirgalleadership@gmail.com